HE MUST LIKE YOU

DANIELLE YOUNGE-ULLMAN

Viking

For reasons that should become obvious, this book is dedicated, with all my love and hope and conviction, to my kind, smart, strong, hilarious, brave, sweet, magnificent daughters, Tessa and Scarlett.

VIKING

An imprint of Penguin Random House LLC, New York

First published in the United States of America by Viking, an imprint of Penguin Random House LLC, 2020

Visit us online at penguinrandomhouse.com

LIBRARY OF CONGRESS CATALOGING-IN-PUBLICATION DATA IS AVAILABLE.
ISBN 9781984835710

Printed in the United States of America

1   3   5   7   9   10   8   6   4   2

ALSO BY
DANIELLE YOUNGE-ULLMAN

Everything Beautiful Is Not Ruined

THE CUSTOMER IS ALWAYS RIGHT

"I have *the item*" is the first thing I hear when I walk into work on Sunday night.

The item in question is my duvet, and the person winking at me about it is Kyle.

Kyle, who is standing behind the host stand in the cheery foyer of the Goat wearing a mini cowboy hat with plush horns curling out of it—the latest in his growing collection of goat-themed apparel. He looks hilarious, cute, and deceptively harmless.

"It's in my truck. I'll give it to you after?"

"Sure. Thanks," I say, with what I hope is a neutral-seeming nod.

I'll have to wash it in hot water. Twice.

"Or we could go for a drive, climb into the back, get cozy," Kyle suggests, with a waggle of his white-blond eyebrows.

My insides take flight like a flock of startled birds, and then I'm doing this awkward thing where I'm cringing and trying to smile at the same time. But smiling might be too encouraging and so I stop, because even after three weeks of my ignoring his texts and generally avoiding him as much as possible, Kyle continues to look at me with those stupidly hopeful, flirty eyes.

Still, I don't want to be rude. We work together, and in that capacity Kyle has been fine. In fact, except for the one (admittedly problematic) incident, he's been great. Not to mention, I'm the one who asked him to bring me the duvet when my mom finally noticed it was missing today. I'm also the one who let him wear it home from my house in the first place.

"I'll just grab it from you after," I say. "I have a lot of homework."

"Your call," he says with a shrug.

"Right."

"What?"

"Nothing," I say, with another too-bright smile. "Um, what's my section?"

"The patio," Kyle says, gesturing at the giant, erasable seating chart that sits on the host podium.

"Alone?"

"Yeah. That okay?"

It's a big section to handle solo, but more tables means more tips, so I say, "Totally."

"By the way, Perry's coming in, and he asked for you specifically," Kyle says, looking at me like he expects this to make me ecstatic.

Perry Ackerman is a handful, and high on the list of people I'd rather not have to deal with right now. But he's a great tipper, and a regular, so I give Kyle a thumbs-up and say, "Awesome."

"I knew that'd make you happy."

"So happy," I say, and walk away taking deep breaths.

On my way through the restaurant I wave at my fellow servers Brianna and Kat, both of whom are working in the front tonight. Kat seems not to see me, but Brianna gives me a thumbs-up and pulls a comically panicked face that tells me she's already in the weeds.

The patio is at the back of the restaurant, and is, in fact, not a patio at all, but a windowless, rectangular space tricked out with fake plants, paper lanterns, an anemic fountain, and painted "windows" on every wall that do not fool anyone.

I have just enough time to tidy the section, tally my float, and gulp down a half cup of hideously bitter coffee behind the wall of the service station before I hear, "Libbyyyyyyyy!"

"You got the ol' perv?" Brianna gives me a wry, dimpled grin as she comes through with a stack of dirty plates. Her amazing crown of black braids adds at least three inches to her diminutive stature.

"Yep."

"All right, tits up," she says, which I've come to understand means some combination of "chin up" and "good luck."

I snort and square my shoulders.

"Libbyyyyyyyyyyyy!" Perry is now advancing conspicuously through the dining room in one of his linen suits, with a shirt almost as pink as his bulbous nose, his silver hair gleaming. He's accompanied by two of his friends, Douglas and Garcia, while Kyle trails behind them with a stack of menus.

I paste on a thrilled expression and step out from behind the station.

"There you are! Where's my hug?" Perry demands with open arms, then closes the distance between us and yanks me into one of his boob-crushing, bone-cracking, full-frontal embraces. Perry Ackerman is Pine Ridge's much-loved town savior, thus the hugging must be endured. It's a bit much, though.

When it finally ends I take the menus from Kyle and

usher Perry and his friends to their table. I get them settled, take their drink order—Ackerman beer to start with, of course—punch it in, and head to the bar to pick it up.

Nita, our bartender and niece of the owners, Dev and Maya, gives me a wave.

"Hey, Nita."

"Perry, huh?" she says, with a knowing look.

"Yep," I say, carefully balancing three beer glasses upright in my left hand, then grabbling the bottles by the neck in my right. "At least it won't be boring."

"That's the spirit," she says, then adds, "Oh, hey, can you try to sell some of the cucumber salad? Or the butter chicken burger? People are really digging the fusion items and Maya and Dev really want us to keep pushing them."

"Sure," I say, and head off.

Perry, Douglas, and Garcia order a ton of food and agree to every upsell and special I suggest. They're going to have way too much and their table is going to be overloaded, but I've become pretty mercenary about this stuff. Every little increase of the bill increases my tips. Not only that, but the more I sell overall, the more shifts and better sections I get. And the more shifts and better sections I get, the higher my bank balance climbs, which is the rather urgent reason I'm working here in the first place.

Kyle is careful not to fill up my section until Perry & Co. are settled, but soon all my tables have been sat, and the pace picks up. I'm checking on orders, cranking the pepper mill, delivering and clearing plates, taking more orders, making suggestions, chatting people up, running bins of dirty dishes to the dish pit, making pots of coffee, getting another round of drinks for Perry because they're switching to sangria, and helping Brianna and Kat any time I'm not busy for more than ten seconds.

Dev makes his way around, overseeing it all and lending a hand where needed. Kyle's there too, on the periphery, bussing and turning tables, but I don't have time to think about him. I don't have time to think about anything.

This state of bonkers, nonstop busyness where the entire world falls away was one of the biggest surprises for me about this job. Restaurant work can be hugely stressful, but when the place is full and everything is going right, it's wild. You get into this zone, like a flow state, where you're thinking and moving so fast, juggling so many things at once, that hours can pass in what feels like the blink of an eye. You come back to reality with your brain melted, feet/knees/back throbbing, smelling like you live inside a barbeque, but also knowing you somehow survived.

And then there are the times when one tiny thing goes wrong, and it causes a cascade, and then sometimes an avalanche of more things going wrong, and you just can't recover.

The tiny thing that goes wrong for me tonight is Perry's salad—the one Nita told me to push. Thirty seconds after I deliver it I hear, "Libbyyyyyyy!" and then Perry is pointing at his bowl and saying he doesn't like red onion.

I had told him there was onion in it, but saying so would be futile.

"I'll get you a new one made right away," I say, and then take the salad back to the line cook, Domenic.

Domenic frowns, but agrees to make me another one.

"Can you do it fast?" I say, giving him my most pathetic, pleading expression because he's got a huge stack of orders to get out and this'll put him behind. "Please? It's for Perry."

Domenic makes a show of grumbling, but he's on it already.

I deliver two soups for Kat and a bread basket for Brianna, grab the new salad, thank Domenic profusely, make the delivery to Perry, and then go to deliver the orders of a family of six.

I'm carrying four heavy plates, one in each hand and two up my arm, and am arriving at their table when I hear, "Libbyyyyyyy!"

I glance over my shoulder and signal to Perry that I'll be with him in a moment, set the plates down, then zoom back to the hot food window to grab the last two orders and deliver them, while Garcia and Douglas start chiming in.

"Libbyyyyyyy!" "LibbyLibbyLibbyyyyyyy!"

Charming.

More customers are trying to flag me down, someone wants their bill, I need to punch another order in quickly because people with small children hate having to wait, I can barely hear myself think, and I'm starting to sweat.

"This isn't spicy," Perry says, waving at the salad. "Isn't this Indian stuff supposed to be spicy?"

Maya's been very careful to introduce her South India-inspired menu items slowly—masala fries, a mild fish curry—nothing too hot for the average Pine Ridge (i.e., small town) palate.

"It's not meant to be spicy!" Domenic shouts at me thirty seconds later when I return with the salad.

"I know. But can you just . . . add something to it?"

"Fine," he says, rolling his eyes.

"Thank you," I say, then I duck out to the computer to print a bill and input the dessert and coffee order for the family of six before returning to Domenic.

I take the salad, now with spicier dressing and conspicuously garnished with chili peppers, out to Perry, and wait to make sure he likes it.

He makes a big production of his first bite, whoops, and finally grins.

"Good?" I say.

"I dunno," he drawls, "you're so cute when you're flustered, I almost want to send it back again."

"Please don't. Domenic would kill me."

"But we're enjoying watching you come and go," Perry says.

I need to leave so I can deliver the bill I just printed and get caught up, but Perry grabs me by the wrist and trails his eyes blatantly down my body. My stomach clenches. I manage a weak chuckle and a playful swat to get him to let go of me, then walk away feeling like there's a target on my butt.

Brianna swoops in to help me with my falling-apart section.

"You okay?" she asks as we slide into either side of a booth to clear and clean it.

I nod.

"A couple weeks ago Perry smacked me on the backside and said 'giddyup' after I took his order."

"Gross!"

Dev has new customers ready to sit in the booth the moment we're out of it, so that's the end of the conversation.

When I arrive back at Perry's table a few minutes later, he's flushed and in the middle of retelling his favorite story: how he saved Pine Ridge.

"Bank closed down and nobody'd buy the building. People had lost their jobs. The bank jobs, plus around that time a lotta people lost their farming jobs, too. Everyone was starting to think they'd have to move somewhere else. And I looked at that big, fancy old building, with the pillars and the vaults, and thought: Beer!"

Garcia and Douglas, who have no doubt heard this story multiple times, nevertheless burst into raucous laughter.

All I want to do is quickly grab some of the dirty plates before moving on to my veritable horde of unsatisfied customers, but Perry turns the beam of his attention on me, trapping me at their table. "Nobody around here even knew the term 'microbrewery' and everyone thought I was crazy. Who's crazy now, right?"

Perry presses on with grandiosity, chest puffing, and I almost expect him to start pounding it. "That's right, I employed all those people, still employ them, and now we got tourists, and we got stores with stuff in them that nobody even knows what it is. Furniture made out of twigs and someone'll pay a thousand dollars for it. I did that."

Amid the next chorus of cheers, I start clearing the table.

There's so much uneaten food I can't imagine they're going to want anything else, but then Perry informs me Dev is buying them dessert.

"Great," I say, pausing, arms loaded with dishes. "I'll bring dessert menus."

"Don't you have it memorized, doll?"

"Sure, but—"

"We want your sales pitch, Libby," he says, with the pronounced enunciation of someone trying not to slur. "Everything sounds so much more delicious coming from your lips."

"Okay," I say, blowing out a breath. "Just let me drop off these plates."

Luckily I only have to take three steps before Kyle is there with an empty bin, which means I can unload and go straight back to Perry.

"Make it good," Perry says, with a leer. "Cause I'm still mad at you about the salad."

"Right," I say, pushing down the urge to point out that there was never anything wrong with the salad. "First we have the cheesecake with salted caramel—"

"No, no!" Perry puts a hand to my lower back. "Not like that. It's what I'm always telling my staff: sell it to me. I want to *feel* the caramel on your tongue. I want to feel like *I'm* the caramel on your tongue."

His buddies chortle and Perry's hand slides lower. I try to shift discreetly away, but the hand comes with me.

I don't know how to do what he's asking, exactly, and I'm super distracted by the fact that his hand is now fully cupping my butt cheek, but I am not going through all of this crap only to lose my tip right at the end. So I just try to imagine I'm acting in a cheesy TV commercial. I slow down on words like "salted" and "caramel," roll the "r" in "creamy," try to look ecstatic about sticky toffee pudding, then finally throw on a bad Russian accent for white chocolate mousse tower.

"Oh God, can you tell me that last one again?" Perry says, with a disgusting groan. "But do it like . . . have you heard of Marilyn Monroe?" And then Perry finally drops his hand from my butt and does an imitation of her singing "Happy Birthday, Mr. President," all breathy and wriggling his shoulders and chest ridiculously, which, of course, makes his buddies roar.

"Do it," he commands. "White chocolate mousse tower, Marilyn-style, but keep the Russian accent. Sing the whole menu!"

Everyone is staring—not just Perry and his loathsome friends, but most of my section, plus Brianna and Kyle, who's standing nearby with a strangely blank look on his face.

This, of course, is awful. But Perry's bill is up over two hundred dollars already. A twenty percent tip will be at least forty bucks, and the faster I do it the faster he'll be gone.

And so I sing the whole damned dessert menu in a breathy voice, with a bad Russian accent, to the tune of "Happy Birthday," skipping all the gross wiggling but finishing with what I hope is a cute tilt of my head.

There's a short silence once I'm done, and then Perry, Douglas, and Garcia start clapping and hooting.

"Yes, yes, give it to me!" Perry shouts. "What's *your* favorite, Lib?"

"The, uh, toffee pudding."

"The *sticky* toffee pudding, you mean. We'll alllllll have it."

"Great," I say, tone brisk and back-to-business. "Three toffee puddings."

"And more sangria."

"Sure."

"And Libby?"

"Yes?"

"It better be the stickiest, best toffee pudding I've ever tasted," he says, reaching out to give me a sideways squeeze, "otherwise I'm going to come after you with my mousse tower."

Ugh. I might vomit. On purpose. On him.

But honestly I'm scared by the look in his eyes and so the best I can manage is to laugh, as if by laughing I can erase it. I laugh as if he's hilarious and then wrench myself out of his grasp, and finally make a beeline for the service area.

My laugh turns into a strangled sound as soon as I'm out of view, and I come to a full stop just as Dev enters from the opposite side.

"What's wrong?" he says, stopping short at the sight of me. "Are you sick?"

"No, it's just Perry."

"Still about the salad?"

"No, still about the being a disgusting, butt-grabbing pervert," I say.

Poor Dev is very proper, so he nearly chokes. He's probably never even said the word "butt" out loud. He's also almost as new at running a restaurant as I am at serving in one.

"Did you mean to say . . . ?"

"That he grabbed my butt? Yes."

"Gracious me," Dev says.

"Honestly, that's the least of it."

I tell him the rest and he listens with a mounting horror and embarrassment that almost makes me feel guilty for putting him through this.

"I knew he was sometimes inappropriate, but I didn't realize the extent of it. You should not have to deal with this type of behavior," Dev says, with a flustered exhale. "I'm very sorry."

"Thank you," I say, so relieved that he's listened and believed me, and feeling proud of myself for doing the thing everyone always says you should do—talk to someone who can help—and having it actually work out.

"What should we do?"

"Do?" Dev says.

"I'd rather not go back out there."

The sudden change of expression on Dev's face at this comment is almost comical—he looks totally panicked.

"Not go? We are understaffed and your section's been a disaster all evening!"

"But . . ."

"Who is going to serve all of those tables? Yes, Perry is behaving poorly, but this is all jokes. He is not going to hurt you. He has a wife!"

"What? Wife? What's that got to do with it?"

"If you're truly worried, I can have Kyle walk you out after your shift, or even accompany you home."

Have Kyle accompany me home.

Awesome.

"Don't worry," Dev says, in what he obviously thinks is a reassuring tone, "everything is fine."

And then he leaves, and I stand there blinking.

Everything is fine.

Right.

Silly me.

Yes, my legs are shaking and I feel like I've been slimed, but there's a job to do. I trudge back to the computer to put in the orders for the desserts and sangria.

When I get to the bar a couple of minutes later, Nita is quartering the oranges for the sangria. "We need to get Perry's keys from him," she says.

"You're kidding, right?"

"Not at all. He shouldn't be driving."

"I am not playing 'find-my-keys-they're-in-my-pants' with Perry."

Nita lets out a choking laugh, and says, "Eww."

"Seriously, no way. I'm not doing that."

"Okay, relax. I'll ask one of the guys to help. Just . . . tell them we'll pay for a taxi," she says, and sets the finished pitcher of sangria in front of me.

"Are we going to pay his mortgage, too? Maybe buy him a

car? Will someone have to jerk him off to get him out of here?"

"Ew. Whoa. What's the matter with you?"

"Nothing," I say, taking the sangria. "Everything's fine!"

And then . . . well, I'm not entirely clear about what happens then.

First I am marching with grim determination back to the patio, and Perry. And there is his face, and the other two faces, all of them flushed and leering as they greet me. The desserts have arrived in record time, and Perry is spooning the sticky toffee pudding into his mouth with relish. For a gross moment things go slow motion and all I can see is his tongue, lizarding out to the spoon, and I'm thinking that I'll never be able to eat sticky toffee pudding again, and how, between that and the mousse tower comment, that's two desserts Perry has ruined for me. And then he's grinning, saying something about how I'm really lucky he likes it.

Meanwhile, I'm looking at his empty glass, trying to figure out how to refill it without getting too close to him because I've had just about enough of his hands on me for one night. Almost like he can read my mind, he smirks, then picks up his glass and places it farther away, where I'll have to lean all the way over the table to reach it.

Later it will occur to me that I could have just made him pour it himself. Later I will have lots of smarty-pants ideas about how I could have handled this differently. But I'm stressed and creeped out and really pissed off, and the only thing I can think of right now is how exposed I will be, balanced over the table trying not to spill.

And all of a sudden I'm pouring the sangria, not into Perry's glass, not into any glass, but onto Perry.

Onto his head, his chest, his shoulders, and finally his lap.

I'm seeing chunks of the orange Nita just sliced bouncing down him, and the fruity liquid soaking his nether region.

And I'm hearing the sound of ice cubes as they hit the floor.

And I'm feeling words roaring out of me, though I don't even know what they are.

And there's Perry's face, and all the faces, shocked, and finally silent.

And it's incredible.

For a moment I feel incredible, I feel amazing, I feel like everything finally *is* fine.

And then I remember.

Life.

My future.

All the reasons I needed this job.

Shit.

THREE MONTHS EARLIER . . .

2

THINKING BUT NOT SAYING

I am sitting at the table in our rarely used dining room on a bitter-cold January evening. My mom has set out the wedding china and the fancy candles that have never been lit.

Something is going on.

That Mom, Dad, and I are eating together at all is unusual, but there's also a lot of smiling. An unreasonable amount of smiling. At me. This, combined with the fact that Mom got all teary before dinner and told me she loved me, and Dad has combed his hair and is wearing jeans and a nice shirt instead of his usual rumpled sweats, is making me very nervous. I'm on alert and at the same time smiling back so hard my face muscles are starting to cramp up.

Then Dad throws his napkin down like it's a gauntlet and says, "I've figured it out."

Mom's smile freezes. In fact her entire body goes as still as her carefully shellacked helmet of golden-brown hair.

"Figured what out, Dad?" I say.

"I've figured out where we went wrong with Jack!"

Uh-oh. My brother Jack is not a good subject—not since he dropped out of pre-med and ran off to Greece with no explanation, taking the remainder of his education money with him.

That was two and a half years ago, only a couple of months after Dad got fired from his real estate brokerage and embarked on his looking-for-employment/festering-miserably-in-the-basement career, which was then made more miserable by Jack's defection to Greece.

There was a lot of ranting (Dad) and weeping (Mom), and then they stopped all contact with Jack and started referring to him in the past tense, as if he died.

Things have been a tad grim since then.

"Uh, what about Jack?" I say in a quiet, carefully neutral voice.

"We spoiled him," Dad says, both arms flying up in one of his signature declamatory gestures. "We gave him too much, helped him too much, complimented him too much."

Sure, Jack bailed on his entire life due to being over-complimented, I think but do not say, because while it could be considered a positive change that Dad's so animated, when he gets like this it's best not to fuel the fire. This means I do a lot of thinking-but-not-saying. I may, in fact, be the champion of thinking-but-not-saying.

"We spoiled him and it ruined him," Dad continues. "There's even a name for it—'entitlement disease'—and I'm telling you, it's an epidemic. Your mother and I worked for everything we have. Paid our own way. Meanwhile, everyone in your generation would fall apart if they didn't have the latest iPhone."

Right. My cell phone is ancient and Dad is the one who gets a new one every year, even in this past year when both Mom and I worked more paid hours than he did. No point saying that either, though—it would just cause him to launch into defending whatever his latest money-making scheme is these days: staging houses, becoming a city planner (when we live nowhere near the city), studying for his brokerage license so he can open his own company and run his old brokerage out of town, media consulting . . . Each idea is pursued with manic intensity for a few weeks before he abandons it and descends into weeks of moping and binge-watching apocalyptic television.

"We're not going to make the same mistake with you," he's saying. "And the fact is, your mother and I need to start thinking of ourselves, about maximizing our investment here."

"What investment? Where?"

"Here! This house. You just turned eighteen, you're almost finished with high school, you need your independence. And meanwhile, we could be pulling in thousands of dollars per month if we Airbnb your room. With all the tourists that come to Pine Ridge for the weekend, it could be a gold mine."

"My room?"

"Yes!"

"A gold mine?"

"Darn right! And Jack's room, too. I don't need to have my office in there. I'll set myself up in the kitchen."

My mom seems to pale at this, which means she's now frozen *and* pasty-white.

"I'm thinking end of June, so we can catch the summer tourists," Dad rolls on. "And we'll need to spruce it up. Same as Jack's room. Get some nice bedding, couple of fancy pillows, and I've got a line on one of those luggage racks, where people put their suitcases! Give 'em that authentic hotel feeling."

I'm still not getting it—I'm too busy trying to imagine how any part of our house could ever have an "authentic hotel feeling."

"We'll need all your stuff out of there by the end of June," Dad's saying. "You're going to have to take your tchotchkes, the stuff from all your abandoned sports and hobbies, your boy band posters—"

Yes, I have abandoned some hobbies, but I have *zero* boy band posters. This fact is easily provable by walking twenty steps down the hallway to my room, and he also knows it, and even still I don't say it.

"We might keep that cool mobile you made, since it's white, but those navy walls, Lib? They'll have to go."

I am most certainly not giving him my origami star mobile—not when he's getting rid of my beautiful walls.

"Tourists want light," Dad is saying. "They want soothing. Not dark walls and stars everywhere."

My room. The only totally "me" place on earth. He's going to de-Libby it.

"Things change, Lib. And the thing is, your mom and I have between us a pretty cool combination of abilities that we can leverage, plus the house itself. I have my realtor experience and your mom's got her customer service skills from the Inn, and the timing is perfect because you need to leap from the nest."

"But . . ." I'm starting to catch on to the central point, finally, "where am I supposed to leap to?"

"You," Dad says, pointing a finger at me, "are going to start building some character! Increasing your resilience, and your work ethic! You're going to get a job and start looking for an apartment. Either that or you can start paying the Airbnb fees starting July 1st. I'll warn you, though, I'm going to charge you at-market rates, and I already know I can get five hundred bucks for a weekend!"

Five hundred? Our town may be dripping with Victorian

charm, but our too-dark, bunker-like split-level house is not. The idea of anyone wanting to pay that kind of money to stay with my parents, any money at all really, is hilarious.

But I'm not laughing.

"Isn't it wasteful for me to be paying rent over the summer when I'm going to have the cost of tuition and somewhere to live in the fall?" I ask carefully.

All of a sudden Dad goes from bombastic to squirmy, and Mom starts strangling a cloth napkin.

Uh-oh. Something's wrong. Something else.

"Did you . . . you've applied to some schools, right?" Mom says.

"Yes. To six schools. The deadline was just a few days ago."

"And you applied for scholarships as well?" she asks.

"Of course. I'll get some money, but it's only a few hundred here, a couple of thousand there. I'm not going to get a full ride anywhere. But Dad showed me the statement for the education fund just a few months ago—last August maybe?—and there's enough in there that, with some scholarship money, and if I work every summer, I should be fine."

Suddenly neither of them will meet my eyes.

"Guys, what's going on?"

"Tell her," Dad says to Mom.

"No!" Mom says with shockingly uncharacteristic sharpness, and then gets up out of her chair and starts backing away from the table. "You tell her."

For a second Dad looks from Mom to me, open despair in his expression, but then he scowls and lifts his chin with familiar belligerence, and says, "We got a little behind on some of our payments—"

"A little!" Mom mutters, shaking her head in a way that tells me this is recent news to her as well.

"Okay, more than a little," Dad says, without looking at her, "and we needed to take that money out."

"The education money?"

"Yes."

Mom has been edging her way, crumple-faced, toward the kitchen doorway. Now she disappears through it entirely.

"I promise you," Dad barrels on, "this is a blessing in disguise. You'll value an education you paid for yourself far more than one that's just handed to you. And maybe this'll make you realize you should study something useful, not this flaky art history stuff."

"Museum studies. And I—"

"Whatever. Waste of money."

"It's not!" I say, in a more strident voice than is wise given that there's no point trying to explain this to him—how for the longest time my dream was to be an artist, but how after tons of hard work that started feeling like banging my head against a wall, I realized that I don't have the talent. I'm good at making stuff but I'm not the real deal when it comes to painting and drawing, and no amount of "believe in yourself" slogans will change that. Plus, I don't enjoy instability, and I'm not sure I have the temperament for toiling in obscurity.

Still, it was a loss. But then I went to my first big city museum on a school trip and was clued in about all the other art-related jobs that exist—art historian, curator, exhibition designer—and suddenly I had a path forward that made sense. Dad helped me transform my room after that, but he never really understood the rest of it.

So all I can do now is repeat, "It's not a waste of money."

"That's the sort of courses girls used to take back in the day when they were only going to college to catch a husband.

If you think about it, in saving you from this fate, I'm actually being a feminist! After all we didn't raise you to be a housewife or some kind of socialite."

"S-socialite?" My head is spinning with the bizarre and terrible turn this conversation is taking. I want to say to him that the point of feminism would be that the choice is mine, not his. I want to grab my lifetime of good report cards and wave them in his face. I want to tell him that I look at his life, and Mom's and die inside at the thought of staying in this town and becoming like them—that I want to run like hell from here, and learn and grow and *do something*, lead a life that *means something*.

I want to say all these things, but they are still not the point. Dad has a way of confusing me about what the point actually is, to the degree that I shut down completely. Even when my future is at stake, which it clearly is.

"One day when you're successful and independent," he's saying, "and you haven't flaked out and squandered thousands of dollars your family painstakingly saved to go live like a wastrel on some Mediterranean island, dashing everyone's hopes and throwing away your future—"

"But Dad," I finally manage to say, hating myself for the pleading in my tone, "I'm not Jack, I'm not going to do that!"

"Damn right you're not!" Dad roars. "And when you haven't, you'll be able to look back and realize we did you a favor. You'll know you did it on your own and you owe nothing to anyone."

Least of all you!

Dad glares at me, and I stare back, furious and despairing and trying desperately to think of something to say that will change his mind, the situation, both.

And then the lights go out and Mom sails out of the kitchen, happy face freakishly restored, and carrying a cake.

A cake!

With lit candles on it and everything.

"Congratulations, Libby," she says, wearing a determined grimace. "Six schools!"

"Huh?"

"You applied to six schools! That's wonderful."

Six schools I probably can't go to anymore.

"I want us to think positively about this," she says, reading my pessimism loud and clear and seeming to smile harder in the face of it. "Make a wish and blow them out!"

What on earth. I glance from Dad, full of ire and bluster, to Mom, who's propping herself up with this bizarre-yet-fierce kind of optimism and looks like she might fall apart if I refuse.

They are so weird and I am so screwed.

But I take a deep breath in, and then blow.

Because this is apparently how things are going to be from now on in my family—give bad news, pretend it's good news, and then force everyone to eat cake.

3

PRIME DIRECTIVE

After this horror show of a dinner I need to get out of the house.

I bundle up for the January temperatures—warmest coat, hat, mittens (not gloves), scarf, and serious boots—and trudge the two blocks through the bitter, windy streets to my best friend Emma Leung's house.

Emma's dog, a rescue mutt named Ben, greets me with wild enthusiasm that cheers me, in spite of the fact that I'm too allergic to him to reciprocate. Emma's dad, John, stylishly rumpled in his signature librarian work clothes— button-down, vest, loose tie, and dark jeans—beams at me with almost equal enthusiasm. He escorts me into the high-ceilinged kitchen of their Victorian house, where, instead of having all gone their separate ways after dinner, Emma's family is still sitting around the table in the midst of some kind of debate.

"Come, sit!" John says.

I was hoping to talk to Emma alone, but just being here with her family has a thawing/warming effect on me. Plus she's in the middle of something with her younger brother Albert. She pauses mid-sentence to wave me toward the empty chair next to her. I check surreptitiously for dog hair, see none, then sit.

Emma's mom, Vivian, passes me a can of sparkling water and gives my shoulder a squeeze before sitting back down. Vivian is one of my favorite adults—she's smart, perceptive, has no patience for idiots, and she's also really sweet—all things that make her one of the most sought-after physicians in Pine Ridge. She and Emma look very much alike with their straight black, shoulder-length hair and athletic builds. I grin at her and then turn back to focus on the conversation.

"I mean, in the original the directive is more of a suggestion anyway," Emma is saying. "And Kirk violated it so many times."

Ah, *Star Trek*. I should have known.

"But I'm talking about the ethics of it. What would happen if we tried to apply it in the real world?" Albert asks, all earnestness.

"Uh, good luck with that," Emma says with an eye roll.

"I know, but just go with it," Albert says. "If you were put in charge of the world—"

"Which I should be—"

"Sure, sure," he says, waving this off. "So if you were in charge, would you institute the prime directive? And how strict would you be about not interfering?"

"I dunno," Emma says. "Sometimes interfering is the lesser evil."

"But in theory you're not supposed to interfere *at all*."

"Sometimes I think they should have interfered more," John throws in, and Albert looks at him aghast.

"That's colonialism!" Albert's face is red and he looks furious, but the fact is he's enjoying every minute of this. They all are.

"Think about the UN," Vivian says in her usual warm, reasonable tone. "The UN interferes with countries for their own good all the time."

"And yet there are often unforeseen consequences," John says, seeming to jump from one side of the argument to the other.

"We're all on the same planet," Emma says. "So I'm not sure it's a fair comparison."

"Perhaps," John says, a definite twinkle in his eye, "the question is whether we would want a species from another planet coming along to impose *their* rules on *us*, or save us if we need saving."

"You would consider letting an alien species dictate your life?" Albert says.

"What do you think, Libby?" Vivian asks me.

They all turn to look.

"Um . . ." Even though I'm used to Emma's family and their debates—which are Trek-oriented today, but might be about cloning or freedom of speech, or the best way to make popcorn tomorrow—I still freeze up when asked to join in.

There's no debating in my house and I don't even know how to do it.

"Come on, throw your hat in the ring," Albert urges me.

"My only *Star Trek* opinion is that the new Kirk is better than the old Kirk," I say, feeling like this, at least, is something I can contribute to.

"Ohhhhh!" Albert clutches at his chest. "You wound me."

"It's the hotness," Emma says.

"Shallow consideration," Albert says.

"It's true he's not ugly," Vivian says with a smirk.

"Mom!" Albert says, scandalized.

"You think Shatner was chosen for his intellect?" Emma says, and then they launch into a new debate, this one about casting and Hollywood reboots.

I sit there, just letting it wash over me. The incessant debating in this house only makes me tense when I'm put on the spot—otherwise I kind of like it. They get mad at each other sometimes, but it's all in the spirit of sharpening their wits and teasing out all the angles of a given subject. It's always been kind of a relief to me, to know I can come here and enter this whole other family reality.

But tonight it's also a bit depressing.

Emma must notice something in my demeanor, because after casting a few glances my way, she abruptly exits the debate, and leads me up to her very pink (with red and black accents) room.

She still has all the color-coded charts and graphs she made to track her college application process, plus her various scholarship options, on her magnet board. She went crazy over the details, even making pro and con charts involving walk scores and cafeteria ratings of various campuses. It's impressive, but she also drove herself into a frenzy and ended up having five panic attacks during the final three days before the applications were due, and only got hers into the portal on time because I came over and did the final steps for her.

I can tell from the shadows under her eyes that she's not completely recovered.

"Are you sure you still want all that stuff up there?" I ask her, and then study her body language—her breathing and how she's holding herself—for signs of trouble.

"I'll still need most of those in order to make decisions," she says, "but don't worry—I'm fine."

"You sure?"

"Yes," she says, dragging me over toward her many-pillowed daybed. I sit gingerly on the edge and keep my hands in my lap and remind myself not to touch my face. I can already feel the sniffles threatening, and it'll be much worse if I get doggy dander in my eyes or nose. "Just tired. Now, what's wrong with you?"

"My dad appears to be taking a 'prime directive' approach to parenting," I say, trying to couch it in ironic terms. "Prime directive in the cut-off-and-don't-help kind of way."

"Uh-oh," she says, seeing through my front immediately. "What happened?"

I tell her everything. I try to keep my tone light—sarcastic/mildly aggrieved, like this is just the latest chapter of antics that we can laugh about, instead of a bomb going off in my life. But the news is really worrisome, and Emma's expression gets more grim by the minute.

"First," she says, "you can live here. I don't even need to ask my parents. You can crash here all summer, no problem."

"Thanks, Em," I say. "But . . . Ben."

"Crap, of course."

"I'm good for a couple hours if I take medication in advance, but not to live full time. Even now, I haven't touched anything and I'm already starting to feel it."

"Okay then, second, I think you should talk to Jack."

"Jack is busy with his hashtag beachlife," I say, feeling myself tense. "What can he do?"

"He's your brother," Emma says. But in her family that means something different than it does in mine. She and Albert can squabble all day long, and he loves to pretend not to know her at school, but they're solid. I used to think that was true of Jack and me, even though we're further apart in age, but the last few years have made me wonder.

"Do you know how many times I've begged him to come home and work stuff out with Mom and Dad?" I ask, my bitterness coming through.

"This is different," Emma says.

"You don't understand. Every time I talk or text with him, I have to keep everything so light. The second I get serious, or start asking questions, he's out. He either starts laughing or just suddenly has to go."

"I'm sure he won't blow this off. He's the only person who knows your parents like you do. Plus . . ."

"Plus . . . ?"

"Maybe he still has some of his education money left. And if he's not using it . . ." She cocks an eyebrow at me.

"No." I shake my head. "No way I'm asking Jack for money. I'm not asking him for anything."

———

But once I'm back home and surrounded by my Van Gogh–blue walls, the star mobile, the string of twinkling lights that Dad helped me hang above my bed like a canopy, it starts to hit me in a different way. I turn in slow circles, seeing the poster prints of famous paintings, the abandoned camera equipment, the guitar I really do plan to learn how to play, my (still in use!) squash racket, my yoga mat, a few ribbons from my short-lived track-and-field career, the soccer cleats and tap shoes up in the closet alongside a box of failed art pieces that I can't bring myself to get rid of even though they never lived up to my vision. And finally, just above and to the right of my bed are the two beautiful sketches my friend Noah doesn't know I grabbed out of the recycling bin after he discarded them at art club. One is of a bird in flight and the other is a kind of cubist self-portrait that merges into a super modern building, with Noah's eyes staring from the wall. (Which sounds creepy, but is, instead, moody and cool and so him.)

What am I going to do with all of this stuff?

Who am I going to be without this room to come back to?

I want out of Pine Ridge, yes, but I always thought I'd be able to come back. Unlike Jack, I don't want to just fly off and leave it all behind forever.

Speaking of Jack, I decide to take Emma's advice after all, and text him.

Super hilarious crisis unfolding here. SOS.

It's really early/late in Greece, so I don't expect to hear back for hours, but he comes right back with: ???

Your fault, you totally ruined my life, lol.

This is hopefully light and jokey enough not to scare him off, but I'm still surprised when my phone rings about five seconds later.

"How did I ruin your life all the way from Greece?" Jack says without preamble.

"Got your attention, huh?" I say, trying to maintain my just-joking tone.

"How did I ruin your life . . . ?" Jack repeats.

"There's a very strong case to be made that you moving to Greece in the first place ruined my life," I say, stalking toward the window and pressing my forehead against the pane. There's no way to really convey this to him—how we've been living with his ghost, and the specter of what he did, how Dad has only stopped picking fights with every other person he sees because he doesn't actually see anyone anymore. How I went from trying like crazy to live up to the legacy of my smart, popular, sporty big brother to having to pretend he doesn't exist. But that's not why I'm talking to him. "To be fair, this time it's more that Dad is using you as justification for *him* ruining my life."

"Uh-oh," Jack says, sounding entirely serious. "Tell me."

Just hearing him say that, and having him not hang up, makes me feel better. I go through the whole story while pacing my room. Emma was right—he doesn't blow it off. He lets me rant and rave and then speculate about what happened to the money and panic over not having nearly enough scholarship money or personal savings, and then finally he says, "Well, it's not fair for him to blame me."

"You did run off with your tuition money."

"Sure, okay. But just trust me when I say you don't know everything," he says, "I had reasons."

"Yeah, your hashtag wrong side of the sunrise hashtag partytime hashtag beachlife."

"Ha ha."

"Jack, please come home," I ask him for the umpteenth time.

"I can't fix this for you, Libby."

"No, but you could fix things with them, and that would help so much. You don't understand how messed up everything's been."

"Let's focus on the current problem."

"Fine."

"I don't know what happened to the money, Libby, but I think you should consider it gone. It sounds like they got into some credit card debt—you'd be amazed at how fast that interest can build up if you don't pay in full every month. Or they just need it to pay the bills, the mortgage. You said he doesn't seem to be working . . ."

"No, just coming up with one useless scheme after another, and meanwhile Mom is putting in tons of overtime. I know her income isn't great, but that's a lot of money, Jack, to just be gone."

"Well," Jack says, sounding uneasy, "he might have put it in the stock market or something. Or lost it in the stock market."

"That sounds horribly plausible."

"Again, though, nothing you can do about it if that's the case."

"Sure, but—"

"Here's the thing: none of it changes what you have to do. Seriously. This might sound crazy, but part of what Dad said is true—you need to become more independent. And part of that is learning to detach from them. Everybody has to do that in one way or another, but with our parents, with him especially, it's really important. Whatever their problem was that they needed the money, that's not actually your problem."

"Except it was supposed to be my money. And six months ago it was still there."

"Yeah, that part sucks. And it does make me worry about them. But wait—what about your own savings account—how much is in it?"

From the time we were old enough to have bank accounts, Mom and Dad made both of us put most of our birthday and Christmas money, plus a portion of any income we made, into our own accounts. I was hoping to save up enough to buy a used car with that money, but obviously that's not happening. I tell Jack how much I have, and I can almost hear his brain doing the math during the pause that follows.

"Okay," he says, "that's not bad, but it won't be enough. What you need now is to get a job, ASAP."

He's right—I could drive myself bananas trying to figure out what's happened, but even if I do ferret out the truth, chances are I'll still be tuition-less.

"I can get back into babysitting and ask for some hours at the gift shop at the Inn—they hired me last summer, and again over the holidays."

"That's not going to make you enough money in time," Jack says. "You need a restaurant job. Something with tips. If you can get a serving gig, and then work your butt off and save like crazy, by spring you should be able to save up enough for rent, and then you go full time over the summer—combined with what you've got already, that might just get you enough for first year."

"Then what?"

"You work part time, you work summers, you apply for every possible scholarship you can find for second year, and if you have to, you go part time."

"That's a lot of ifs, mights, and should-be-able-tos, Jack."

"Well, the other option is to just give up. Is that what you want?"

"No."

"Then go get a job."

Jack has a way of cutting to the chase, which is one of the reasons I still rely on his advice on the rare occasions he chooses to give it, even though I'm permanently mad at him for leaving, and permanently mad at him for not telling me why.

I hang up, make a list of places to apply, and get to work on my résumé.

4

SHIT DISTURBER'S DAUGHTER

Applying for jobs turns out to be more challenging than expected.

We have a total of three restaurants—and one pub that also serves food— in Pine Ridge, plus two full-service coffee shops. Only one of the coffee shops is worth applying to, though, because the second one is so deliberately low-end that the owner actually named it Just Coffee, with the passive-aggressive message WE AIN'T GOT NO FANCY LATTES HERE on the sign under the name. (And in true small-town petty humor, the nicer coffee shop that this was aimed at then proceeded to rename itself Fancy Lattes.)

So there are exactly five places for me to apply. I am, of course, aware that before his basement "sabbatical," my dad was in the habit of getting into little kerfuffles all over town, including at some of the places I'm applying, but I can't afford to be picky. And he hasn't offended anyone for at least a couple of years now—at least not that I know of. Plus I have to have some faith that people can see that he and I are not the same person.

I start at Fancy Lattes, its dark wood-paneled walls, vin-

tage chandeliers, tin-tiled ceiling, and art from different local artists featured every few weeks making it the only place
in town that feels like it might be somewhere else—Paris,
maybe, with Picasso coming in to brood and argue about cub-
ism. I hand my résumé over the counter to the owner, Reg,
an aging rocker type with long, iron-gray hair and chains
hanging from his jeans.

"What's this?" Reg says, eyes narrowing.

"I wondered if maybe you might be hiring . . . ?"

"You serious?" Reg says.

"Very," I say.

"Aren't you Rick Stowe's kid?"

"Um, yes . . ." I say, wondering why he suddenly looks so
annoyed. Should I have bought a coffee first?

"I can't hire the daughter of the man who boycotted me
and then trash-talked me all over town," Reg says, looking
distinctly unfriendly.

"Oh, but . . ." That was a long time ago and I've been a
customer here many times since. I'd assumed he was over it.

"All about the size of our take-out cups!" Reg says, voice
rising. "He stood here, in my place, screaming his stupid
head off at me. Then stood out front screaming his head off
some more. And now you want a job?"

"Well . . . yes," I manage to say, despite my fast-warming
face and all the people now staring at me.

"No way," he says, practically shouting. "Hard pass."

"Oh. Um." If I could find a way to vanish in a puff of
smoke right now, that would be great. As it is, Reg is handing
me back my résumé, and all I can do is take it with a mum-
bled "thank you anyway," and get out of there as fast as possible.

Out on the street I hustle down the block, hot from embarrassment despite the icy air. I pass Just Coffee, recalling how Dad took his business there after boycotting Fancy Lattes, and briefly consider putting it back on the list of places to apply. But Dad got banned from there eventually, too.

Right then. I take a few breaths, watching the fog of each exhale dissipate, and decide to go to Maggie's Diner next. Surely Maggie won't yell at me—Maggie is sweet. And she does give me a lovely smile when I pass her my résumé and ask my question about employment.

But then she says, with a less lovely smile, "I was on Town Council with your father."

"Ah . . ." I say in a one-size-fits-all tone that I hope can be interpreted as anything from "Ah, yes, my dad spoke so well of you" if by some chance she's a fan of my dad to "Ah, well, that's unfortunate but look what a friendly, inoffensive person I am in comparison . . ." if she's not. Because I don't know what happened with my dad and the town council, only that his tenure was short.

The slight wince Maggie makes before saying, "Would you consider yourself to be a team player?" tells me she's in the non-fan category.

"Yes, definitely. Like my mom! You know my mom, Andrea, don't you? She's concierge at the Inn? I worked in the gift shop there, and . . ." I trail off, feeling almost too pathetic to live.

Maggie gives me a pitying look and says she'll get back to me in a couple of months.

Awesome.

At 50 Mile, which is connected to the Inn, and where they only use ingredients that come from within a fifty-mile radius, they tell me straight up that they have nothing against my dad (as though this needs to be clarified), and love my mom, but that they only hire servers with a minimum of two years' experience.

At Crawler's Pub, things start out more promising. Lyle, the string bean of a man who manages it, takes one look at the last name on my résumé, starts laughing uproariously, and says, "Rick Stowe's kid? Your father is a first-rate shit disturber. What the hell's he been up to?"

"He's . . . uh . . ." *Plotting my downfall via Airbnb.* "Working on a few things."

"The guy's a legend. Knows how to stick it to the man, that's for sure," Lyle says, then points to a barstool. I sit, he pours me a soda, and then he starts regaling me with stories about my dad.

"You know that big moose statue in front of the library?" Lyle says.

I nod.

"Your dad tried to unseat the mayor with that moose."

"What?"

"This was maybe before you were born," Lyle says, clapping his hands together and rubbing them with remembered glee. "Mayor was up for reelection, no one running against her, and your dad thought that was wrong. 'Everyone should be challenged,' is what he said. 'Helps them grow.' "

I roll my eyes—this sounds all too familiar.

"But he didn't want the job himself and couldn't convince anyone else to run," Lyle continues. "So he registered the moose as a candidate and ran a campaign—with slogans and a real platform and everything. 'Mr. Moose for Mayor.' "

"Oh my God."

"It was a good campaign too—pointed and kinda funny. Mr. Moose even got some votes! I thought that was great but your dad—he got a little too caught up in it all, and he took it hard that the moose didn't win. I dunno how he ever thought that's what would happen, but I had him in here drowning his sorrows for weeks after that."

"Wow," I say, thinking that, as with everything about my dad, this story is a mixed bag—surprising, hilarious, but ultimately sad.

Lyle continues with the anecdotes—some I've heard, many I could do without. It's not a typical job interview, but I feel like it's going well until Lyle tells me he has no openings at the moment.

"Still, if anything happens, I'll keep you in mind," he says as I head for the door, trying not to let my shoulders slump in disappointment.

I thank him and trudge over to my final destination—the bistro next to the brokerage Dad used to work for and where he used to have lunch a couple of times a week. We went there as a family, too, after Jack's football games back when we were normal-ish and did things together.

I've saved this one for last, thinking it might be my best chance. Because whatever else, Dad is always nice to servers, and a good tipper. In fact, he loves to say you can judge a person's character by the way they treat dogs and waiters. I'm pretty sure this bit of "wisdom" is problematic for both dogs and waiters, but in this case he means well.

My hope rises when I see the HELP WANTED sign out front, and rises further when the manager—the same one who's been there for years—gives me a big, welcoming smile.

But then I tell her why I'm here, and her smile wilts and suddenly she's glancing nervously toward the wall the bistro shares with Dad's old brokerage and saying, "I don't want any trouble," and then muttering something about politics.

My heart sinks as I realize she must be one of the people

who received Dad's infamous email—the one that ended his career. Agents get fired by clients sometimes, but it takes a lot to get fired from your brokerage—they're usually happy to keep you even if you're a deadbeat and all they're collecting is your desk fee. But Dad used the brokerage's newsletter list to send out a fiery partisan email during the last election, making it look like the brokerage was endorsing one party over another, infuriating everyone, and that was it. Neither of the other two real estate companies in town would take Dad on after that, and when he tried to go independent he couldn't get any clients, because by then everyone—even those who agreed with his politics—considered him a loose cannon.

"We're not hiring, hon," the manager says.

"But . . . the sign . . ." I say, pointing to it.

"Oh it's, uh, just stuck there," she says, with the most unconvincing shrug ever. "Sorry."

Right.

———

I'm about to give up on the serving idea and start applying for retail jobs, which won't get me to college, but will hopefully help me pay rent, when Noah (of the stolen art on my wall) remembers the Goat.

The Goat isn't in Pine Ridge. It's out on the highway, between Pine Ridge and the next town. It's part gritty roadside pub, part failed chain restaurant, and under new ownership since last spring. I make a call, the owner agrees to meet me, and it feels like a miracle.

It's snowing on the day of the interview, and Noah offers to borrow one of his dad's snowplow trucks to drive me there.

I tell myself that the extra makeup and the cute dress with black tights and impractical-for-snow heeled boots, not to mention the nerves, are for the interview. I can't even bring myself to look at Noah as I climb in, so there's no way to notice whether he notices, which he shouldn't because he has a completely perfect, albeit long-distance, girlfriend.

But then, in his usual, overly blunt way, Noah says, "Whoa, you look hot."

He doesn't mean anything by it.

Well, he *means* it, but Noah would say the same to Emma, or our friend Yaz, or even Boris (Emma's boyfriend, and my ex—long story) if Boris ever managed to look hot, versus wet-behind-the-ears cute. Noah tends to be a bit filter-less, but he's also annoyingly honorable and would never cheat on Ava, so it's not a come-on.

Still.

"Thanks," I say, then finally look over at him, and in an effort to be casual add, "And you look . . . a tad scruffy, hair verging on a mullet, but clean."

"You don't like my almost-mullet?" he says, putting the truck in reverse.

I do like it. He could do whatever he wanted with his hair—dark brown, straight with tips that start to curve up at the ends when it gets long—and I would like it. Just like I like his soulful brown eyes, aquiline nose, winter-pale skin, narrowish face, and all the other features that somehow over the last couple of years transformed (in my eyes anyway, and unfortunately while I was supposed to be in love with some-one else) from ordinary to remarkable.

"I'm just bugging you," I say.

"Ya gotta try harder than that," he says, starting off down my street. "Like, attack my character, or argue that Georgian architecture is better than Gothic."

"Oh, I would never!" I say, feigning shock.

We lapse into comfortable silence—well, as comfortable as it can be when I'm breathing in the cinnamon soap/beautiful boy smell of him and having visions of leaning over and kissing his neck, and then mentally slapping myself for the thought.

We turn out of my neighborhood toward the highway. I watch the big, fluffy snowflakes land on the windshield, each one just starting to melt before the wipers dispatch them, and try to chill out. It's not too far to the Goat. Close enough that as soon as the snow melts I'd be able to save money by riding my bike there. If they hire me, that is. And that's a big if.

"You nervous?" he says.

"Huh? Oh, yeah, a bit. I'm just hoping they'll give me a chance."

"Want me to come in and vouch for you? I happen to know you're a very upstanding human being."

"No, but thanks. Any idea why this place is called the Goat? I don't go out much these days."

"Apparently the goat used to be a donkey—"

"I remember the donkey."

"Yeah, it's memorable. And because it was so visible from the roof, the new owners didn't want to take it down. But apparently, the old chain restaurant owns the right to the image of that particular donkey, so they couldn't keep it as is. Instead, they decided to modify it. Had someone come in and add horns and turn it into a goat. It's pretty funny, actually, though I dunno if the funny part is intentional. We'll be able to see it in a minute or two."

The goat on the roof comes into view soon, and it is indeed funny—kitschy and weird and rather endearing.

We make up a series of names for it, laughing all the way down the highway and into the parking lot, where Noah wishes me luck and waits while I go in.

And finally something good happens: They do not know my dad at the Goat, and they don't mind my lack of experience.

Noah and I go to Just Coffee to celebrate (Reg was so horrible to me that I'm actually considering following in my dad's footsteps and boycotting Fancy Lattes), and I start working two days later.

5

KYLE

Within a week I've memorized the menu, done my three shadow training shifts, and am working as much as they'll let me.

The job is challenging, but mostly in a good way, and my coworkers are friendly enough once I start to prove myself. The only minor annoyance is Kyle, whom I start out disliking on principal after he tells me he's only working "for fun" and for extra cash to "pimp" his "ride"—i.e., the perfectly good truck his parents bought for him.

Kyle is, overall, just too carefree for his own good, walking around the Goat with his shaggy, bleach-blond hair and ocean-colored eyes, looking for all the world like a surfer who's lost his beach. Nobody should look like that in the middle of winter.

But . . . there's nothing actually wrong with Kyle as a person, and despite my overall feeling that he's too attractive/privileged/charming/chill to be real, he starts to wear me down. He works hard, he's fun, he busses a lot of my tables in his capacity as host, and he saves my butt on multiple occasions by delivering food and drinks when I'm in the weeds.

And then I take as many extra shifts as I can get during the March Break, and lo and behold, so does Kyle.

"Most of my friends are on vacation somewhere," I say to him the first Friday night as we sit in a booth doing the last batch of cutlery roll-ups. "How come you're not?"

"Eh," he says with a dismissive wave, "my mom and sister went to Florida to see my grandparents, but I didn't feel like it. I've been a bunch of times."

"Poor you."

"No, no," he says, missing or ignoring my sarcasm. "I just wanted to stay home with my dad this year. We leave our dirty socks everywhere, eat pizza, binge-watch bad TV, act like bachelors. That's its own kind of vacation."

"Dirty socks on the floor equals vacation? Sounds stinky."

"Exactly." He gives me a dazzlingly unapologetic grin. "How 'bout you?"

"No vacation to beg off from and I need the money from the extra shifts for school next year—tuition, books, housing. Or, failing that, for the year after. Turns out I have, uh, less money saved than I thought and now I'm scrambling."

"You shoulda told me! I can hook you up!"

"With what?"

"The best tables, obviously. I am *the host*," he says the way someone else might say, "I'm the king!"

"You can't do that," I protest. "Other people need the money too."

"Don't worry, I'm not going to shaft anybody," he says, twirling a roll-up in one hand like a mini baton. "But I'm starting to know who the big spenders are, and I can send some your way."

"Thanks, but I'm good."

"Okay, I won't," he says, and then winks, looking ridiculous in a baseball hat with goat horns seeming to grow out the top of it.

He does, though. He gives me fewer kid birthday parties, more couples on dates, more thirsty postgame sports teams, and lots of men, including Perry Ackerman.

Eight days later, on my final March Break shift—a Saturday night—Noah comes in with Ava, who's visiting from the city. Just what I need at the end of a ten-day stretch in which I've worked five split shifts (lunch + dinner) and three closing shifts (dinner until close—as late as two a.m. by the time the cleaning up is done), done zero homework, and had no sleep. I am haggard, smell like a deep fryer, and feel about as sexy as a dead cactus.

Ava, whom Noah met while staying with his mom last summer, is painfully adorable and about as opposite from me in looks as a person can be. She's short and tiny-but-curvy with curly black hair and blue eyes so big and round they could belong to an anime character. I'm not hideous or anything, but I feel like a bag of sand next to Ava. I feel very medium compared to her—medium height, medium build, and sand-colored all over. Even my eyes can't decide between being brown and green and therefore come out looking almost the same shade as the rest of me, only shinier.

But you'd have to have a heart of stone not to like Ava. She's sweet and smart and tonight she seems a little down. They both do—probably because she's leaving tomorrow. And so, as part of my ongoing efforts to not act jealous, or give my feelings away whatsoever, I take it upon myself to cheer them up. I'm so successful that they stay for hours, laughing and canoodling and lingering over dessert and coffee.

Which serves me right, I suppose.

They do eventually leave, but not before Ava hugs me

about a million times and Noah thanks me sincerely enough to make me feel like the worst person on earth, since all I really want is for her to go away and never come back.

Finally, when the last stragglers are gone, the sections are all cleared and wiped down with vinegar, ketchups are married, roll-ups are rolled, sugars, salts, and peppers are filled, and chairs are put up, it's over. My feet and knees are throbbing, my brain feels like it's just survived a hurricane, my heart aches, and I have that end-of-shift tired/wired feeling that sometimes takes hours to come down from no matter how exhausted I am.

I scarf down a bowl of lemon rice made with fresh curry leaves, ginger, green chilies, and lentils. Maya makes a big pot of something simple for the staff every day that we can help ourselves to, and it's always ridiculously tasty. (Plus I never knew until I started working here that curry came in any form but powder.) Feeling nourished and slightly less jangled, I drift over to the bar, where Nita, as she does sometimes on weekends, pours beer for the remaining staff. Kyle and I are underage, but all the customers, plus Dev and Maya, are gone, so she winks and pours each of us one too. It starts to turn into a bit of a party, but Nita's too cautious to let it continue very long, which is how I end up inviting everyone to come over and hang out in my basement.

"My parents are at a funeral," I tell Brianna and Kyle.

"At one in the morning?" Kyle says. "Cool funeral."

"Ha ha. It was today, but they're gone overnight. First time they've left me alone, actually."

"Well, then we've gotta come over, babe," Brianna says. "On principle."

A few people stop to grab more alcohol from their places on the way, and we also do a careful raid of my parents' bar, but the party is low-key until Kyle spots the old vinyl record player.

"Whoa, does this thing work?"

"I think so."

Within a couple of minutes he has it up and running, '70s disco playing, volume cranked. Brianna has a strobe light app on her phone, and somebody rolls back the rug so we can dance on the tile floor.

Kyle turns into a hilarious dancing maniac. He jumps and slides and gyrates, and pulls out one record after another. Soon we're all dancing. I grin and laugh and sway, my aches and pains forgotten, my money and future worries forgotten, my impossible crush and guilty feelings about my crush shoved aside, and lightness stealing over me.

Things eventually start to die down, people leaving in twos and threes, and then I'm alone.

Alone with Kyle, that is.

"I don't think I should drive," he says, the manic gleam still in his eyes. "Can I crash here?"

"Sure, um . . ." I'm not entirely sober myself. "You can sleep down here on the couch. But won't your dad worry?"

"As long as I don't drink and drive, he's cool. I just have to text him."

Kyle sends the text while I stand there waiting, swaying a bit on my feet.

"Let me get you a pillow and some blankets," I say.

"I'll help."

"No, that's—" He's following me up the stairs anyway. "Oh. Okay, thanks."

I feel him close behind me as I head down the dim hallway and push open the door to my room.

"Do you want a T-shirt too, or—"

I never finish the sentence because all of a sudden Kyle is kissing me.

He's kissing me, and I'm kissing him back.

It is not part of the plan.

And I have a split second of thinking I shouldn't be kissing Kyle, because of Noah.

But Noah's with Ava. Right this second he's with her.

And damn, can Kyle kiss. Kyle can kiss so well he could give lessons. For the good of humanity he *should* give lessons.

I let my arms wind up around Kyle's neck and let him press in closer. We make out in the doorway until standing starts to seem counterproductive, and then we stumble over to my bed.

"No sex, okay?" I murmur in his ear. "I just want to mess around."

"Fine, sure," he says, and strips my shirt off of me.

All right, then.

Kyle comes on strong, hot, and hard to stop, but he's also really fun.

I lose most of my clothing and so does he, and there's a lot of rolling around and heavy breathing, but everything's playful and unserious until suddenly I feel him right up against me.

I pull back. "Wait, no, wait."

And he says, "Sure, sure, okay. Relax," and applies his lips to my collarbone and his hands to other places.

I close my eyes and say, "Okay," and relax, and then relax some more.

And then all of a sudden it's happening. The thing I said no to.

I gasp.

"It's okay," he says, and continues.

It's okay . . .

"Condom," I manage to whisper, and we stop while I get one from the back of my bedside table drawer.

I didn't want to do this, but now it seems too late.

Oh well, I think but do not say, *I guess we're doing it.*

6

NAKED IN THE DRIVEWAY

The next thing I know I'm trapped under Kyle's arm, watching him sleep.

I can barely breathe.

It's the weight of his arm, I figure. Or maybe the smell of him—the now-stale beer on his breath, the sweat, a whiff of restaurant mixed with day-old cologne. Or maybe it's just that there's a naked boy in my bed . . . and I am so thoroughly disgusted with myself.

I pry his arm off of me, escape from the bed without waking him, grab some clothes from the pile on top of my dresser, and make a beeline for my never-been-renovated, genuine vintage, mint-green-and-peach-colored bathroom. Once inside, I lock the door, brush my teeth, and take the kind of shower that would have my dad pounding on the door and threatening to turn the water off if he were home.

Finally I get out, wrap myself in a bath sheet, and stare at my foggy outline in the mirror.

I feel scorched and soiled, and I hate what I see there.

Someone who let that happen after saying it wasn't going to happen.

Someone who didn't even put up a fight.

Still, it's over.

I put on deodorant, get dressed in the sweats and T-shirt I grabbed, and stick my hair up into a messy bun. Not wanting to be anywhere near Kyle, I head down to the basement with garbage and recycling bags to clean up. It doesn't take long, and soon I'm outside the kitchen door, shoving the garbage in the garbage cans and the empty bottles in our neighbor's recycling bin, crossing my fingers they won't notice the addition.

Then my eyes fasten on Kyle's truck, sitting conspicuously in the driveway.

Crap.

The early birds are starting to chirp and soon it'll be light.

I need Kyle out of here. Now.

I rush back inside to wake him, but he won't budge. I try poking him, rolling him, saying his name, but all that happens is he jams himself into the corner and throws an arm over his face.

Yikes. I need help.

Emma only got back from vacation yesterday, and it's an insane time to call anyone, but I go to the front hall and grab my phone anyway.

There's precedent for this. I went to her house in the middle of the night twice last year to help when she was having a panic attack and didn't want to wake her parents, and we've always promised to be there for one another, no questions asked.

Well, she *will* have questions.

But she'll save most of them for later. I hope.

I hit CALL, wait while the phone rings once, then I hang up and dial again knowing her Do Not Disturb setting lets the second call through. I'm just about to give up when she answers.

"Libby?" she whispers groggily. "What's wrong?"

"My parents went out of town overnight, and I sort of accidentally had a small party with some of my coworkers."

"Uh-oh. Is your house trashed?"

"No, but there's a boy in my bed."

She whistles. "You devil. What boy?"

"Just someone from work. He didn't think he should drive, so I let him . . ."

have sex with me

wtf

" . . . uh, crash here. But I need him out of here in case my parents come back early, or the neighbors notice his giant freaking truck in the driveway, but he's dead to the world."

"Is he breathing?"

"Dead *to the world*, Em, not actually dead."

"I'll be there in five."

True to her word, Emma arrives, on foot, five minutes later. She looks far more alert and put together than seems fair, dressed in cute, color-coordinated tennis wear, her eyes snapping with curiosity, and only a pillow crease on her cheek giving any hint that she was fast asleep ten minutes ago.

"How drunk was he?" she whispers as we head down the hallway toward my room.

"Drunk but capable," I say, and then feel myself flush and rush to add, "like, not stumbling around or passing out."

"Will he be safe to drive?"

"I . . . think so?"

"Do you have his keys?"

"They're probably in his pants pocket. Hang on." I creep into my room, grab his pants from the floor, and drag them back into the hallway.

Emma's eyes widen. "You didn't mention he wasn't wearing them!"

"Oh, yeah, um . . ." I focus hard on the pants, give them a shake, and hear something that jingles like keys. "I guess I should probably warn you: he's not dressed."

"You mean he's *naked*?"

"Well, last time I looked he had the covers pulled up to his chest."

Emma snorts and I shush her.

"I'm sorry," she says, trying to stifle her laughter, "it's just . . . the look on your face . . ."

I start to laugh too, but it turns into more of a shiver, and Emma's amusement evaporates.

"Hey, whoa, Libby. You okay?"

"I'm fine," I say, holding the pants away from my body and trying not to look at them. "I'll be fine once he's out of here."

"Okay, let's get it done, then."

I get the keys from Kyle's pocket, hand them to Emma, and we go in. On my way to the bed I casually kick my very-obviously-discarded-on-the-floor clothing to the side, hoping she won't notice it . . . which she does not, due to the fact that she's now stopped in her tracks and staring, wide-eyed, at Kyle.

"Oh my," she whispers.

Kyle is uncovered from the waist up with one leg also thrown out toward the edge of the bed and looking extravagantly debauched. I busy myself with finding the rest of his clothing, folding it neatly, and setting it on the end of the bed with the pants, and try not to look.

Meanwhile, Emma reaches over to give Kyle a gentle push, to zero effect. She tries again, and then harder, and finally gets a moan out of him. Then we both poke at him, and this time he groans, says "Piss off," and then rolls away, putting his back to us.

"Nice manners your boy has," Emma says.

"He's not my boy."

"We could just whip the duvet off," she suggests.

I shake my head. I need him covered almost as much as I need him out of the house.

"Or douse him with cold water." Emma leans in close and sniffs. "He still reeks of booze, Lib. You know where he lives?"

"Not in Pine Ridge—I think Bayview."

"We could drive him."

"But then we'd be stuck there with no way to get back."

"Shoot. Okay, so we just get him and the truck away from your house, and leave them somewhere nearby."

"Let's just worry about getting him up."

Emma zips out to get a cup of water from the bathroom just in case we need it, then we get to work, finally having to roll Kyle right off the bed before there's any response from him. He lands on the floor with the duvet, groaning and cursing.

"Kyle!" I say. "You have to go."

"I'm sleeping," he mumbles, making a baby face.

"Cute faces aren't going to cut it, dude," Emma says, and then starts flicking water at him.

He squeezes his eyes shut and stays put.

"Here," I say, then I reach for the cup and (unaware this is soon to become a theme) dump it on his head.

"What the hell . . . ?" Kyle roars to life and we leap back.

"You have to leave," I say.

"Fine." Kyle gets up, keeping the duvet wrapped around him, and heads out of my room. We catch up with him in the foyer, where he's shoving bare feet into his sneakers.

"Wait!" I sputter. "You can't just . . . Your clothes!"

"Give 'em here," he growls.

I shove the bundle toward him and prepare to turn my back while he dresses. But he just pulls the clothing to his chest, opens the front door, and marches out onto the driveway. Then he opens the door of the truck, which he must have left unlocked, and stuffs himself, duvet and all, into the driver's seat.

"Where's my keys?" he says, dopey and petulant. "Who stole my keys?"

Out of the corner of my eye I see Emma tucking them behind her back.

"We need to know if you're sober enough to drive," I tell him.

"Is this how you treat all your lovers?" Kyle says, looking both wounded and peeved.

"Only the ones who won't leave when asked," I say, and avoid looking at Emma.

"Look, we can drive you," Emma offers, and then we exchange a glance, during which we decide via best friend telepathy not to tell him our plan to leave him somewhere nearby to sober up. "I'm sure you don't want your 'lover' to be grounded for life because someone sees you, or God forbid her parents come home early and find you here in the driveway . . ."

"Sure, sure, but I'm fine," he says, and then launches himself back out of the truck onto the driveway, still wearing the duvet. "Watch."

He lines himself up along the edge of the driveway and marches forward with excess deliberation. Then, clearly pleased with his performance, he closes his eyes and lifts his arms for a higher degree of difficulty . . . which of course causes the duvet to land on the pavement, which means that instead of being gone quickly and inconspicuously, Kyle is now naked in my driveway.

"Enough!" I hiss, scooping the duvet up and throwing it over him.

"No driving for you, mister," Emma says, and helps me propel him to the passenger side of the truck and then push him inside, where he immediately starts snoring.

"Is he asleep?" Emma asks me.

"Yep," Kyle says, "he is."

We drive to the gas station with the separate coffee kiosk inside (officially the cheapest date location in Pine Ridge) and park around back.

"Kyle," Emma says.

He doesn't respond.

"You think he's faking?" she asks me.

"Who knows?"

We get Kyle coffee and a doughnut and leave him a note on the dashboard. Then we give the keys to Emma's cousin Jimmy, who works in the kiosk, instructing him not to give them to Kyle unless he's sober.

"And dressed," I say under my breath.

Jimmy winks at Emma, and we decline his offer of more coffee and leave.

"You trust Jimmy?" I ask her as we start walking.

"I kept it secret when he was growing pot in his parents' attic a couple of years ago, so . . . yeah, mostly. You okay?"

"I—sure," I fumble. "But . . . can we forget this ever happened?"

She gazes at me, a million unasked questions in her eyes, then says, "I can if you can."

7

TEA

Forgetting about Kyle is easy.

My attraction to him has conveniently vanished, and been (inconveniently) replaced by distaste bordering on revulsion. I've been checking the weekly schedule Dev posts and swapping and/or giving away shifts where we're both scheduled, and it's not that hard to ignore his texts. Though he does keep sending them. Whenever I do have to work with him I'm perfectly friendly, but not friendly like someone who's ever so much as kissed him.

And as for the sex, I just don't let myself think about it.

Admittedly, if I do accidentally think about it, I start to feel queasy. And if his arm brushes mine at work, or he gets close enough for me to smell him, it's an effort not to flinch or wrinkle my nose. Not that he smells bad, but it reminds me, and then I feel like an idiot for having such a weird reaction. I mean, I had sex with him, and I regret it, but life goes on. No big deal.

And then comes a day that messes up everything.

It's a warm Friday in April, and "social issues" week at school, which means daily assemblies, each highlighting a different issue.

Boris, tall, thin, and weed-like, with his big eyes and a wild shock of gelled-up, light brown hair, is hovering alongside Emma and me. We're being bumped and jostled toward the gym, having just come from class together. Then I spot Yaz and Noah trying to push through—Yaz's long, bright red hair and glowing pale skin visible from afar, and Noah easy to spot because of his height and because my eyes can always find him. They reach us just as Boris opens a chocolate bar and Emma swipes it and takes a bite.

"Hey, give that back," Boris says.

"You want it back, you'll have to come and get it," Emma says, then sticks her tongue out with the partially masticated hunk of chocolate on it, and Boris moves toward her like he's going to take it from her with his mouth.

"Eww, you guys," I say before I can stop myself, "spare me!"

They practically jump away from one another, Boris flushing and Emma looking at me with stricken eyes.

"We're so sorry!"

"Oh, for God's sake, I'm not jealous, I'm grossed out," I snap. "If you could see yourselves you would be too."

I can tell by their chastened expressions that they don't believe me, but I push my irritation down because this situation is my own fault. I'm the one who was too cowardly to break up with Boris when I realized I just wasn't into him anymore, and instead messed with his head until he broke up with me, and then pretended to be heartbroken about it. I know—not my best moment, but my intention was to spare his feelings. (Word to the wise, this doesn't work.) Instead it drove Boris to Emma—looking first for advice, then for solace, and you can imagine the rest—their pained, guilt-ridden confession that they'd fallen in love, my also-pained, chagrinned acceptance of it, and all the ensuing awkwardness as we all tried to move forward.

Anyway, their relationship still bugs me, but not for the reasons they think.

"Sorry, didn't mean to be harsh," I say, trying to soften my tone.

"It's fine," Emma says.

"Yeah, we're sorry," Boris says, looking at me with his puppy-dog eyes and causing me another wave of irritation.

Boris is a perfectly nice person, I remind myself.

Luckily, the logjam in the hallway starts to clear, and soon we're all finding spots on the gym floor. I make sure to get Yaz on one side of me and Noah on the other. Emma starts out in front of me, where I can conveniently see right over her head, but then Boris squishes in closer to her, which causes me to have to crane my neck to see the podium.

Boris is not trying to annoy me. He's not even thinking of me. But still, ugh.

The lights dim, and we're all expecting the usual thing—a play with earnest twentysomething actors, or statistics and slogans by a well-meaning adult—the same stuff we've been hearing for years.

I'm fully intending to snooze through the session, maybe with my head on Noah's shoulder (what? He has a good shoulder), but the presentation starts with loud, dramatic music that seems set to foil my plans. Then all of a sudden there are massive photos of couples making out being projected onto the gym wall, followed by a video of the same.

Noah goes, "Whoa," Yaz claps a hand over her mouth, all over the gym people are giggling and whooping, and Emma turns back toward me and shrieks, "It's a sex talk!"

The teachers are shushing us to no avail, then suddenly a

powerful voice booms from the loudspeaker, cutting through the noise.

"How do you know when someone wants to have sex with you?"

This prompts nervous laughter and a few whistles.

The images on the wall appear faster and faster, but now, interspersed with the sexy parts are crying faces and couples arguing, and the music goes discordant, and finally it all stops and the lights come up.

At the front, with a microphone, stands the owner of the booming voice. She's mid-thirties, medium height, dressed in a crisp button-down, blazer, and jeans. She has golden-brown skin and eyes of arresting intensity, but what's most striking is that she's so obviously filled with purpose. It's in her stance, her tone, and the way she looks at us. She's here for a reason and you get the feeling she'll stay until she's achieved it.

"How do you know when someone wants to have sex with you?" she asks us again. "The answer should be simple. They *tell you*. How do you know when someone *doesn't* want to have sex with you?"

No one answers.

"Come on now, you all know at least this much," she says, voice dripping with disappointment. "They say 'no.'"

I swallow.

"So, when someone says 'yes' to having sex with you, that means they *consent*. When they say 'no' that means they *do not consent*. But there's more to consent than yes and no. I am Dahlia Brennan, your public health nurse, and I'm here to clear a few things up."

She proceeds to go through some sexual assault statistics, accompanied by big graphs projected on the wall. I stare at the numbers, unable to look away.

Then some idiot at the back starts chanting, "Bring back the porn!"

"You 'bring back the porn' people are the ones who need this information the most," Ms. Brennan says. "Consider this: Do you want to be any good at sex?"

That shuts them up.

"Because communication is an essential part of being good at it. And the first and most basic communication you need to have is that you both consent. For that you need to know what consent is and isn't. Let's go through some scenarios. Obviously if someone says 'no' to sex and you physically force them to do it, that's rape, which comes under the legal umbrella of sexual assault in most places. But how about if someone is drunk—let's not pretend that nobody in high school ever gets drunk—" she says with a knowing look.

At this there's a chorus of snorts and snickers.

"So in the most extreme, if someone is drunk and then passes out. Is it okay to have sex with them? Give me a show of hands for yes."

Nobody raises a hand.

"How about asleep? Okay to have sex with someone who is asleep?"

No hands go up.

"Exactly. Passed out or sleeping, a person cannot consent to sex. This means—in case anyone's looking for a loophole—that if they said they wanted to have sex with you but then passed out or fell asleep, it's not okay to have sex with them. Also if they pass out *while you're having sex with them* and you continue to have sex with them, that's also not okay. But what if they're just a little tipsy?"

Another idiot behind us whispers something about "beer

goggles" and a few people chuckle, but Ms. Brennan silences them with a look.

"How drunk is too drunk? Err on the side of caution. I would say that too drunk to drive is too drunk to consent. Stumbling, out of balance, slurring, incoherent is too drunk. Of course sometimes it's hard to tell how drunk someone really is, which means you could have what you think is a great time with someone, only to find yourself accused of sexual assault. Or you could wake up one morning and realize that you had sex you really didn't want to have, with someone you'd never have done it with sober. And that's not a good feeling."

It certainly isn't.

"This stuff gets ugly, people, and it gets complicated," Dahlia Brennan is saying like she's read my thoughts. "You don't have to physically force someone to have sex for it to be a crime. Which is why you need to make sure you have consent—enthusiastic and *ongoing* consent. Check with the person, ask if they're okay with what's happening, stop if they seem uncomfortable, and above all you need to hear a 'yes.' And you might get a 'yes' in the beginning that changes to a 'no' later when things are really moving. In that case and always, the 'no' reigns supreme."

I want to crawl out of my skin.

But all I can do is sit, staring straight ahead, hoping no one looks at me.

"Moving on from the alcohol questions, can someone consent *without* saying 'yes'? They can, but nonverbal signals are too easily misinterpreted and could lead you to make a mistake that could change your life forever, so I advise you to get a definite and enthusiastic yes. On the flip side, can it be assault if the person never says no? Yes it can. If someone is pulling away from you, or is pushing your hands off of them, or freezes, or becomes rigid, or if they are *crying while you're having sex with them,* time to stop. Even if they're just lying there not seeming into it, it's time to check in, and probably time to stop. If you then find out that they're crying from joy because you're such a hot lover, awesome. If not, you damned well better stop. Because sometimes somebody is too afraid or too overwhelmed and/or things are happening faster than they have time to process it, and they are *not consenting* but just haven't found themselves able to say so."

This gets worse by the second but Dahlia Brennan's not done.

"I've got one more tricky one. Just because someone has had sex with you before, does it mean they have to have sex with you again? Call out the answer."

"No," A bunch of people say.

"Even if they're your girlfriend or boyfriend?"

There's some muttering and whispering at this, but again a bunch of people say, "No."

"That's right. No. And here's another thing to think about: If someone—your girlfriend, boyfriend, lover, whatever—says no repeatedly and you whine and wheedle, beg, threaten, or otherwise pressure them into saying yes, that's not consent. That's called coercion and can be considered sexual assault."

Something is now exploding inside my head.

"Whining, wheedling, begging" is exploding inside my head. "Aversion" and "whining, wheedling, begging, pressuring" are exploding inside my head.

Understanding is exploding inside my head . . .

And now I'm staring at the back of Boris and wishing for a transporter beam, a tornado, a flying carpet, a shrinking pill—

She keeps going, turning the lights back off and playing a video with an analogy about offering someone a cup of tea and how you wouldn't pour it down their throat, or force them to drink it if they'd said no thank you. How you wouldn't make the tea in the first place if someone said they didn't want it.

I can't even breathe.

I'm going to break out in hives, go up in flames, die.

———

The very second the presentation is over I leap to my feet, cut through the crowd, and make a beeline for the gym doors, escaping before anyone else has really even moved. I zoom through the entrance hall and out the front door like I have something very important to do out there.

Which I do.

It's called hiding.

If there was a clump of bushes, I would dive into it, but I settle for tucking myself into a recessed area to the right of the doors where I'm at least out of sight of any people who might come out of them.

I crouch against the wall, panting like I've just run a race, and try to calm down. This is hard to do when Dahlia Brennan basically just reached into my brain, grabbed a bunch of my memories from where they were filed (mostly under "crappy sex" or "boy acts like jerk" or "Libby is an idiot"), threw them on the floor, and told me I have to refile them under "coercion," "sexual assault," and "rape."

That doesn't seem like a fun job.

I'd prefer to put everything back the way it was, where it felt manageable.

Although, in the case of Kyle, maybe it wasn't entirely

manageable. Because it's not like I haven't been thinking about the fact that I said "no" right before we had sex. It's just that my mind has been shying away from the "r" word because what happened didn't feel like what I thought of when I thought of that.

But I did say no.

So now I don't know what to think.

And how manageable is it, really, having to be around Boris all the time with that one weird part of our relationship always sliding back to the front of my mind when I least expect it?

Still, this is something I do not need right now. What I need is to keep working, and save money, and get out of this town. Because once I'm out, I won't have to see Kyle or Boris, and I won't be living in a place where my father is an infamous shit disturber.

I'm about to apply myself to the task of pulling myself together and going back inside when the front doors open and I see Dahlia Brennan coming out of the building. Up close she is taller than I thought but also somehow less intimidating.

She pauses to check her phone, turns slightly to the side while doing it, then looks up and sees me, standing there like someone has pinned me to the wall.

"Hello," she says.

She is officially the last person I want to talk to. But my mom has drilled politeness into me so hard that I find myself saying, "Hello."

"No class this period?" she says, coming closer.

"Oh," I say, "just getting some air."

"Are you all right?" she asks, giving me an assessing gaze.

"Sure. Of course," I say, trying for a breezy tone but not quite selling it. "Why do you ask?"

"Were you in the gym for my presentation?"

I nod.

"What did you think?"

"It was very nice."

"Nice?" She raises an eyebrow.

"Yeah, I mean, it was good," I say, feeling my face flush. "Super . . . informative."

"Anything in it . . . surprise you? Or . . . bother you?"

"Me? No, I'm not bothered," I say, trying for a casual shrug. "Do I seem bothered?"

"I don't know you so it's hard to tell. But I've been doing this presentation a lot and often I find someone hanging around afterward, looking like they have questions."

"I'll bet it's never the idiots who need the information the most."

"You'd be surprised. Sometimes they're worried they pushed somebody too far and never felt good about it but didn't understand why. Sometimes those people need to talk, sometimes they're trying to figure how to cover their asses. I'm Dahlia, by the way."

"I know. I mean, nice to meet you. Uh. I'm Libby."

I say all of this with my back still pressed to the wall like I can use it to disappear into if anyone comes out and turns around and sees me talking to her. And I'm hoping she won't insist on shaking my hand or getting all visibly chummy, which she doesn't.

Instead she comes and leans on her own piece of wall, close enough for us to keep talking but far enough that it could look like we're both just here coincidentally, doing our own thing.

She's good at this. Smooth.

She glances sideways and says, "It doesn't look like you got the flyer with my contact info and the crisis hotline . . ."

"I'm cool. There's no crisis."

"That's good, but just in case . . ." she says, and then discreetly passes me the flyer, low down like it's a note in class, and I decide it's easier to just take it. "I am happy to listen even if it's not a crisis. I'm trained to help with all kinds of situations."

"It's not even a situation," I say, realizing a second later that she's tricked me into admitting that there is something.

"Okay," she says in a soothing voice. "Still, if you're upset . . ."

"I'm not upset!" I snap, and then, with an eye roll at myself, mutter, "Wow, that was so convincing."

She laughs, but more with me than at me.

"Look, it's nothing I can't manage."

"Okay," she says again, and then just stands there.

"You do realize that people *get drunk specifically in order to hook up*, don't you?" I find myself blurting just to get rid of the silence. "To get up the courage? How're you going to change that? And then when both people are drunk, how is anyone supposed to even analyze what happened? Both people could say they weren't sober enough to consent, and then what?"

"Then it can be a big mess," she admits. "Is that the kind of non-crisis, non-situation you're dealing with?"

"That's not what I said. I—look, nothing terrible has happened to me. I haven't been hurt or really . . . forced or anything. And I don't want to go accusing anyone of anything. I have other things going on right now that are much more important, and doing that would screw up my whole life."

"No one's saying you have to. I was just suggesting it might help to talk."

"I can barely think right now, much less talk," I admit.

"It doesn't have to be now. It's whenever you're ready."

She's so warm and calm and nonjudgmental that it's getting to me.

"Thank you for offering," I tell Dahlia, swallowing hard. "But I really should go."

"Me too," she says. "I'm going to be holding office hours here over the next few weeks, though. If you don't want to talk here you could come to the health center. It's free and completely confidential. All the info is on the flyer. Think about it at least?"

"Sure, okay," I say, just wanting to get rid of her at this point. "I will."

8

PRACTICALLY TRAGIC

Of course I have no intention of thinking about it.

I have college to think about.

Exams to study for.

High school to finish.

Money to make.

Dredging up the not-so-great details of my past and recent-past sex life is not something I'm interested in doing.

And so I go home Friday night and throw myself into studying.

To prevent myself from getting off track, I stick Post-it Notes on the white board above my desk with the words FO-CUS and FUTURE on them. I also open tabs to pictures of college campuses on my laptop, so that I'm not tempted to stray into googling sexual assault laws and definitions.

I work until I'm bleary-eyed on Friday night, then fall into bed and lie awake trying not to think about the things I'm trying not to think about, before falling asleep and dreaming about them.

Saturday I meet Yaz and Noah at the library, where we study for a few hours before Emma shows up and invites us all to come to a movie tonight with her and Boris. Noah and Yaz accept, but I beg off, not wanting to spend the money and also unable to stomach an evening with Boris just now, even with Noah's presence as incentive.

"What are you going to do instead?" Noah asks.

"Ignore my parents, check my bank balance, and then maybe binge-watch something mindless."

"If that's what you want," Emma says, with a doubtful frown.

It's not such a terrible plan for a Saturday night. I like time alone and I'm really good at ignoring my parents.

Later, Noah texts me an extensive list of his favorite mindless TV shows and films, presumably from the car on his way to the movie. I'm reading it when the doorbell rings.

I open it to find Noah on the front step with a huge bowl of popcorn.

"I popped this myself," he says. "And it's either special delivery for your evening of solo guilty-pleasure binge-watching, or . . ."

"Or . . . ?"

"Look," he says, lowering his voice, "I know you don't have people over much, so I didn't want to invite myself . . . but I was sad you weren't coming tonight, so I thought I'd bring you something. Plus if you want company, I'm in. Which means I sort of am inviting myself."

"You bailed on the movie."

He nods.

"Yaz will have to be third wheel," I say.

"Yaz will get on her own cloud, as she is so good at doing, and Em-Boris won't phase her, even at their worst."

"Emboris?" I smirk. "That sounds like some kind of plague."

"Or a really disturbing verb—like to embarrass, but worse."

"Like you could get Emborissed?" I say. "Embarrassed by way of Boris."

"Yeah, or, like, encase, entomb, emboris . . ."

"To entomb with Boris!" I say, cackling but then turning abruptly serious. "If this caught on it would be the worst."

"Agreed." He nods, mirroring my seriousness.

"We must vow to never say Em-Boris aloud in their presence, or anyone else's." I hold my hand up, palm forward, and he touches his palm to mine.

"Promise," he says.

"Promise," I say, and then step away. "Phew."

"So," he says, holding the bowl out to me, "if you just want the popcorn, that's cool too."

"No, come in," I say quickly, stepping back to make room for him and wishing I'd put on something more attractive than fleece lounge pants and a ripped T-shirt when I came home from the library. And ideally some makeup. But it would be too obvious now if I changed, much less went to the bathroom and came back all made up and anyway Noah knows what I look like. And is here as a friend. And has Ava. And I have a disastrous record with boys anyway, and really should consider calling a personal moratorium on love and lust and everything in between until I can trust myself not to behave like an idiot.

"We'll have to watch in my room."

"That's fine," Noah says.

I don't announce him to my parents, and I feel a little self-conscious as I take him through the house where we have turned on no lights for the evening, and couldn't anyway because half the bulbs in the house are dead and no one ever bothers to buy new ones much less change them out. Dad didn't even come up to grab food earlier, and is instead un-showered and eating chips on the rec room couch while watching what could be his fifteenth zombie apocalypse show of the day, and Mom has wisely disappeared into a book.

At least my room is clean. Of course there's no furniture to sit on besides my desk chair, and something about the idea of being on the bed, on the ratty blankets I've been using since Kyle took off wearing my duvet—whyyyyy must I keep thinking about Kyle?—feels odd. And as usual, the worry about it feeling odd when it should just feel totally normal (because Noah is my friend—just my friend!) makes me feel more odd, and then I don't know whether to just jump onto the bed and start gobbling popcorn, or what.

"I could grab some couch pillows," I suggest after a too-long moment. "Then we'll have the side of the bed to lean on, and I can set my laptop on the chair right in front of us."

"Sure," Noah says.

When I come back with the pillows, I find him standing in front of his two drawings, a puzzled frown on his face.

Shoot, I forgot all about them. Now he's going to know that I've got his discarded art on my wall—beside my bed no less! And that I rooted through a recycling bin for them.

He turns to look at me and I clutch the couch pillows to my chest, my entire body engulfed in a wave of mortification.

"When did I give you these?"

"Uh . . ."

"I'm surprised I let you have them. This one—" He points ruefully at the self-portrait/building, "I was trying to think of a different way to do a self-portrait, and I decided to model it on this famous sculpture of Che Guevara on the side of a building in Cuba. Didn't turn out so great, though. You don't find it creepy to wake up and see that staring down at you?"

Creepy is *not* what I find it. I shake my head.

"I have a much better draft of this bird, too," he says. "I'll give you that instead."

"Okay," I say, knowing I'll keep both. "Thanks."

We make a comfortable nest on the floor and start working our way through Noah's binge-watch list, starting with a cooking show, moving on to a reality thing with archeologists and a hilarious narrator, and then some early 2000s comedy.

"Does it actually qualify as binge-watching," I say, during a break, "given that we're only watching one of each of these?"

"We're binging my list, not the individual shows," Noah says.

"Ah."

"You feeling any better?" he asks, turning to look at me.

"Better? I'm not sick."

"No, like, better. Earlier today I thought you seemed a little . . . off."

"You mean when Emma invited us to the movie?"

He shakes his head. "Before then. You were pretty intense with the studying, and it took you a second or two longer than usual to laugh when something was funny . . . and there was a lot of frowning and sighing."

"Frowning! That's probably because of calculus," I say, wanting to joke my way out of this and keep all thoughts of Boris and Kyle and consent and sexual assault at bay and away from this—from Noah here with me, having a nice time.

"How's the job?" he asks.

"Harder than it looks. Things move really fast. There are a million things to stay on top of, and you have to do them all while also being charming."

"Charming's not a stretch for you," he says, with one of those slightly crooked smiles of his.

"Ha. You should have seen me Wednesday night. Someone asked me for a water refill and I just pointed to the sink and said, 'There's the sink.'"

"Nooo!"

"In my defense—"

"There's a defense?"

"Yes! I had a group of fifteen small children—different table—and one of them had puked all over the floor and the parents just stood there watching me clean it up. Did not lift a finger, either of them."

"Are you serious?"

"Dead. And then, you'd think if you clean up puke for someone, while continuing to be charming of course, you'd get a nice tip. But no. Still, I like my coworkers and we help each other out and make the best of it. For example, we have this one VIP regular who's all flirty and insists on these really long, gross hugs. The female servers keep a running tally and at the end of every month whoever's logged the most seconds of being hugged wins the 'Most Appreciated' award."

"What?"

"The prize is actually pretty good—a three-course, staff-discounted dinner that everyone chips in for. Still, you really don't want to be the winner because it means you've been rubbed on a lot."

"Rubbed on! Wait," Noah says, his dark eyes outraged, "your bosses know about this and all they do about it is let you run a contest?"

"No, they just think we vote on who's been the most helpful or whatever. They have no idea."

"Wow, so the job actually sucks."

"No. I know I'm making it sound that way, but most of the time it's actually fun in a crazy way. The Singhs—Dev and Maya—are good people. They used to run this huge Indian food factory—wholesale, retail, catering. So they know what they're doing when it comes to food. Plus the rest of the staff is pretty nice once they know you're a hard worker and not an idiot, and I'm making good money."

"Still, it makes me appreciate working for my dad," he says, shaking his head. "Snowplowing's quiet, and so's land-scaping. No people, no puke, no hugs. Plus charm is not one of my charms."

"You arrived here tonight with popcorn you popped your-self. That's pretty charming."

"That's not charm, that's just trying to finagle an invite. I'd start telling people to piss off on day one."

"Oh, come on, there are lots of people who'd appreciate your unpolished appeal."

"Unpolished appeal?" he says, grinning suddenly. "Do I need a shave or something? Is it my cow-tipping habit? The chewing tobacco?"

"You don't chew tobacco."

"But you think I tip cows."

"No."

"Or do you mean unpolished in a sort of ruggedly hand-some sort of way?"

"Stop fishing for compliments," I say, willing myself not to blush. "Besides, maybe *unfiltered* is more the word. Like, if someone asked you if the chicken was good and you didn't think it was, you'd probably just say so. You never, like, massage your opinions to make them more palatable."

"Ah, but maybe I need to *massage* my appeal."

I roll my eyes.

"What part of it do you think needs to be massaged?"

"Definitely not the ego part."

"Oh, burn," he says.

"And not the id either."

"Oh, hey, I took that psych elective too, smarty-pants," he says. "Nobody touches my id."

"Ha."

"I'd tell those people with the puking kid to clean it up their damned selves. Anyway I like a job where I can think about other things—think, daydream, imagine stuff I want to build. Your job doesn't sound like it leaves room for that."

"None," I say. "But I'm not so into daydreaming these days."

—

On my way to sleep I replay the evening, happy and unhappy at the same time. Because there's always a vibe between Noah and me—a fun banter, a kind of knowing, and trust. If I'd responded to his overtures a year ago after Boris and I broke up instead of thinking I had to wait some respectful amount of time in order to save Boris's feelings, maybe Noah wouldn't have gone off and met Ava over the summer, and we'd be together now.

Things would be different: I'd resent Emma and Boris less for falling for one another while I lost my chance with Noah, and Kyle wouldn't have happened.

And now I'm awake and grabbing my computer and finally giving in to the search I've been resisting since Dahlia Brennan's consent/sexual assault chat.

Because I need to know.

After some horrifying reading (dangers of internet research!) I get out of bed and search for the flyer Dahlia gave me, and wind up on the website about healthy relationships.

I'm expecting it to be cheesy, condescending, and full of moralizing, but it's actually full of entirely straightforward information. And it confirms that while what I've experienced is far from some of the violent, messed-up things that happen to people, some of it has been outside the definition of "healthy." Quite a bit outside.

Having confirmation makes me feel both worse and better—worse because I feel stupid for having let these things happen, and confused even about what part of the blame is mine and what part is Kyle's or Boris's for that matter. But at least now I know I'm not crazy to have been feeling so screwed up.

I sleep poorly and wake up Sunday morning feeling jagged and raw and obsessed.

I'm in the middle of an epiphany—a shitty one. And the revelations don't arrive in straight, clear lines, they come like cyclones, like explosions. It's like I have to break apart before I can be put back together, as if I'm Humpty Dumpty or a cubist painting—no part of me fitting back quite right to the other parts.

I'm in flux, fragile, and made up of sharp angles.

And I'm pissed off, not to mention confused.

One of the things that's making me craziest is wrapping my head around what to do about these not-okay things that have happened. Having just read the results of a bunch of sexual assault cases is a huge deterrent to taking any kind of legal action.

But I am trying to face the situation, which is something.

Beyond that, I guess I just need to be smarter in the future—be smarter, fight harder, avoid situations where I might be vulnerable, and be super clear with myself and anyone I'm with about what I want and don't want. Set strong boundaries and be prepared to defend them. Of course boundaries might not help with someone like Perry, or someone worse than Perry, but with guys like Boris or Kyle they should. Or might, anyway.

I don't want to go through life assuming the worst, either. That doesn't seem fair—not to me, or to the many completely decent and evolved boys/men who exist. But until the Dahlia Brennans of the world fully get the message out, I guess it's a bit like what you learn in drivers ed—"defensive driving" but applied to sex and men in general.

It isn't fair, but I have to be tougher, more perceptive, and alert for signs of trouble.

And so I will.

Sunday afternoon, Dad is in some kind of zombie-TV-induced fog. He doesn't appear to have moved from his spot in front of the TV, and when I mention it to Mom she just shakes her head and says, "At least he's quiet."

Then she asks about my missing duvet and I tell her a big story about Emma borrowing it for a science project, and resign myself to having to get it back from Kyle.

Every time I've seen him since that night I've felt so gross and embarrassed and mixed-up, and now I know why. He raped me. Kind of. Only it wasn't "kind of." I said no and he did it anyway. The fact that we were drunk and naked and doing all the other things we were doing doesn't change that.

The fact that I paused things to get a condom and then just sort of gave in and participated also, supposedly, doesn't change that. But it does confuse me.

Because what was that? Thirty seconds of rape and then the rest of it consensual? Even though I never actually consented?

I'm mad at Kyle and disgusted with myself.

Still, I need the duvet back.

9

BURN RUBBER

"I have *the item*," Kyle says when I walk into work Sunday night.

Then comes "Libbyyyyyyy" and Perry and the hugging, and the salad, and the mousse tower and me finding out how fast my decisions and paltry self-declarations can fly out the window in the face of someone like Perry—his demands, his complaints, his eyes and hands and words coming at me, landing on me—until I feel like I've been slimed.

And then there's me, losing it.

Me, and the pitcher of sangria.

Me, Perry, the sangria, and the skittering ice cubes and chunks of orange and then total, stunned, shocked silence.

And finally there's me, realizing what I've done, and starting to move.

The next thing I know I'm out in the parking lot, hands shaking as I unlock Betty—my vintage three-speed—then shove my helmet on, swing my leg over, and ride out of there like the hounds of hell are chasing me.

Ten minutes later I turn onto the far side of my driveway

and stop in the dim space between the car and the branches of our neighbor's willow tree.

I'm just stepping off of Betty, and still gasping for air, when I see the headlights approaching from the same direction I just came, and a fresh batch of adrenaline floods me.

Perry?

No, that's irrational.

And yet it's irrational that he would grab my butt in front of dozens of people, too.

I nudge Betty's kickstand into place and back into the darkness of the willow branches. What do I do if it's him—crawl into the bushes? Hide in the backyard? Run to the front or side door, lock the doors behind me, and tell my parents to call the police? My keys are in my backpack, which I've left near the bike, so I'd never make it. My phone is in there too.

I'll just have to run.

If it's Perry and I'm not just being a paranoid freak, lurking here in the foliage.

The car pulls up in front of our house, turns off, then a door slams and there are footsteps. I peer through the willow branches and then breathe a sigh of relief when I see who it is: Kyle.

Oh, the irony of that being a relief.

He's headed to the front door. I step out of the tree cover, intercepting him.

"Hey!" he says in a too-loud voice.

"Hi," I say in a loud whisper, and put my finger to my lips, then jerk my head toward the house to indicate that I don't want to draw my parents' attention.

"Sorry," he says, nodding and using a lower voice. "I texted.

Said I was coming to see if you were okay, because I saw what happened. That was awesome."

"I'm all right," I say, though I'm clearly not. "But it wasn't awesome, it was stupid."

"No, it was great. Totally deserved," Kyle says, brimming with indignation. "I know everyone in Pine Ridge loves the guy, but he's a turd. And now thanks to you he's a wet turd. Ha ha!"

"Eww. And shhh," I remind him. I'm tempted to drag him into the shadows in case Perry does show up, but really shouldn't, lest he get the wrong idea (as we've seen he's prone to).

"Sorry," he says.

"It's fine," I say.

"Dev's pretty upset with you," he says, turning abruptly serious.

"Yeah, soaking a customer who's giving you trouble isn't exactly one of the strategies suggested in the server manual."

"I'm studying that manual right now and it doesn't cover people like Perry. The dude needs to be outfitted with, like, a shock collar or something."

"This is a nightmare."

"Listen," Kyle says, "everybody in there knows what Perry's like. Dev included. The guy was so out of line tonight. That garbage about the desserts and his hands on you all the time, and acting like you were a dish that's on the menu. You were provoked, Libby, and by the way I said so."

"You said that to Dev?"

"Yeah, straight up. And Nita and Brianna backed you up, too."

"Wow, thanks." I pause and give my head a shake, trying to rearrange my already-rearranged thoughts about Kyle's actions toward me to include this. "Dev'll still fire me, though."

"Maybe. I think he's scared of Perry. You shoulda seen him—hustling around, patting at Perry's suit with paper towels trying to soak up the stains, and apologizing over and over. I'll bet you could press charges. You've got a ton of witnesses."

"This is Pine Ridge—no one here is going to say anything against Perry."

"I would."

I can tell he means it, and that fact is making my head hurt. How is he this person, and also the person who pushed past "no" without a single thought for my feelings?

"Listen," he continues, fired up, "my mom's a lawyer and she's all over this sexual harassment stuff. I could ask her for you."

"I've got enough going on right now without having to deal with police or lawsuits. Plus every one of these cases you hear about—they're total crap for the women. They get their whole lives picked apart, and they never win."

"Not never."

"Almost never."

"How about I just ask my mom for information?"

How about you ask her what it means when you have sex with someone after they said no?

"I feel bad that I didn't help. I could see you were having trouble, and I didn't do anything. I should have told him to lay off, or, even, I could have gone to Perry and been like, 'Hey back off, she's mine.'"

"I'm *not* yours," I snap, in what is probably an over-the-top reaction.

"No, I mean just to—"

"I'm not!"

"Whoa." Kyle takes a step back. "I just meant—it might have helped."

"If you'd said that and it did help, that's almost as bad. Should I have let you take a pee on me too? Maybe put a sticker on my forehead?"

"Listen, if the positions were reversed—"

I snort.

"If the positions were reversed," he says, pressing on, "and you said I was yours, in order to protect me or help me out, I wouldn't have minded. I woulda liked it, to be honest. And actually, I think it's pretty big of me, considering how you've just . . . blown me off."

"How I've blown you off?" I say, gaping at him.

"Yeah," he says, up in his feelings all of a sudden. "One night together, a pretty good time, I think we can both agree, and I did all the right things after, texting you that I wanted to see you again, not being the typical guy, and you just blew me off. And here I am trying to be a nice guy anyway!"

"Oh, somebody get this boy a medal!" I choke out. "The Trying Nice Guy medal!"

"Fine, fine," he says, hands up and backing away. "You're upset. You've had a bad night and you're upset."

"Yes!"

"Great. I'll just . . . get your duvet and leave you to it."

He stalks off to his truck, retrieves the duvet from the back, brings it to me, and drapes it over Betty. This causes me to realize I did not think through how I was going to carry the thing home tonight when I asked him to bring it. Duh.

"You're welcome," he says, scowling at me and clearly expecting an apology.

"Just go, okay, Kyle?"

And, unlike the last time I asked him to leave, this time he does.

———

It's hard to be inconspicuous while carrying a big, fluffy duvet, but I'm not in the mood to have to explain why, when I told Mom that Emma borrowed it, I appear to be bringing it home from work, so I enter the house as quietly as I can.

It's been sad, the way the three of us live most of the time like not-very-friendly roommates since the Jack fiasco and worse now since the Airbnb thing, with Dad alternating between total space-out on the couch and frenetic activity on his computer into the wee hours. Tonight, though, I count myself lucky for it as I tiptoe through the house.

I heave a sigh of relief when my bedroom door is closed behind me, then drop my backpack on the floor and shove the duvet into the closet because I really am planning to wash it. A lot. But not tonight.

I pull my phone out of my backpack, read the texts from Kyle, and another few from Nita freaking out about what I just did. Then I check my voicemail, where there is, as I feared, a message from Dev, telling me what a disaster I've caused, and how much money the dry cleaning bill for Perry's clothing is going to cost him, and how disappointed he is at my actions, and then firing me.

I knew it was going to happen, but it still hits me like a kick in the stomach.

Fired.

Determined to get through all the bad news at once, I go on social media to see if the story has spread. Because it will spread—it's just a matter of time, and a matter of whether it spreads faster by old-school word of mouth, or via the internet. Luckily I don't see myself tagged anywhere, or any mention of the Goat, or Perry, and none of my school friends have texted me yet, either. I'll give Emma a heads-up later, but for now I turn the phone off and go to my desk.

It sounds crazy, but maybe I'll study.

Ever since things started to go downhill in my family life, I've found schoolwork to be surprisingly calming. It's a way I can shut everything out, and of course has the benefit of having made me a much better student than I was before.

But I already worked a ton this weekend in an effort to avoid thinking about my little history of being sexually assaulted (now not quite as little—ha ha!), and when I sit down to read I find my eyes won't fasten on the words.

I keep thinking of the duvet, jammed into my closet, with Kyle cooties all over it.

That, at least, is something I can do something about.

I grab the duvet and head to the basement.

It's cool and musty-smelling down here, but in a way I find pleasant. It's kind of an old book smell, a happier time smell. When my socked feet hit the linoleum tiles, I march purposely across the rec room toward the laundry room, passing Dad's office door on the way. It's open a crack, but he doesn't look up.

In the laundry room I plug the giant sink, stuff the duvet into it, and turn the water on to hot. The washing machine could do a better job but I need to do something physical, and short of wringing my own neck or someone else's, this is my best option.

Soon hot water is pooling and I add a generous amount of soap, then plunge my hands in. It's scalding but the burning sensation is clarifying. I stir and pummel and scrub that duvet. I pull it, press it, wrestle with it. I imagine pounding the Kyle germs out of it. I imagine it's Perry's smug face.

Finally, after a thorough working-over, I rinse the duvet in water so cold it makes me gasp. I'm sweating and my arms are bright pink past my elbows when I let the third tubful of freezing water out and start the difficult process of trying to squeeze/press/wring enough of the water out of it to put it in the dryer.

"What'd that thing ever do to you?" says a voice from the door.

I let out an undignified shriek.

"Dad, jeez."

"What are you doing?" he says, leaning bleary-eyed against the doorframe.

"Laundry."

"By hand?"

"Yes." *In preparation for my future as a laundress, or homesteader, since those are going to be the only options left to me.*

"Washing something by hand is usually worse for the environment than putting it through a high-efficiency machine," Dad points out. "I'll bet you used more water than the machine would have."

"Huh."

"Good night at the restaurant? Or . . ." His gaze sharpens as he seems to notice something in my demeanor. "Bad night? That the reason you're beating up a poor, innocent duvet?"

"I . . ."

Suddenly the truth is on the tip of my tongue to tell him. He's not a Perry fan. He might not even be mad. In fact he might be delighted by what I just did.

Maybe even proud.

I suck in a sharp breath.

"What's wrong?" Dad says. "Talk to me."

He would be proud because it's exactly the kind of thing *he* would do.

"Was someone rude to you? Or stiff you on a tip?"

Stiff me on a tip. Ha.

"You know, even the bad nights are good nights in the end," Dad continues. "Because you get through it, and you learn something."

I just stand there. I never know what to do around him anymore, and never know what to expect. Here he is being his old self—what I think of as an almost normal father—sympathetic, caring, a bit dorky, and clueless with advice, but well-meaning. But if I were to tell him, I really have no idea what he'd do. Without my telling him anything at all, I still don't know what he'll do, what he'll be like just five minutes from now. And that hurts. It hurts to love somebody and not be able to trust them, hurts to know you can't ever let yourself need them. Even when you're desperately in need and they're standing right in front of you, willing to be needed.

"This is boots-on-the-ground learning, Lib," Dad continues, still standing in the laundry room doorway and blocking my exit. "The school of hard knocks. And you'll learn more useful stuff about life in that place than you ever will in school. That's what happened to me."

Sure, Dad. Hard knocks.

"I'm proud of you," he says, and the words are like a sucker punch.

"I have to go," I say, and abruptly push past him, and out into the rec room.

"Whoa! Where?"

"Homework," I mumble, hustling toward the stairs.

"Wait, Lib, honey . . ."

But I'm not stopping. I'm flying up the stairs, then down the hallway to my room, just barely resisting slamming the door and instead shutting it firmly and quietly, and then standing in my room, fists clenched at my sides, legs shaking.

Because the hard fact is that I don't get to have a crisis.

Not one that anybody knows about, anyway.

Mom and I are the counterbalance to Dad, the anchors. It's not that we've ever talked about it, or planned it out, it just happened—we hold the line of normalcy. We are steady, unruffled, smooth with a force of will that seeks to pull Dad back into a normal orbit.

I still have to relearn the lesson occasionally, though. Like the time in eleventh grade that I came home in tears about the C+ I got on an English essay. Dad, after listening sympathetically, went to the school and freaked on my English teacher, demanded a meeting with the principal, where he freaked again, and then spent the next month and a half writing letters to the school board trying to get both my teacher and the principal fired. All this achieved, of course, was embarrassing me and causing my English teacher to despise me. And, looking back, the C+ was deserved.

The lesson? Any meltdown I might have will cause Dad to melt down too, and melt down *more*.

It isn't fair, but I'm not sure he can help it.

Luckily, because of Emma's panic attacks, I've done a bunch of research on how to disrupt fight-or-flight feelings, and I have a lot of helpful apps on my phone. I grab it and pull up a breathing app, plop down on the floor in a cross-legged meditation pose, and breathe along with the expanding and contracting icon until I feel calmer.

If only I'd had this image laser-beamed into my head when I was dealing with Perry.

Finally I get up, go to my desk, and open my laptop so I can start working on some kind of plan, and then of course procrastinate by checking my inbox.

And that's when I see it—an email from my first-choice college.

Holy cow.

I stare at it for a few long moments, then click to open it. Then I'm reading the words and clapping a hand over my mouth, leaping up out of my chair and feeling a few amazing moments of joy before sitting heavily back down and shaking with silent, mostly hysterical laughter, and then finally texting Emma.

You're not gonna believe this.

　　??? she texts back.

Call me?

Give me a minute

K

And so I wait for her, thinking all the while that of course, *of course*, this would be the day that I would get my first acceptance notice, and from my first-choice school . . . just when I have thoroughly torched my chances of going anywhere at all.

10

SHIELD

Monday morning I get up early to revise and print out more copies of my résumé so I can start applying for jobs again.

It won't be fun, and neither will school today, but I'll handle it.

And I'll find another job. Maybe Lyle at Crawler's needs someone by now and will consider my recent shit disturbing to be a bonus. Or maybe I could work as a tutor, or do retail. Because I want, more than ever now, to get out of this town, go to college, and make something of myself.

At the front door I put on my combat boots, my biggest sunglasses, lipstick, and my black baseball cap as if I'm some kind of badass celebrity in disguise. None of this will actually disguise me, but it makes me feel better.

Outside, the warm spring air hits me. Yaz is perched on the edge of the porch, grinning her sweet, slightly crooked-toothed grin, and Noah's striding up the driveway.

"What are you guys doing here?"

"Emma texted us after you talked to her last night," Yaz says. "Told us what happened."

"Oh, okay," I say, relieved I won't have to tell the whole

story to each of them. "Did you, um, have either of you . . . heard it from anywhere else yet?"

Noah, at the base of the steps now, shakes his head and Yaz says, "Not yet."

"I take it Perry's the creep you told me about?" Noah asks. "The hugger?"

"Yep," I say, nodding. "It was a bit of a disaster."

"A bit of you kicking some righteous ass, you mean," Noah says.

"Still, a disaster," I say. "And probably going to get worse."

"Nah, it'll just be people talking," Noah says. "That's not worse, just more. You're already fired, right? And you already messed up your chance of getting a good reference, and already pissed off Perry Ackerman. The worst things have already happened."

"Is this supposed to be a pep talk?" I say, and Yaz gives him a disapproving look.

"It is!" Noah says. "That stuff is over, and it's all uphill from here."

"Except the part where everyone hears about it and thinks I'm psycho."

"So what?" Noah says. "Screw 'em."

"Noah!" Yaz looks scandalized. "We're supposed to be supportive!"

"Please recall that nobody comes to me to get sunshine blown up their butts," Noah says with a cocky grin. "Some people will think she's psycho. Who cares? They don't matter."

"I need a new job, though," I say. "That matters."

"Welllll, you might be in a bit of crapola there," he concedes.

"Never mind that right now," Yaz says, shooting Noah a look. "The point is that this is just . . . a setback."

I snort.

"No, really," she insists. "That's how you need to think of it—as a setback."

"Or," Noah says, "as a personally costly, but very satisfying, dispensation of overdue vigilante justice."

"*Setback* is less wordy," Yaz points out.

"*Satisfying dispensation of overdue vigilante justice* is better," he says. "And doesn't she look like she's ready to kick some ass in those boots?"

Oh, Noah. If he is ever single and interested in me again, I will jump his bones.

After getting his enthusiastic consent, of course.

"Anyway," Yaz says, "we're here to escort you to school."

"You didn't need to do that," I say, throat feeling tight.

"Yes we did," Yaz says, and at the same time Noah says, joking, "We can go if you don't want us."

"No, I want you!" I say way too fast, and then, because I said it while looking right at him, descend into awkwardness and stammer, "Er, to walk me. Both of you. Thank you."

"You all right?" Yaz asks, looking at me quizzically. "Need a hug? Some quick reiki?"

"Better not," I say, taking a step back. "The reiki is never actually quick and the hug might make me cry."

"How about an arm?" Noah says, offering said arm, bent at the elbow, like an old-fashioned gentleman, and I descend the stairs to where he is, and take it.

Yaz follows me down the step and links elbows with me on the other side, and we head toward the sidewalk arm in arm.

Emma meets us one block later and Boris catches up with us at the crosswalk in front of the school. By the time we go through the doors, I have Emma in front of me, Boris behind, and Noah and Yaz flanking me, like they're some sort of

military force, or a well-disciplined marching band at the
very least.

Of course, it's overkill, particularly since I don't detect
anyone looking at me strangely yet, but I love them for it.

The strange looks finally start midmorning, and it's
almost a relief. I'm coming out of European History when
I get a text from Emma, who's on the other side of the
building.

Get ready. It's on.

Where?

Crotchety Complainers. A video.

Ffffff.

You have study hall?

Yep.

I'm so sorry I have a test! Wait for me to
watch it with you at lunch.

Waiting will just make me feel worse. I'm fine, I tell her,
and this is mostly true. Of course, I also feel like I'm going to
keel over from the suspense, so I head to the nearest bathroom, lock myself in a stall, and go online to get it over with,
sure I'll feel better afterward.

Crotchety Complainers is our nickname for the Pine
Ridge Residents group on Facebook, where people are supposed to share information about community events, post
about lost dogs, et cetera, but which has turned into a hot-

bed of controversy. It's full of un-neighborly spats, people bickering about crosswalks and fence-height bylaws, parent-shaming and counter-shaming, and general bad behavior. It's like reality TV, but less glamorous, which is the reason half the high school students in Pine Ridge have joined—purely for entertainment purposes. Some have even taken to baiting the grown-ups—some of the more intense helicopter parents, this dude Roland Rickland who'll go off in spectacular fashion about almost anything, and one or two of my mom's co-workers who can't resist a dustup.

Thank God my dad is anti-Facebook, otherwise he'd be infamous on there by now.

It takes me a minute to open the app, during which time Emma texts, DO NOT READ THE COMMENTS.

I'm not that stupid, I text back.

The video is right at the top of the feed. It captures the just-soaked Perry perfectly, and the back of me as I wave the empty pitcher around wildly, shouting the entire time. For my second viewing I grab earphones and put the sound on. The audio only catches every fifth word, most of them curses. Then you see me whipping the pitcher onto the floor so hard the plastic cracks (I don't even remember doing that—yikes!) and then I turn, pause long enough to be clearly identifiable (*as a lunatic*), and storm out.

Watching the video does *not* make me feel better. Shocker. But I can't stop. I spend the entire period watching and re-watching, feeling worse and worse.

And then, even though Emma warned me not to, and even though you should NEVER READ THE COMMENTS, and even though I would be better off drinking water from the toilet or jabbing my thumbs into my eyes, and even though I told Emma that I'm not that stupid, it turns out that I am exactly that stupid.

I'm still scrolling through, almost at the end, when Emma calls.

"Hi," I whisper, though I don't think anyone else is in the bathroom. "You done already?"

"You read the comments."

"I've said, like, three words—how can you tell?"

"I just can. Why did you do that?"

"I figured someone might have stood up for me, or that what I was imagining people saying was worse than what they were actually saying."

"And was it?"

"No."

"Comments sections are where people's best selves go to die, Libby. Where are you?"

"South end bathroom."

Two minutes later I see her red converse high-tops under the door, and then she's hissing, "Let me in!"

I open the door and she crams herself into the stall with me.

"You look like hell," she says.

"Thanks."

"It's your eyes. You have screen-time eyes. Comments-section-I-didn't-listen-to-my-best-friend eyes."

"I'll be okay," I say, my voice admittedly shaky. "I've been through this type of thing before—no big deal."

"Listen to me," she says, so intense it's almost comical. "Remember how when I'm having a panic attack you tell me it's going to be okay, and that it will be over soon, and there is no emergency?"

"Yes . . . ?"

"And you know how our deal is that I agree to *believe you no matter what* every time, and how this has basically saved my life?"

"Yes . . . ?"

"I'm invoking that."

"Oh, it can be invoked?"

"It can and it is. I need you to trust me now. Do you trust me?"

"I guess."

"A little more certainty, please."

"Fine, I trust you."

"Okay. So. Of course you can handle the people who're going to start acting like idiots here at school. But this online stuff will make you lose your mind. Seriously. If nothing else, it's a time suck, but at worst it's an abyss. So. If you trust me, which you have stated legally that you do—"

I snort, but she keeps going.

"—then you will turn off the Wi-Fi on your phone and on your laptop, and block texts from anyone but your close circle, and make a solemn promise to me that you won't go back to the video, or to any social media, for at least forty-eight hours. Get an app to lock yourself off if you have to. Or give me your phone and I'll do it."

"I see your point. But if I'm being attacked, don't I need to know?"

"If you're being attacked and you don't know about it, are you actually being attacked?" Emma responds.

"Uh, yes. And the tree also falls in the forest and the glass is half empty."

"Well, since we're getting philosophical, if someone says something about you and you don't learn about it, then for you that's the same as it not existing. It's like that person took a swing and their punch landed on air. And then they're just a crazy person punching the air, and you don't even feel it. If you don't read or hear the words, they can't hurt you."

"That's not true—my reputation—"

"Okay, Taylor Swift . . ."

"Seriously, it matters. Especially because I need to get another job, like, today."

"One thing at a time. Not commenting, at least for a couple of days, will not make things worse in that regard."

"But I have to defend myself."

"Just promise me two days. I'm not saying you shouldn't do anything, I'm just saying hold off, see what happens. Somebody else from the Goat might come forward, or someone might say they saw Perry grabbing your butt, and that does the defending for you. Even if no one else comes forward to support you or accuse Perry, something totally unrelated might happen—some other scandal—and everyone will just move on."

"Except me."

"Especially you."

"All right, but—"

The lunch bell rings, which means the bathroom is going to be filled with people in a minute.

"Okay," Emma says as we start hearing lockers banging in the hallway. "Just to relieve your anxiety, how about I monitor everything for a couple of days—all the online stuff—and if there's anything you need to know, I'll tell you. I'll be like a filter, or a shield."

My throat tightens and my eyes start to mist up.

"No, no," Emma hisses, "no crying."

"Okay. But you're amazing."

"Well," she says with a grin, "between this and the naked boy eviction you really are giving me opportunities to build up my friendship karma."

"Yeah, well," I say with an eye roll as I reach out to unlock the stall door, "obviously that's why I did it."

11

AN ART TO IT

The rest of school on Monday is, admittedly, a bit of a trial. There's the usual snickering and staring that comes with being part of/adjacent to a scandal, but I have at least one friend in each of my afternoon classes, and it's high time I practice my withering glare—it's been getting rusty.

Plus this Perry thing has done me the favor of driving the other things that were bothering me (e.g., my little trash heap of nonconsensual sexual situations) almost all the way out of my mind.

Yay.

And, Monday is Art Club with Noah, who, astonishingly enough, has not been driven out of my mind even a little bit. This is the only one of my extracurriculars that I didn't quit when I started working back in January, for obvious reasons.

The art teacher has left a selection of supplies out on a big table. I grab a bunch of random pieces of fabric and a pot of glue, and then head to our usual spot by the window where we can watch the more sportily inclined students run around on the still-muddy back field. Noah is already there, working on something in his sketchbook.

"Hey," I say.

"Hey," he says, with something distinctly downtrodden in his tone.

"Uh, you okay?" I ask him.

"Me? You're the one having the crap day."

"A bit crap," I concede, and then start sorting through the pile of stuff I grabbed, settling on a large piece of burlap. "But it could be worse."

"True," he says, then focuses back on his work.

Okay, so he doesn't feel like talking.

And I don't feel like doing art.

Which means I find myself sitting there pulling the fabric apart, thread by thread, while either staring out the window or at him.

He's holding his charcoal pencil way too tightly and he looks gloomy.

"What's that going to be?" I ask finally, trying unsuccessfully to get a peek at what he's drawing.

"The Death of Hope," he says, and I can't tell whether he's joking.

"Hello, melodrama," I say, and this gets me a tiny smile from him. "You're calling a building 'The Death of Hope'?" Lately Noah spends Art Club working on architectural drawings—some very brass tacks and mathematical, others more conceptual.

"This one isn't a building," he says, then looks over at the mess I'm making. "And, uh, what's that supposed to be?"

"The Death of All Ideas of What to Do in Art Club?" I say, and he laughs, but it's a pained laugh. "Okay, Noah, what's with you?"

He studies me, then shakes his head. "You don't need to hear my problems today. You got your own."

"Maybe hearing your problems will help take my mind off mine."

"Oh, so my problems are what—a cheap distraction?"

"Cheap? I would have said *free*."

He laughs.

"Start talking," I say.

"Ava and I are going back and forth about something, and I just got a text from her."

Ugh, it's about Ava. Still, I did ask.

"She doesn't want to do the gap year thing with me," he adds.

"Was she going to?"

"Yeah, we were planning on it."

I get four nearly simultaneous, conflicting feelings about this: 1. a stabbed-in-the-gut feeling re the two of them planning a romantic year traveling together; 2. a wash of entirely selfish joy/relief that it's not happening; 3. another stabby sensation of guilt over my feeling happy about something that's making him miserable; and 4. plain old empathetic pain over his being in pain, because, of course, I want him to be happy.

"Wow," I say, my fingers working harder than ever to destruct the burlap. "What . . . uh . . . changed?"

"She was into it and then her parents convinced her to apply to college anyway. Now all of a sudden she's gotten accepted to some programs, and she doesn't want to travel anymore, and I'm pissed off that she caved to her parents and hurt that she just . . . changed her mind like that."

"She has the right to change her mind."

"Sure. But now she's saying I should stay, too. For her."

"But you've been saving and planning for this forever!"

"I know. It's just the long-distance thing sucks. We're doing it already, and this would be so much worse. It would've been good to just be together, you know? And then after, if we were at different schools it would have been okay because we'd be solid. Or the trip would show us we weren't solid, and then we'd both be free. But to be apart next year? It'll just make us both less committed to where we are, to be constantly trying to stay connected to someone so far away."

"I see the problem."

"What would you do?"

"Uh, if I were you, or if I were her?"

"I meant me, but . . ." He's been waving his pencil and tapping his foot and looking all over the place talking about this, but all of a sudden he's dialed in on me in a way that makes it hard to breathe. "But yeah, what would you do if you were her?"

"If I were her I'd go with you."

"Really?"

"Yeah," I say, and then lift one shoulder like I feel totally casual about it. "I mean, you get a chance like that once. If you're lucky. To travel, see the world with someone you're madly in love with? Absolutely."

"But aren't you dying to go to college?"

"Oh, are we talking about actual me in this hypothetical situation?"

"Yeah," he says, "uh, if you had someone like that. Would you go to college, or would you go with him?"

"Actual me probably can't do either of those things," I say. "Actual me will probably be stuck in Pine Ridge next year working and trying to save money, and I guess if actual me scraped together enough money to go to college, actual me should probably go, and not spend it on travel because then at the end of the traveling, actual me would be right back where

I started. But if the money wasn't a problem? Hypothetical me would seriously consider the gap year with the actual you."

"Huh," he says, and I have to look away because I've said wayyy too much.

But he seems not to have noticed, because after a moment he says, "Okay, then, what if you were me?"

"Easy. I'd go on the trip."

"Right. So the only problem with that is that Ava and I sort of agreed that if we're not in the same place next year, we won't . . . continue."

"Oh. That's hard. Are you considering staying? Are you tempted?" I ask, wishing I didn't feel so invested in the answer. "I mean, there's a purpose for this trip for you. It's not like you're planning to just go wander randomly around—"

"Well, there may be some random wandering."

"Right, but don't you have a list of architectural wonders or whatever that you want to see in person?"

"Yeah," he says.

"And yet you have this wonderful girl," I say, trying not to sound bitter on "wonderful." "I can see how you'd be torn."

"That's what's really bad, though," Noah says, looking at me with troubled eyes. "I don't think I'm torn enough. I think I'm torn about not being torn, if that makes any sense. What does that say about me? That I'm not even tempted to stay? Am I that selfish? Or do I not care about her like I thought I did? Anyway now I have to tell her there's no way I'm changing my plans for her. And then what?"

"What do you mean?"

"Do we stay together right up to the time I leave in August, and try to spend the summer together, or do we just break up now? We don't need to break up yet. But if the decision was that easy for me, what am I doing dragging it out? And dragging it out long-distance, no less? And how is it I so badly wanted her to come with me, but then I'm not tempted *at all* to stay here with her? Did I just want a travel companion?"

"Well, she wouldn't have been *just* a travel companion," I point out. "She'd have been a travel companion you could snog."

"Yeah, that's a loss for sure," he says, and then laughs for the first time. "Anyway, nothing you can do about it."

Oh yes there is—take me . . . ! I want to shout. *Pick me!*

But gap years cost money, unless you spend them at home, working. Plus he is my friend, in pain and confusion, and this is not the time to be imagining myself making out with him in every zillion-year-old cathedral and modern art museum in Europe.

"What do you think she'll want to do?" I say, trying to focus.

"I dunno," he says. "I need to sort myself out before I talk to her, but I'm not great at hiding my feelings even long-distance, and I know she's already getting weird vibes from me."

"A suggestion?"

"Yeah?"

"Maybe don't lead with the Death of Hope theme," I say, gesturing toward his sketchbook.

I drop off ten of the updated résumés on my way home—to all the places I applied before plus some stores along Main Street, including the shop with the expensive stick furniture. The only place I can't bring myself to go back to is Fancy Lattes. Even so, I get a mix of reactions that range from amusement to shock to a lecture on Perry's wonderfulness to calling me a "hussy" and telling me never to set foot in their establishment again.

It's even more exciting than my job search in January.

Still, it feels good to do something.

And it occurs to me that I may have inherited one worthwhile character trait from my dad: stubbornness.

My last stop is Crawler's Pub. There are only a few people there and Lyle is behind the bar moving crates of glassware. He stops everything when he sees me, puts the crate he's holding down on top of the bar, and says, "Well, well, well."

"Hi, Lyle," I say.

"You here for a drink?"

"Things are not yet so tragic that I would be belly-up to a bar right after school," I say, "but stay tuned."

He gives a bark of a laugh and I pull my résumé out and hand it to him.

"Guess what? I have experience now. *Lots* of experience."

"So I hear," he says, looking at the piece of paper. "You got some balls putting your three months at the Goat on your résumé, given the story I just heard."

"Everywhere I apply is going to have heard anyway," I say. "And I do know how to serve tables now, which I didn't before, so it shows my experience, and . . . that I'm honest? Plus I am a good server. Even Dev would have to admit that, I think. In fact, he even said the words 'you're an excellent server' on the voicemail message where he fired me! I have it. I could play it for you."

"That's gonna be your strategy?" Lyle says, the corners of his mouth quirking upward. "To play the message in which your boss is firing you?"

"Only the part where he says I'm excellent," I say, and start pulling my phone out.

"No need," he says, stopping me. "I believe you. And I hate Ackerman's guts, but I still got nothing for you. Might have a dishwashing position in a few weeks, but nothing right now."

"You'd hire me for that, though?" I say.

"Yeah, I'd hire you," he says. "You can holler at the dishes. Entertain the staff back there. I don't mind my people on the salty side."

"Would I have the chance to move up?"

"Never say never," he says. "Keep in touch."

All is quiet when I get home, and I head to my room, flop on the bed, and send up prayers to the universe that my parents have not heard about last night's fiasco yet, and that I can have a nice, calm evening.

This hope is dashed when Mom comes home.

I can tell by the way she closes the front door that something's up. When you have a family like mine you learn to tune into the tone of their comings and goings. In this case, Mom does not so much slam the door, as very carefully *not* slam it.

Yikes.

A minute later she's inside my room and sitting gingerly on the end of my bed.

"I think we should talk," Mom says in horribly quiet voice, hands clasped in her lap.

"You heard?"

"Heard, yes," she says, her normally smooth expression pinched. "And *saw*. So handy, everyone having a phone these days, and access to everything. This way, when your least favorite coworker tells you your daughter has made a spectacle of herself and attacked a pillar of the community for no apparent reason, and you give them a gentle lecture on how they shouldn't believe everything they hear . . . that person can then come back with a video and prove you wrong."

Oh boy. I can just picture the scene at work, where my mom has been the sole voice for discretion in a sea of busybodies who think the only reason she doesn't like gossip is that her husband has so often been the subject of it. (Which may be true and who could blame her?) I only thought about how she might be angry, worried, or disappointed when she found out, but not about how she might be humiliated.

I should have. She and I have been living in the rubble of Dad for years—the rubble of Dad, and then the rubble of Dad plus Jack.

And . . . she's crying.

"I'm sorry," I say.

She doesn't even duck her head, just swipes angrily at the tears with the back of her hand.

"I'm especially sorry you found out like that."

"*I* am sorry," she says, swiping at a tear and sitting up straighter, "that you caused such a scene. I thought you knew better."

"I do, but . . ."

"Yes . . . ?"

"People are saying I just flipped out for no reason. But I had a reason."

"Of course you did," she says, finally turning to look at me, gaze pointed.

"I—I—" I stop, stumbling over the halted torrent of words I was about to unleash in my defense. "What?"

"Perry Ackerman is a saint in this town, but every woman under seventy-five, and maybe a few over, knows he's also a sleazebag."

I just stare at her, mouth hanging open.

"Don't look so surprised, Libby. Women have been dealing with this forever. You don't need to tell me what Perry said, or what he did to set you off. That man has done his routine everywhere. He's a walking boner."

"Ewww. *Mom.*"

"You can't go around having tantrums every time some ridiculous man insults you or hits on you, or both. It's naïve, not to mention foolish."

"Foolish!"

"It is," she says, her tears already a thing of the distant past. "I thought you understood from watching your father the stupidity of that variety of behavior. And the pointlessness."

"But—"

"You have to think about *what you're trying to accomplish*, and whether it's feasible that you can *actually accomplish it* when you do something like that. You have to think about the consequences and whether you're able to withstand them. Yes, it's unpleasant having to deal with men like Perry, and I'm sorry you've had to go through it."

"Are you?"

"Yes."

She's not, though. Or she is, but she's actually more upset that I didn't do a good job handling being sexually harassed than that I was sexually harassed in the first place. This shouldn't surprise me, shouldn't hurt, but it does.

"This is the reality, though, Libby," she continues. "You have to think—every time!—about who you are in the world, and what your position is. About who has the power. Perry employs half the town, owns a ton of real estate, has shares in most of the businesses, including a controlling share of the Inn, which is my place of employment in case you forgot. So it's not just your job on the line here—it could be mine."

"You never mentioned . . ." I feel the blood draining from my face. "But, Mom, he's not your boss, is he?"

"He's not running things day-to-day," Mom says. "But in the big picture, yes. He's the boss of my boss, which makes him my boss. And he could make life very difficult for me, or even have me fired. That's my point, Libby. Here in Pine Ridge Perry has power. And what you did is just going to make him want to flex it."

"I know, I just—I couldn't handle it anymore. What was I supposed to do?"

"Find a way to manage him, hold on to your dignity, and bide your time."

"Managing him *and* holding on to dignity are mutually exclusive in this situation, Mom."

"There's an art to it, dear."

"Seriously?"

"Of course. What do you think I do at the Inn? Figure out how to calm people down, make them feel special, important, and taken care of. I deal with every variety of person, and all sorts of situations. It's a skill, and when done really well, an art."

"There shouldn't be an art to being sexually harassed. That shouldn't be a thing."

"That's life, Libby. And it always has been. I'm not saying you have to just let it happen. You find ways to protect yourself. You dodge the unwanted hand, play dumb about the comments, and of course you need a signal you can send out to another woman when you really need help. I'm sorry I didn't instruct you on any of this but I thought you knew."

"I do now," I say. "But I shouldn't have to."

"But you do," she says with a resigned shrug.

"The other thing you said—about biding my time. Until when am I supposed to bide?"

"Until you are in a position to do something."

"That means never." I drop back onto my pillow.

She reaches over, pats my arm, and says, "Maybe . . . maybe there'll come a time when it just won't matter anymore."

"That is the most depressing thing I've ever heard. Mom, it should matter," I say, sitting back up. "Or do you get to your age and just find you've become so tired and disappointed with life that you stop caring when things are wrong? Because I do know that you can't go around swearing and throwing stuff. I know it doesn't accomplish anything positive. But what you're saying is my options are either that, or do nothing."

"You're not going to change someone like Perry, dear. That's what I'm saying. And there will always be someone like Perry. And now your position is worse than it was before. Now you have to fix this, when before there wasn't anything to fix."

"How am I supposed to fix it? What if I don't want to?"

"Then I don't think you're going to like the consequences."

BARKING DOGS

Things get more exciting on Tuesday, if that's even possible.

First thing in the morning I text my friends and let them know that I'm fine to walk to school sans entourage, because I figure the worst is probably over. After a couple of minutes, Emma texts back, suggesting we all meet in front of the school and go in together, which I agree to.

Then Noah texts me separately: How about just me? I'm not an entourage.

True. I'm fine, though. Seriously.

It's a long walk in for you.

My stepmom can drive me.
I'll bring you a coffee . . .

You keep bringing me stuff.

Is that a yes?

My fingers hover over the phone. Noah and a coffee sound like an excellent start to the day. A bit too excellent. If he wants to talk about his relationship with Ava again, I'm not sure I can handle it. It's so tempting to encourage him to dump her, which makes me such a bad friend. And feeling like a bad friend might cause me to go overboard in the opposite direction and convince him to stay with her, which might be the wrong decision for him, which again would make me a very bad friend. Plus, let's be real—I'd be so mad at myself.

And what if they do break up? Am I a better option for him? My life is a mess right now, and I seem to be some kind of magnet for bad relationships, and I can't go traveling with him next year either, not that he's asking. So, no.

But I still text, Yes.

He brings the coffee in a reusable mug with the Ted's Snowscape logo on the side.

"I put some of that hazelnut stuff in. That's the flavor you like, right?"

"Yes." I beam at him with far more enthusiasm than the situation warrants. I mean, he probably remembers how Boris, Emma, and Yaz like their coffee too.

"I made it myself, I'll have you know," he says. "In our French press."

"Ooh, fancy."

"I even ground the beans."

"Now you're just bragging."

The first part of the walk is comfortable and quiet, with no one else around, but as we get closer to school there are other people walking in the same direction, and I start feeling the stares.

"Wow," Noah mutters, noticing. "I hate people."

"You think we wouldn't do the same?"

"No. No way," he says, and then adds, "I hope not."

"There's nothing I can do about it," I say, with a rueful shake of my head.

"I hate to think you have to just hide out until this is over, though. I'd go nuts. You should come to my house and do the Stomp."

"The Stomp?"

"It's a trail my dad and I made on our property. I named it the Stomp because when I'm upset, or just trying to figure stuff out, I like to get outside and stomp around."

"Literally?"

"Yeah, it's a thing, like . . ." He looks sideways at me and demonstrates a hilarious, stomping walk. "Some people run, I go out in the yard and stomp. And I climb the landscaping stuff—the rock heaps and whatnot, and stomp on those too if I need to."

"How did I not know this about you?"

"Oh, it's a carefully guarded family secret," he jokes. "But seriously, we've got ten acres and no close neighbors to stare at you, so if you want to come stomp around it's an open invitation. Actual stomping optional. It'd get you out from under all these eyes, and . . . out of your house, too, in case that's something you need."

"I may well take you up on that."

"Good. Because I don't make the offer to just anybody," he says, and then gestures to the small parade of fellow students walking toward school in tandem with us, "certainly not to any of these asswipes."

I wonder if he's taken Ava on the Stomp, but we've had an Ava-free morning so I decide not to ask.

And then we're in front of the school and Yaz and Emma are there. We walk in together like we did yesterday, with the three of them sticking close to me and Emma staring daggers at anyone who so much as glances my way.

"Anything I need to know?" I ask Emma in a low tone as we head to our lockers.

"Nothing," she says. "You really didn't look?"

"I said I wouldn't. No chance someone's caused a new scandal and everyone has moved on?"

"Sorry, hon," Yaz says. "Not yet."

"I'll cause a scandal," Noah offers from behind us. "What do you want me to do? I could toilet-paper someone's house, set off some smoke bombs in the park? Oh, we could steal the Fancy Lattes sign and put it on Just Coffee, and vice versa. They'd both be so pissed and it would get the Complainers going with all kinds of conspiracy theories."

"Let's not get you arrested," Emma says, shaking her head. "That would be the opposite of helpful."

All morning things go quiet every time I walk into a classroom, but it's not like I'm getting waves of hatred. It's tolerable. Then on my way to lunch I pass Rod Catena, one of my least favorite people, and he gives me a very deliberate, aggressive smirk.

Ugh.

Two minutes later, as I'm digging my lunch bag out of my locker, I hear barking.

I turn around, half expecting to see an actual dog, but instead there's a group of boys—Rod and his crew of idiot friends, standing there cackling. Why anyone would want to be Rod's friend is beyond me. He has no discernible talents or ambitions beyond partying, slacking off, and being the biggest possible jackass. But maybe being the biggest possible jackass is its own special talent.

Rod barks, looking right at me as he does it, and his

friends echo him with a chorus of yips and howls. They are just the tiniest bit scary when they're all together like this, but we've all learned the hard way that it's best not to cower, or show any weakness at all with these jerks, and I've had extra practice dealing with them due to my dad's antics. So I grab my lunch, then slam my locker shut with a purposely loud bang, give them my most withering glare, and say, "Go hump a landmine, Catena."

The sound of barking follows me all the way down the hall, and I'm relieved to get outside to the picnic table we always have lunch at as soon as it gets warm.

Emma, Boris, Yaz, and Noah are already there, and I set my lunch down and survey them for hints that they know what's going on. Emma's peeling an orange, Yaz is eating seaweed, Boris is on his phone, and Noah's halfway through a massive sandwich.

"Anyone want to tell me why people have started barking at me?" I ask when nobody volunteers any information.

"Barking?" Yaz says.

"Yeah, like dogs?"

"That's random." Yaz has never been a good liar—everything shows on her face.

"It doesn't feel random," I say, and she's suddenly concentrating really hard on her seaweed.

Boris and Noah are both staring fixedly at Emma, who grimaces.

"Em . . . "

"Okay. You know the video? From the Goat, the one of you and—"

"Yes, I know the one," I say, cutting her off.

"You know how the audio only caught a tiny bit of what you said to Perry after soaking him . . . really just the swear words and the word 'pig' I think. Well . . . someone made a doctored version of the video and dubbed in the sounds of a dog barking, exactly in sync with you speaking."

I wince.

"And there's a tail involved," Boris adds. "Uh, on you."

"She didn't need to know that part," Emma says, rounding on him.

"I was just trying to help."

"How, exactly, does that help?"

"Well, if people start asking her to go fetch she'll . . . uh . . . know the reason?" Boris says, digging himself deeper.

"I. Am. The Boss. Of. This. Boris," Emma says, pounding on her chest for emphasis.

"I'm sorry, Em, I . . ." Boris mumbles, and then turns to me. "Sorry, Libby."

"It's fine. Being a laughingstock is the least of my worries."

"Lots of people are actually laughing *with* you," Emma points out. "With you, and *at* Perry. At least . . . they are regarding the original video. Because the look on his face is hilarious, and him sitting there soaked is also hilarious. Now, eat. You need to keep your strength up."

"Uh-oh, did I also put you in charge of my nutrition?" I say, then grudgingly open my lunch.

"Whoa, what's that?" Noah says, looking at my overstuffed lunch box that contains a large burrito, guacamole, and a colorful compartment of fruit salad.

"Weird thing—ever since I started working at the Goat my dad's been making me these crazy lunches. Not every day, but once or twice a week I'll go in the kitchen in the morning and he's packed me some massive lunch. He hasn't done lunches since I was in sixth grade."

"Sweet," Yaz says.

"Well, I think it's a guilt lunch," I say. "So that detracts from the deed a bit."

"Still, yum," Noah says.

"A guilt lunch will keep your strength up just as well as a normal lunch," Emma says. "And probably taste just as good since it's his guilt, not yours. Eat."

"Who do you think made the video?" I ask, then take a bite of the burrito, which is, in fact, delicious.

"I dunno," Emma says.

"That maggot-burger, Catena," Noah says at the exact same time, then throws his hands up when Emma glares at him. "What? Libby hates him already. We all hate him. Now we can hate him more."

We would hate Rod Catena anyway, as he has always been awful, but we all hate him particularly because of what he did to Yaz. In junior year, before she realized she prefers girls (and possibly hastening that realization), he showed up newly hot-looking after the summer and convinced Yaz to go out with him. Then he got her alone and proceeded to slobber all over her face while trying repeatedly to grab for her boobs and butt, even after she pushed him away. When that caused her to immediately dump him, he told everyone at school that she had "let" him do those things and spread all sorts of gross, false details about their supposed hookup.

"Sorry again," Emma says, taking in my expression. "These people are not listening to me."

"Rod's always been despicable. It's no surprise."

"Want me to kick his ass?" Boris says out of left field, like he believes he's suddenly become some kind of bruiser. "I'll kick his ass."

Emma groans at this, Noah laughs, and Yaz looks worried. Because in no way would Boris be able to kick Rod's ass.

I mean, maybe if he came up behind him, and used his trumpet to bash him over the head, and then ran away really fast, but otherwise no.

"I could at least talk to him," Boris says with bizarre eagerness. "Ask him to take the video down."

"Oh please, man, let me come along to witness this travesty of a conversation," Noah says.

Boris, like always, is trying to be nice.

Or, he's actually being nice.

"Let me at least try," he says to me, all earnestness, and suddenly I'm so irritated. Worse than irritated—I'm all-out-of-proportion enraged, my body in fight-or-flight mode.

"Not *you*," I snap at Boris. "Not about this."

Everyone gapes at me and Emma says, "Libby!"

"Sorry. I just." I stand up, shaking all of a sudden, wanting to kick something, wanting to run. "Can't."

And then, making it fight-*and*-flight, I grab my stuff and take off.

———

Emma follows me, as does the charming sound of barking once I get inside. The new video has obviously spread like wildfire during the lunch hour.

Fun.

I seriously consider barking back. Maybe howling.

"Libby, what the hell?" Emma says, catching up with me just in time to foil my excellent plan of spending the duration of lunch slumped in the same bathroom stall I hid in yesterday.

"Give me some space, Emma," I say, continuing forward.

"No," she says. "Talk to me."

"You don't want to hear what I have to say right now."

"What if I do?"

"You don't. And even if you do, I don't want you to."

"Why not? Is this about Boris? You're so weird about him. Talk to me."

"I . . ." Crap. Suddenly I'm about to cry. What is wrong with me? "I can't."

"Why?" she demands again.

"Because I can't handle any more . . . stuff. I don't want to fight and I don't want you to be upset with me. I can't lose you."

"Lose me?" she says, incredulous. "A little faith here, please. That's not how this best friend business works."

"Look, I just need a break from Boris sometimes," I say, deciding to be blunt, if not thorough. "He annoys me, okay? I know I acted brokenhearted when we broke up but honestly I was sick to death of him. I stayed in the relationship far too long because I just . . . couldn't find the words to end it. I thought he might get mad, or be hurt, and any thought of conflict just . . . freezes me."

Emma looks confused and I know I'm not explaining this well. I'm only starting to figure it out myself—how literally impossible it feels for me to speak up in certain circumstances. I do freeze but that's not all. It's as if, as things got worse at home, I started to submerge myself—to see trouble coming and slowly sink down into an existential swamp, with only my nose and eyes above the water line, safe but incapable of speaking or taking action. Maybe that's why half of my relationship with Boris feels like it occurred underwater.

"The point is, Em, I was a coward. And I care about Boris, but I needed a break from him."

"And you never got it because of me."

"Yes."

"You should have told me," Emma says, eyes suddenly flashing.

"You said you wouldn't be mad."

"I said you wouldn't lose me, not that I wouldn't be mad. I can be mad."

"Fine," I say, folding my arms together across my chest and squeezing like I can physically hold myself together.

"Why didn't you at least tell me when he and I started falling for each other?"

"What could you have done about it at that point?"

This gives her pause.

"Plus I would have been a hypocrite to tell you not to go out with him given that I didn't want him. I'm sorry, though."

"I'm sorry, too." Her shoulders sag. "I'll try to limit your Boris exposure."

"No. We have, what, two months of school left? We're all friends and I don't want that ruined right at the end of high school after all these years. It's my issue to deal with, and most of the time I'm fine. Let's just go to Geography."

She looks at me for a long moment, then says, "Sure, okay."

All things considered, this didn't go as badly as I feared. Then again, I haven't told her everything about Boris and me. Nor do I plan to.

13

MERCY SHAG

Speaking of Boris exposure, I find him waiting by my locker after school.

"Hey," I say. "Sorry about earlier. I'm a little on edge, I guess."

"No big deal," he says, and steps out of the way so I can get my stuff. "It's been a rough few days for you."

"Thanks."

"So," he says, as I'm shoving books into my backpack and grabbing my sunglasses, "I told Emma I was going to offer to walk you home, since she and Yaz have basketball, and Noah has to work, but she got a weird look on her face and told me not to. She said you might need some space."

Shit.

"It's fine, Boris," I say, and inwardly roll my eyes at myself because now I'm going to end up overcompensating and spending more time with Boris instead of less, because I feel badly that he might feel badly . . . even though he actually should feel badly, but not about the thing he thinks he should feel badly about. If he actually thinks that, which he probably doesn't.

Ugh—someone please save me from my overthinking brain.

Rod Catena walks by and barks, and Boris starts to turn toward him, but I grab his bony arm.

"Steady there, tough guy," I say while tugging him in the opposite direction from Rod. "A walk home would be lovely."

I make some efforts at small talk, lobbing subjects toward Boris, which he lobs feebly back, but pretty soon we're out of conversation and the short walk to my house starts to feel really long.

It got like this when we were together, too—nothing to say.

Once in a while he would go heavy into physics, composition theory, or the many odd things he knows about geology, and I would do my best to keep up. Or I would try to talk about art, tell a funny-but-dark story, or dive into something deep, and the result would be either blank confusion from him, or worse, he would start laughing nervously, and then literally pat me on the head, and be like, "Hey, whoa, calm down."

In other words, Boris and I are not soul mates.

"I always think of you when I pass here," he says out of the blue as we're walking by the tiny park where he turns left to go to his house, and I continue straight on to mine. When we were dating, we'd stop and play on the teeter-totter, or sit on the grass and smooch.

"You want to sit?" he asks, and points to an empty bench.

I don't want to be guilty of being mean to Boris twice in one day, so I say "Sure" and follow him over.

It's only when we sit—me on one side, him about midway, that I notice his hands are shaking. It's chilly in the shade, and we're both a little underdressed, but I don't think that's the reason. I look up at his face then and see him looking at me with a very serious, very nervous expression.

"I have to talk to you about something," he says.

"Listen, if it's about you and Emma don't worry about it. Seriously."

"It's not that," he says. Jeez, he looks like he might cry or something. "It's . . . Libby, I wanted to ask you about . . ."

Oh God. Everything in me goes rigid and I stare fixedly at the kids on the play structure, suddenly wishing I could switch places with one of them.

Because I think he wants to talk about *that*.

And I can't. I can't do it. I won't.

But no. Boris is so clueless, it can't be that.

Still, if it is, could talking about it possibly make me feel any worse? Well, given that it feels like my every muscle has tensed and my organs are turning to stone, yes. Much worse. In the short term. But in the long term?

"About what . . . ?" I manage to say without keeling over and dying.

"About the mercy shag."

Submerge, submerge, my brain is screaming.

But I can't. Won't.

———

Boris and I were together for almost a year, and he seemed the right boy to lose my virginity to. He was sweet and thoughtful and did all the romantic things high school boys are supposed to do—flowers, good night texts, hand-holding, declarations of devotion, et cetera.

We spent a lot of time making out, then rolling around and making out, then fooling around and making out in various levels of undress. I wanted to have sex. I was curious. Still, we didn't rush, and the not rushing activities were quite interesting and fun.

When we finally did the deed, though, it was distinctly less fun than everything that came before. Still, I knew the first time wasn't necessarily going to be the best, so I didn't panic. And it did get a little better after that—less awkward at least. But I soon realized that none of it was really doing it for me. I didn't hate it, but given a choice between sex with Boris and a really good plate of waffles, I'd have chosen the waffles.

Boris, though, was having the time of his life. I swear he was glowing, and he looked like he'd grown a foot. He would probably have given up waffles for life in order to keep having sex.

Meanwhile, I felt progressively worse—like a fraud and a failure. Because if he was having such a great time and I was only moderately into it, it must be my fault. He was a perfectly nice, considerate, cute, clean boyfriend, and instead of being ecstatic, I found myself sighing every time I saw him walking toward me.

Boris wasn't doing anything wrong from a technical standpoint, at least not that I could think of. He wasn't "bad" at sex. He was enthusiastic, bursting with love and gratitude, and had lots of energy. After our first time, he composed an almost-good trumpet solo and named it after me.

And, to be fair, Boris didn't know I wasn't having a good time, because I didn't tell him. For one thing, I'd been pretending to like it in anticipation of eventually liking it, so I would've had to start out by explaining that my moans of ecstasy were exaggerated and/or outright fake, which did not put me in a good light and was frankly too embarrassing. Plus male egos are famously fragile about this stuff, and I didn't want to be responsible for scarring Boris for life.

So I started making excuses not to do the deed. At first he was understanding. Then he got whiny. Then he started in with "a man's got needs!" and "have mercy on your poor, neglected, horny boyfriend."

Mostly as a joke.

Except he made the jokes too often for them to be actual jokes.

One day when we were alone at his house after school and I was studying for a test I had the next day, he made another one of these mercy comments.

My inner censor must have been sleeping, because I said, "Oh, so you want a mercy fuck?"

He blanched. Boris was a "make love" kind of guy.

"Mercy shag, then?" I amended.

"Um. Well . . ." he stammered.

"What?" I said, getting up from his desk, where I was set up to study, and coming toward where he was sitting on the bed. "Are you saying you don't?"

"Well," he said. "It sounds . . . I mean . . ."

I pulled my shirt over my head and tossed it over the back of a chair, then undid my pants, took off my bra, underwear, and socks, and lay down on the bed.

"Let's go," I said. "But make it fast—I really need to study."

Boris did, at least, hesitate, and take a moment to look confused. But then he laughed, and muttered, "Mercy shag, huh? You sure?"

"God forbid we fail to meet your needs," I said, but I said it with affection, with humor. "C'mon. But don't expect much from me."

"You're hilarious," he said. But he took me at my word and reached for the condom box, and thus was born the mercy shag.

I found I could give a mercy shag without too much distress, maybe because I kept my real self somewhere deeper than Boris ever got to anyway.

After that Boris made a lot of winking jokes about mercy shagging, and it was clear he'd convinced himself that I actually enjoyed them, and was only toying with him by pretending not to.

From then on, they were all mercy shags.

It's only now that I'm starting to realize I put myself under Boris in a way that I couldn't undo, in a way that made me feel I was always under him, his breath in my face, his sweat dripping on me, trying so hard to detach from my body and burrow deeper into myself. Every time I saw him, even months after we broke up, that's how I felt. That's, I guess, how I still feel—not all the time, but in unexpected flashes that sneak up on me and leave me feeling gross and violated.

And now there's Kyle, which was (confusingly) both a better and a worse experience than I ever had with Boris. Maybe if I hadn't allowed all those mercy shags, I would have known how to say no more forcefully to Kyle. Or I wouldn't have been so twisted as to have a body that responded to Kyle at all. Through everything, too, is the feeling that I did this to myself.

But that's not true either. Well, it is and it isn't.

Regardless, Boris has said the words and now the subject is out in the open and I have to deal with it.

———

"What about the mercy shag, Boris?" I manage to say.

"That assembly last week made me think about it. All those times we did it, you basically . . ." he takes a gasping breath then continues. "You told me you didn't want to. It sure wasn't enthusiastic consent."

I'm dying here. Tense and sick and wishing I could somehow vacate myself. Take the real me and exit, leaving just the shell here to get through this conversation. I did it during every mercy shag, why can't I do it for this?

"Am I wrong?" Boris asks, and I can hear the wishful thinking in his voice. "I would love to be wrong."

"No, you're not wrong," I say, the words coming out in a ragged whisper.

Boris crumples backward on the bench like someone just punched him.

"Okay, let's just get it out," he says, seeming to gasp between each word. "Was it worse than not being enthusiastic? Because I . . . did . . . a whole bunch of the things she listed. Whining. Pushing you. Bugging you, pressuring you, trying to make you feel guilty."

"Yeah, you did," I say, my hands gripping the bench.

He lets out a low moan.

"But," I concede, the words starting to come easier, "it's not like you were threatening me or anything. And no offense, but it's not like you, yourself, are threatening, physically speaking."

"That's gotta be the first time it's ever been conveyed as a plus," Boris says. "Uh. Not trying to make light of anything."

"It's fine."

"People do 'quickies' and I told myself it was the same thing. I told myself you were only acting like you weren't into it to tease me. But you weren't teasing me, were you."

His expression is stark, and he doesn't state it as a question, but I've made a start, managed to get this far in the conversation, and so I need to answer. It's hideous and awkward, but I have to answer. And yet, I am amazed and horrified to observe in myself, still, the urge to smooth this over, to make it better for him, the urge to tell him that I didn't lie there under him hating it and just waiting for it to be over, to tell him that it didn't mess me up and make me hate us both.

I still somehow feel badly for him. I still feel guilty and gross and sad.

Because what he did was ugly, but what I did feels ugly to me, too. I didn't just lie to him about the mercy shags, I started lying way before that—pretending to be enjoying sex when I wasn't. And that was on me. Yes, I did it to protect his ego, and not hurt his feelings, but it was also because I was a coward and, like always, because I just could not speak.

"I wasn't teasing," I say.

He nods, then drops his head and says, "I'm so sorry. I have no excuse. I have reasons—like I didn't have any experience, and I was partially blinded by just wanting you, and I thought part of the whole deal was, you know, that you sometimes had to convince somebody, seduce them . . ."

"By whining?"

"Ouch. But fair. Whining is not a legitimate tool of seduction."

"It's not the hottest."

Boris gives a pained chuckle, and then winces like he thinks he shouldn't be laughing.

"Listen, I've been thinking about this, too," I say, turning to face him. "It's true that you shouldn't have taken me up on the mercy shag offers. But I *did offer*. I offered, which means in some way I consented—not enthusiastically, but still, you can't take all the blame for your confusion. I could have said no. I could have stopped offering. I should have, but I didn't."

"But I still did what I did."

"Yeah."

"Well," he says after a too-long silence, "this is truly awful."

I don't know why, but this makes me laugh—another one of those pained laughs, which causes Boris to give me the most wounded of looks.

I press my lips together and try to channel a more serious demeanor.

"How do I make this right, Libby? Is there something I can do? Do you want me to . . . take a break from Emma?"

"No, you cannot dump Emma. Are you kidding?"

"Well, I'd rather not but . . . I'm trying to show you I'm serious."

"Short of turning yourself in to the police . . ." I say, and he blanches. "Oh, come on, we both know that you'd get laughed right out of the station."

"Still. What can I do? Uh, ideally besides that. I can make myself scarce for a while—give you space. Would that help?"

"Actually, yes. Not in an extreme way, though. I don't want any drama and I don't want to have to hash this out with our friends. But some space would be lovely."

"Done," he says, clearly relieved to have a concrete task. "What else?"

"You're doing it, I guess. It was brave to talk to me about it, and I appreciate that. It's a relief having it out in the open. But we don't get to erase our mistakes. Just . . . don't do that to anyone again."

"I won't!" he says. "I really won't."

"Good."

"Would it help—do you want to meet again to talk more about it?"

"No!" I say, more forcefully than is necessary.

"Oh . . ." he says, his hurt look giving me my usual twinge

of Boris-related annoyance, but without the usual after-twinge of guilt over the annoyance. "You sure?"

"Hard pass, Boris. If you need to talk about it, I encourage you to find a professional. As for me, I'd be delighted to never talk about this again. Ever."

Boris looks a little downcast at this, and I get the sense he was hoping for more—either more time for punishment and self-flagellation or more of a big, emotional moment of forgiveness from me. But I'm not up for participating in either or those, so all he can do, finally, is nod and say, "All right."

14

THE FIXER

The conversation with Boris leaves me feeling strange—like I have expanded inside, but also like there's an empty space there. It hurts, and feels like grief, and at the same time I feel like if I ran fast enough I might be able to take flight. Like I might stretch my arms out and glide above the earth and leave it all behind me.

Finding two more college acceptance letters in my inbox when I get home only adds to my aching/flying sensation, but then I notice the acceptance deadlines—May 1—and come crashing back to earth.

Less than a month.

And then I get a text from Kyle letting me know about the video (like it could have evaded my notice) and asking if I'm okay. I considered blocking him but he is my best source of news from the Goat. At the same time I'm not in the mood for a lengthy exchange, and I'm tired of reassuring everyone that I'm okay. So I send him a thumbs-up emoji and then turn my notifications off, and park myself on my bed to do some reading.

And that's where I am when I hear Mom coming in an hour later.

"I'm home!" she sings out, sounding significantly more cheerful than she did yesterday.

Within moments, she comes bursting into my room.

"Look!" She sets an armload of stuff down on the bed beside me.

"Um . . ."

"Towels!" she says, with the excitement a normal person might reserve for things like winning the lottery. Not only that, but she's dressed to kill, Mom-style anyway, in a burgundy wrap dress, heels, full makeup—and are those false eyelashes?

"Towels?"

"They're bamboo!" she says.

"Okay . . ."

"Just wait," she says, and bustles back into the hallway, returning a moment later with a giant, clear plastic case with a picture of a super flowery, overdone bed on it.

"A duvet set!" she says, triumphantly.

"You missed your calling as one of those game show host ladies," I say. "You know, the ones that show off the prizes?"

"This is something I know you need," she says, leaning in and giving me a knowing look.

Suddenly my heart seems to skip a beat and I'm gripped with the irrational conviction that she knows about Kyle. She knows and this cheerful thing is an act and I'm in so much trouble.

But of course that's absurd.

Still it's hard to shake the suddenly pinned-in-place, exposed feeling that's come over me, the feeling that's been ambushing me at random times ever since the Kyle thing happened.

"Uh . . . why?" I ask, carefully.

"Isn't it super?" she says, gesturing at the picture of the made-up bed on the package. "Very lively and pretty, and it even has some of that indigo blue you like so much."

"Right . . . nice . . ." The only super thing about this duvet set is that it's super ugly, but I like Mom in this mood much better than I liked her in yesterday's post–Perry video mood. Obviously she hasn't seen the barking version.

"It's for your new place," she says, cheerily.

"I have a new place?"

"No, but you will. In July."

"Oh—that new place," I say, and now I can't help the snark that seeps into my tone. "You must mean my new place on Emma's basement couch, wheezing and sniffling with her slobbering pooch. Or maybe I can build a tent with this? And sleep on the towels?"

"Let's have some optimism," Mom says, patting the duvet.

"I have my regular duvet back already," I point out.

"Oh, I know," Mom says, waving a hand. "You left it wet in the sink but Dad got to it in time and rewashed it for you."

"Oh. Oops."

"It's okay!" she chirps, and I start to wonder if she's on some happy drug, or if maybe she's had a psychotic break. "The old one can serve as an extra, or you can leave it behind. It's just that seeing your bed with only those ratty old blankets on it made me realize you should have something new and fresh. There's the duvet, a cover for it, plus two shams, and even a little heart-shaped throw pillow."

"Heart-shaped throw pillow," I say, thinking how bizarre this is after the conversation I just had with Boris. "That solves everything."

"I think the phrase you're looking for is 'Thank you,'" she says, but she keeps smiling this twilight zone smile that reminds me of her cake-with-tragedy smile from January.

"Okay, what's going on?"

She walks over to my dresser and picks up a framed photo of Emma and me from sixth grade, puts it down, then turns back toward me, throws her arms wide, and proclaims, "I've fixed your situation!"

"Really? Which one?"

"I know I'm not perfect," she says, ignoring my actually sincere question. "I know you think I just stand by and let your father run roughshod all over us. And that may be true in some ways, but I also work hard to keep us afloat, Libby."

"I know you do. But where are you going with this?"

"Where I'm going is that I know how to talk to people, help people. And today, I wanted to help you. I know you need that job at the Goat. I know it probably wasn't easy to get a job in Pine Ridge in the first place because of all your father's . . . issues. You need money in order to be able to move out, and your boss, even if he wanted to, probably can't just . . . give you your job back. *And* I know how to talk to certain types of men. So."

"So . . . ?"

"So, I put on some lipstick and went to talk to Perry."

"I'm sorry, what?"

"That's right," she says, looking entirely too pleased with herself. "Your mother does still have some charm, you know."

"Charm!" Yikes, the dress and makeup make a terrible kind of sense now. "What did you *do?*"

"I just spoke gently to him," she says, and then puts a hand on one hip, thrusts that hip out flirtatiously, and bats her extremely voluminous eyelashes.

"Oh jeez, Mom . . ."

"I explained nicely that our family has been under a great

deal of stress, financial and otherwise, and that this is your first job, and you're saving for college, and you were simply not at your best the other night."

I stare at her.

"Fortunately he likes me. And you, as a matter of fact."

"Oh, is that what that's called? 'Liking'?"

"Save your sarcasm for someone who didn't just put herself on the line for you," she says with a sudden and skewering glare.

"Sorry," I say. "He likes you, he likes me. Go on."

"The long and short of it is that he agreed to give you a second chance," she says with an ecstatic and rather smug smile.

"A second chance at what?"

"I stood right beside him while he called your boss and encouraged him—very strongly and eloquently—to hire you back."

I may need smelling salts—I'm feeling a bit faint.

"Your boss was very receptive to the idea. Apparently you're one of their best servers!"

"Really?"

"Really. I believe you'll be getting a call soon."

"But Mom . . . Perry is so . . . how can you stand it? How did you even do it?"

"Oh, it's nothing," she says with a feminine wave of her hand. "You'll learn as you get older that most men just want to feel good about themselves, and they don't seem to be able to get that feeling on their own. They need to feel powerful, needed. It doesn't hurt if you can make them feel attractive and manly while you're at it."

"Ugh! Stop!" I say, throwing my hands up as if to ward her off.

"There's an art to it."

"Ugh, not the 'art to it' stuff again."

"But there is," she says, plowing on. "There are differences in how you approach each man . . . but essentially they're all the same. They're easy to get on your side if you know what to do."

"Seriously, I might puke."

"I didn't do anything untoward, Libby. I only told him the truth, and let him cast himself as the potential hero—the savior of us both."

"While looking hot and crying."

"Something like that," she says, and pats her hair. "But with more nuance, I hope."

"Blech. This stuff is from the dark ages."

"Then we are still in the dark ages. And again, I think the phrase you're looking for is 'thank you,'" she says, and then sweeps out of the room.

Wow.

I'm admittedly a little traumatized at the image of my mom in Perry's office, making him "feel manly." But it's done, and I have three colleges awaiting my response, and, aside from the relentless sexual harassment, I liked my job at the Goat. I don't just need it back, I want it.

This is what I'm thinking about when my phone rings.

A glance shows me it's Dev and, heart thudding, I pick up.

"Hello, Dev."

"Libby?"

"Yes."

"Do you realize you forgot to cash out on Sunday night?"

"Oh! Sorry."

"It's fine. I did most of it for you, but you'll have to bring the remaining cash from your float."

"Thank you. I'll do that."

This is not coming across like a job offer. Perhaps Mom overestimated the power of her charms. Still, Dev is at least speaking to me, and I just saw, with Boris, how a sincere apology can go a long way.

"Listen," I say, "I'm really sorry about what happened. I shouldn't have freaked out like that. It was unprofessional. And I'm sorry about the dry cleaning bill and . . . for the trouble."

"You cannot lose your temper at customers," Dev says. "We wouldn't exist without them."

"I know. I'm sorry."

"And you certainly cannot verbally abuse and physically assault them."

"Even when they've been abusing and assaulting me?" slips out of my mouth before I can stop it, and I wince.

"Even then," Dev says. "You know this already. You are a good server, Libby. A hard worker. I was very surprised at your outburst."

"So was I, if that helps."

He sighs heavily, and I stay silent, hoping I haven't screwed this up.

"Normally it would be one strike and you're out," Dev says finally. "But the fact is it's spring and the restaurant is getting busier, and I am short-staffed, and so . . . I have decided to give you a second chance."

"Really?" I leap to my feet.

"Really."

"Dev, thank you so much. I promise you won't regret this!"

"You are officially suspended for the week," he says, not quite matching my enthusiasm. "I cannot bring you back with no consequences. But you may come for your shift next Monday."

"Thank you," I say, almost ready to jump up and down. "Thank you so much. You have no idea how grateful I am. I promise I will never dump sangria on anyone again, and I will hold my temper, and I will work so hard, and—"

"There's just one thing," Dev says, interrupting me.

"Anything."

"You must apologize to Perry."

My joy and relief screech to a stop.

"Whoa, what was that again?"

"You must apologize to Perry," he repeats. "It's only reasonable. In fact, it was he who convinced me to give you this chance."

"Ohhh."

Of course Perry has to get something out of this, besides my mom turning up looking pretty and flirting with him. He gets an apology, *and* the credit for being magnanimous, generous, and forgiving. Mom must have known this part, but decided to let Dev tell me.

"Libby? Are you still there?"

"I'm here. I don't suppose this apology could be in the form of a letter, or an email?"

"Certainly not," Dev says. "Perry will be here with his friends on Monday evening, and he has agreed to let you apologize then. Once you do it, and of course you must do it well, then he is willing to put it in the past."

"What if I went to see him this week, or . . ."

The thought of going to Perry's office at the brewery is awful, but I could take Emma, or even Mom, and then at least the moment would be private.

"No, he was very clear. He wants the apology at the scene of the crime, so to speak. You must understand he has been somewhat embarrassed, with that video going around," Dev says.

"He's not the only one."

"No, indeed."

"Dev, I really want to come back, but I don't know if I can do this."

"Certainly you can. You had no problem apologizing to me just now, and this will be no different. You were in the wrong—"

"And he wasn't?"

"Perry Ackerman is a customer and an upstanding member of the community, Libby. He is powerful and influential. I have put every cent I had into this enterprise," Dev says, in a suddenly low voice. "My money, my wife's money. I feed my family from this. I make our future from this. My children's educations. I cannot . . . I'm sorry, but someone like Perry, if he decides to . . . he could ruin everything for me. Do you understand?"

"Yes, but—"

"Please, apologize to Perry, and do it well. He even said he will let you serve him afterward."

"Let me! How generous."

"Indeed," Dev says, either ignoring or not noticing my acidic tone. "Will you do it?"

The idea makes me sick. But my second-wave job search did not go very well yesterday, and the idea of having no income also makes me sick.

It's not like I have to work at the Goat forever. If I can just get myself through this, and through the summer, eventually I'll be in a better, more secure position where no one can do these things to me, and maybe where I can prevent them from happening to anyone else.

And a lot might happen between now and Monday night. Perry might get the flu, or not show up for some other (ideally nonfatal but I'm not too picky) reason. He could have a full-scale attack of conscience, and realize how wrong his behavior was and decide, instead, that *he* should apologize to *me*. (Not holding my breath for that one.) Or I might find another job after all. In the meantime, wouldn't it be the most practical thing to say yes?

"All right, Dev," I say, "I'll be there."

"And you'll do it?"

"Sure, I'll do it," I say, crossing my fingers that I won't have to.

15

THE WORLD IS MY OYSTER

So I have my job back, or will soon.

I'll make the apology if I have to, and life will go on, and people will stop barking at me in the hallways at school, and my bank account will start rising again.

Admittedly, apologizing to Perry will probably feel like swallowing fireworks, but I decide to not think about that right now. Better to tackle a more immediately solvable problem instead.

Housing, for example.

Dad was on about the Airbnb thing again last week, even dragging me down to the basement to look at the "concept board" he's created with magazine clippings. His energy took a dive over the weekend, but I have no doubt he'll be back on it soon.

So I need to make sure I have somewhere to live come July 1, ideally before May 1, when I have to notify colleges about whether I'm coming or not. Once I know what my living expenses are going to be, then I'll be able to crunch some final numbers and decide.

I do my best to shake off the phone call with Dev, then

park myself in front of the computer to begin the search for an apartment, or room, in or around Pine Ridge.

It doesn't take me long to discover that while rental prices in Pine Ridge are drastically less expensive than practically everywhere else, there isn't a plethora of options. Most of the places for rent seem to be entire houses, and a $1,600/month house with four bedrooms, while perhaps a good deal for an entire family or group of roommates, isn't what I need.

Fortunately, there are a few studios and rooms for rent, and by the end of the night I've made appointments to see two of them tomorrow after school. Neither looks fabulous, but I'm not expecting fabulous.

I call Emma to ask if she wants to come with me, and also to tell her about Dev's call.

She goes really quiet.

"Maybe I won't have to go through with it," I say, hating the feeling that I'm overjustifying. "And I am really being kicked out of here at the end of June, so . . . ."

"Yaz and I have both offered—"

"I'm allergic to both your houses. I'd be wheezing twenty-four-seven."

"What about Boris? No pets there, and—"

"No! And not Noah, either. No way."

"Why not Noah?"

"Just not comfortable, okay?" I say, glad she can't see my face. "And look, I can apologize for my actions—the ones that were out of line. I can live with that if it gets me the job and my independence back. I don't have to grovel or tell him he's a saint or anything."

"Don't count on it."

Wednesday morning Emma practically bounces up to me at my locker, as though none of the barking or side-eyeing of our fellow students even exists.

"Good news," she says.

"Did Perry get abducted by aliens?"

"Sadly not," she says. "But you didn't sound too excited about the places we're going to see, and I have something that'll hopefully cheer you up. I hope it's okay, I invited Yaz to come too."

"Of course," I say, then frown. "Is that the good news?"

"Oh, no, the news is that when I told her, she remembered she has this new neighbor, a city guy, who's bought that old B&B and is renovating it. Apparently he's planning to rent one of the rooms out full time . . . and so she emailed him last night, and he said we can come see it today."

"Oh, amazing!"

"You're getting first dibs on it 'cause he's still renovating. The rent would also be cheaper to start—because of noise, obviously. Yaz says he's a really nice guy. It is a basement," Emma admits, "and I know you don't want a basement, but . . ."

"Hey, if that's what I have to do, I'll do it."

———

The first apartment is at the back third of the second floor of a meticulously landscaped, cranberry-colored Victorian house I've always admired.

"It's not all three of you trying to rent?" the landlady says, looking at us skeptically as we stand on the front porch.

"No, just me," I say. "They're here for, um . . ."

"Moral support," Yaz says.

"All right," she says, not moving to open the door any farther, and suddenly peering at me with new intensity. "You're the girl who threw a fit at Ackerman."

"Well, yes. But I promise I would not throw any fits . . . as your tenant. I'm actually a very quiet, responsible . . . uh . . . person."

"She totally is," Yaz says.

"And there were extenuating circumstances," Emma adds.

"Yes, I've seen Perry's extenuating circumstance," the woman says, and finally cracks a hint of a smile. "I'm Sarah."

We head upstairs to the small-but-cute bedroom at the back of the house. Everything seems fine until Sarah informs us that I can only rent the room if I agree to let her cover the windows overlooking the backyard with black garbage bags and duct tape, from the outside.

"I could just bring some dark curtains," I suggest.

"No, I don't want the feeling that people could be looking down on me when I'm out there naked. That's why I haven't rented the room until now."

"Oh!" I say, trying very hard not to look at Emma or Yaz.

"Naked?" Emma squeaks out.

"Yeah, sunbathing or gardening or whatever. I'm a part-time nudist."

Sarah is a very pale-skinned redhead, like Yaz, and should probably be slathered in a very high SPF all year round, not cavorting naked in her backyard, but I say, "Cool."

Yaz has turned beet red.

"Do you ever worry about drones?" Emma asks, her lips twitching.

"Drones! I shot two of them down last summer and I haven't seen any since. Whether it's drones or grabby-handed

perverts, you can consider us well protected on this property," she says, like this is a bonus she should be charging
extra for.

We extricate ourselves quickly and somehow manage not
to collapse into shrieking, crying laughter until we're a full
block away.

———

The next place is better, in the sense that it has a seemingly
normal landlord, and again isn't a basement.

It is, though, above the fish market.

*I'll just keep the windows open. And bring extra blankets for
winter . . .*

Then I see a line of massive ants when I open the cupboard under the kitchen sink.

I'll just get some ant traps . . .

Yaz and Emma march me out of there, grim-faced.

———

"You cannot move to either of those places," Emma says as
we head toward Yaz's street.

"Yeah, no," Yaz says. "Bad vibes at the first place, bad bugs
and smells at the second."

Yaz's neighbor, and the potential landlord-to-be, is
Trevor—a fit, thirtysomething Eeyore, with a fashionable
shock of hair, expensive-looking jeans, and a permanently
woebegone expression on his face.

We tour the entire house, surveying the renovations in
progress, before heading to the basement. On the way Trevor
tells us the story of how he moved here from the city after
his wife left him and at the end of the ensuing breakdown-

slash-midlife crisis. He'd quit his job and taken off to wander around in Australia and then New Zealand, where he'd briefly considered starting a Lord of the Rings commune, then come back to finalize his divorce and finally get his capital from the sale of their house.

And then on a visit out to his friend's hobby farm just outside Pine Ridge he saw this neglected B&B.

"It was lonely, like me," he says, "and the town seems pretty idyllic."

"Maybe if you haven't lived here your whole life," I say doubtfully.

"Keep in mind, we're in high school," Emma says. "High school is the opposite of idyllic."

"There'd still be some work going on when you move in," Trevor says as we make our way through the completely gutted kitchen. "You'd have to put up with some noise, some dust . . ."

"I'll just get some earplugs," I say.

"I'll just get . . ." is threatening to become my phrase of the day.

Still, I'm feeling optimistic until we go to the basement.

"Some of it's unfinished," he says as we cross a dark, cavernous expanse, "but you'd have the whole space down here to yourself. It's just the room you'd be paying for, but if you wanted to use this zone, that's cool too. I only come down here to check the furnace filters and, you know, turn off the electrical or the water when needed."

He pauses to pull on a chain attached to a bulb and harsh, bald light floods the area. Something skitters away just behind him and Yaz stifles a gasp.

"See?" Trevor says, clueless. "You could get a rug to define the space, then some bean bags, a lava lamp . . . and you could hang out down here. You could even have some low-key social events. I wouldn't mind."

The only kind of "social event" I could have down here is a Halloween party, with the basement acting as a haunted house. Still, Trevor is so earnest that all I can do is nod.

The bedroom is small, with a dropped ceiling, yellowish-beige carpeting, baseboard heaters, and one small, filthy window, and the walls are a dusty salmon color that cannot be improved with art.

"Damned spiders," Trevor mutters, batting at the air in front of his face.

I shudder.

"Although," he says, shifting gears like he's just realized he's not being the best salesperson, "they say spiders in a basement mean it's dry—no mold. And of course they eat other bugs. Not that I have other bugs. And I got rid of the mice already. Some people just put poison traps out and consider it done, but then they keep coming in. You have to find the entry points and seal them. Believe me, they are *not* coming back in. And there was only the one rat."

"Rat?" Emma squeaks, looking like she's going have a panic attack.

"They're supposed to be really sweet, and I swear I went into a depression over having to kill it," Trevor says. "I almost tried to make it into a pet."

"Maybe . . . try a dog?" Emma ventures.

Trevor, missing the irony gene, looks at her with the utmost seriousness, and says, "I might. Anyway, you're welcome to paint. Any color you want. I think it's important to have your surroundings reflect what you want to manifest."

I shiver. It's hard to imagine what I could manifest here,

or spending any time at all in this place without becoming warped and depressed.

The worst thing is that of the three places I've seen today, this is actually the best—a creepy, unfinished basement with spiders, skittering things that are hopefully mice, and the ghost of a dead rat.

As nice and unintentionally comedic as Trevor is, I can't live here.

⎯⎯

But I can't keep living at home either, as I'm reminded when I get home to find my father, back on his feet and in my room with a large book of paint swatches.

"I'm moving my office out of Jack's room," he announces as I stop in the doorway, "and I found my color wheel! I've gotta get these rooms ready."

"You said end of June," I say, feeling slightly panicked. "We're still in April."

"Yep, end of June. You might need to park on the couch for a few nights before that, though, to avoid the paint fumes."

"You're not really going to put your office in the kitchen, are you?"

"I had a better idea," he says with an enthusiasm that should be infectious, but is instead just worrisome. "I'm setting up behind the bar! All the computer stuff fits perfectly up there, and I remembered that old stool—the tall one. I think I'll like being high up like that, with a bird's-eye view."

"The better to spy on your renters coming and going?"

"I'll be discreet," he says. "I won't bug them. I could even make a screen."

"No one will find that creepy," I say, crossing my arms and leaning on the doorframe.

Dad starts looking peeved. "A little positivity would go a long way, Libby."

I imagine myself lifting my fists in a cheer, giving a deadpan recitation of every cheesy inspirational quote ever written. *Be the change you want to see. Believe in yourself. You can be anything you want. If at first you don't succeed, try, try again.*

"I'm sure it's all going to turn out fine, Dad," is the best I can do.

"Exactly." He pulls me into the room, then flourishes the color wheel. "Look at all these grays! You might think gray is just gray but you would be wrong. I have fourteen shades of gray here, including Designer Gray, Gray Wisp, and Lily of the Valley Gray. You have to choose your gray carefully because people who know about these things *really* know about them. Gray is a serious matter. Want to weigh in?"

I stare at the plethora of grays and feel a sudden pang. Dad and I have stood looking at this color wheel before. It was maybe three years ago after that life-changing field trip to the museum. I came home buzzing about it, and though Dad wasn't too interested in my new career aspirations, he offered to help me transform my room. He even checked out books on fine art and museums from the library, and we pored over them together. I chose *Starry Night* as the inspiration, but we stood here with this same color wheel, trying to figure out which color was closest before deciding it would need to be a mix of two different blues. Then we painted the room together.

I wonder if he remembers. I wonder if he feels sad about it too.

"I don't know, Dad," I say. "They kind of all look the same to me."

"Maybe we can paint it together," he suggests, giving me another pang. "If I recall, you and I are a pretty great painting team."

"Great and terrible at the same time," I say with a pained chuckle.

"Exactly. Whaddya say?" he says. "Tell you what, you help me with this, and then I'll help you if you need to paint your new place."

"Uh, maybe," I say, thinking grimly of Trevor's basement.

"Oh ho," Dad says, catching something I didn't intend him to hear in my tone. "You okay?"

"I'm all right."

"Yeah?" He turns his eyes on me and they're like ice-blue tractor beams—piercing, keen, and perceptive. For good or bad, and whatever else my dad is, he's a force. And when he turns his attention to something, or someone, it's undeniable. "How's the apartment hunt going?"

He can also be freakishly perceptive when he's paying attention.

"Funny you should ask," I say with a heavy sigh.

"Well?"

"I need to make a lot more money."

"That's not what I asked."

"That's the answer, though."

"Oh," he says, and rubs his palms together like he finds this totally exciting. "You see a couple of dives?"

I flop down on my bed, now covered in the overwrought duvet set that makes me feel like I'm about to be attacked by flowers, and stare at the ceiling.

"You spend some time living in a dive, and it will be the making of you! It'll be so character-building."

"If I don't die of tuberculosis first."

"I know you feel that way now," he says, and comes to sit on the edge of the bed, "but I'm telling you, it's going to be great."

"Yeah, it's amazing," I say. "The world is my rat-infested oyster."

"You know rats are apparently very nice creatures. Smart, friendly . . ."

"You are the second person to tell me that today!"

"Then it must be true."

I just look at him, one eyebrow raised.

"Aw, it's just a little adversity," Dad reaches out to grab my hand as if we're going to have a heart-to-heart in which he says something that's actually wise and helpful, and then says, "Adversity will make or break you."

"Really?" I say, too tired and overwhelmed for a moment to keep my inner voice on the inside. "What has it done to you, Dad—make or break?"

Dad lets go of my hand and stands, suddenly unable to meet my eyes, then grabs his color wheel and heads to the door.

"Gotta get to the hardware store and get them to mix this for me," he says. "I'll do Jack's room first."

"Thanks," I say. "Have fun."

And then he's gone.

I try to focus on homework after that, but something is worrying me—specifically, my dad being out and about in Pine Ridge is worrying me.

Yes, he's become antisocial, but on the other hand anyone who saw him would assume he knows about the Perry issue already, which means they might bring it up. And this is the type of thing that's almost guaranteed to bring my dad out of "retirement."

While my Dad Problem spidey senses are tingling, I decide to go to Emma's.

"I have a worry," I say without preamble when she opens her door.

"Just one?" she says, one corner of her mouth quirking up.

"Ha ha."

"Come," she says, and we go inside. We pass through the kitchen, where the slow cooker, no doubt set up by Emma's dad before he left for the library this morning, is cooking something delicious, and Albert is sitting at the island punching numbers into a calculator and making notations.

"Hey, Albert," I say. "Nice shirt."

Albert has a substantial T-shirt collection, and today he's wearing a black one with a gallery of Star Trek captains in multicolored neon bubbles across the chest.

"Thanks," he says, barely looking up.

"I still have first dibs if you ever decide to get rid of the one with the Jack Russell terrier Patronus, right?" I ask him.

"Sure, sure," he mutters, still not looking up.

"Good luck with that," Emma says, then leads me up to her room. "He threatened to vaporize me when I borrowed his 'The Answer Is 42' shirt without asking last week."

"Oh, he has vaporizing powers now?"

"You never know with him," she says with an eye roll. "But they would be scientifically based powers, not magical."

"Of course."

Emma goes to put music on while I wander toward her desk and stop short. All the charts are gone, and in their place on her magnet board is just one thing—a photo of

Emma's top choice school . . . which I recognize because it is/ was also my top choice.

"You got in!" She'd never put a photo up otherwise—she'd be too afraid to jinx it.

"I got the email same day as you," Emma says gravely, and studies me. "But that was Sunday night, and you were having an epically bad day so I didn't want to say anything."

"Em, you're allowed to be happy. You should be celebrating."

"I am happy. Of course. But it's hard when I know you got in, too, and maybe can't go."

Because of tennis, in combination with her grades, Emma has serious scholarship money coming to her, not to mention her pick of schools. Plus her parents have good jobs, so even without that she'd be fine. Still, we always planned to go together. We made Pinterest boards for decorating our dorm room and everything.

"I'm sorry," I say.

"It's not your fault," she says, but tears are suddenly welling in her eyes.

"Oh, Em . . ."

"Still, everything's changing."

"I know."

"I mean, that's life," she says, trying to blink the tears back. "But now and then it just hits me. I mean, I shouldn't complain. Not with everything that you're going through."

"It's not a contest," I say. "It's not like because I have this crappy drama going on that you therefore don't get to be sad and feel conflicted about the fact that our entire lives are about to change forever. It's hard."

"Yeah. Planning and dreaming is one thing, but all of a sudden it's real. And I admit I felt better all this time thinking we'd be going through it together. You maybe don't realize it, but you steady me. Like, you have other good qualities, of course—"

"Oh, vast numbers of good qualities," I say. "Too many to count . . ."

"Seriously," she says.

"I know," I say, and take her by the shoulders. "But Em, we will never not be best friends. We will always be in each other's lives. I'll come sit in the courtroom while you win case after case, and you'll come hang out with me in Trevor's basement with my lava lamp—"

"At your gallery openings," she says.

"Or . . ."

Her gaze sharpens. "Or what?"

I shrug. "I might do something else. Psychology, or social work, or . . ."

"Ah," she says, "this Perry incident has changed you."

"Yeah. Not to sound woo-woo, but it's made me feel a different sense of purpose. And maybe I can find a way to merge my interest in art with those things."

"Okay, speaking of those things," Emma says, dragging me over to sit on the bed. "You said you're worried. What's up?"

"It's my dad."

"Uh-oh," she says. "Did he find out?"

"Not that I know of, but . . ."

I explain my concerns while she listens avidly. Luckily Emma knows all about my dad and doesn't feel the need to bullshit me via telling me not to worry.

"He's anti-Facebook, though, right?" she says.

"Yes, thank God." I nod, absentmindedly playing with the fuzz on a hot pink throw pillow.

Emma reaches out and puts a hand on mine. "You're going to pluck that thing bald."

"Sorry."

"Plus it's going to make you sneeze."

"Right." I set it down.

"Okay. The best you can do for now is go home and see if anything's happened. Wouldn't he say something to you?"

"Maybe, maybe not."

"Then keep a close eye on him, and I'll also keep eyes and ears out—in town and online too, just in case. If he does find out, though, Lib, I'm sure he'll be on your side."

"Doesn't matter," I say. "It'll be a dumpster fire no matter what."

"Okay, but wouldn't it be a bigger dumpster fire if he wasn't?"

"We'll see."

DICKS FROM ALL OVER THE WORLD

Something feels different on Thursday. The weather is worse—muggy and drizzling—but there's less barking at school, and people seem to be looking at me differently. Although they are still looking.

"Holy crap, sit down," Emma says when I arrive at our back-of-the-library table for study hall—the one period of the week we all have together.

I sit down in the empty chair beside Noah, then notice Boris, sitting conspicuously alone, one table away. Noah follows my glance, and says, "Apparently he's got serious work to do and he anticipates us being too distracting."

Boris looks up right at that moment, catches my eye, then looks away quickly and practically burrows into his textbook. Oh, good grief. This is him keeping his distance, obviously, but of course he has to be so Boris-ish about it.

"Never mind him. Do you remember a girl named . . ." Emma glances down at her phone, "Martina? Who worked at the Goat until . . . early March?"

"Yeah, she was traveling for a year, visiting her grandparents here for a few months, and then off somewhere else before going to grad school, I think. Why?"

"Well, Martina's grandmother is in the Pine Ridge Residents group. She saw the video, then sent a link to Martina. Meanwhile, Martina has a very popular travel blog. It's fun—mostly photos and stories about her adventures."

"I remember her talking about the blog."

"Right. Well. Martina isn't from here and is not worried about upsetting Perry Ackerman. So . . ." Emma says with a flourish, "she's written a huge post about him, and his harassing ways."

"Are you serious?" I say, suddenly breathless.

"Dead. When she saw the video she knew exactly why you dumped that sangria on Perry. He was the same with her—the hugging, the side boob grab, the gross flirting, the personal questions, the dick jokes," Emma says, waving her phone at me, but too fast for me to actually see anything.

"Holy cow."

"Yeah, and there's more. Listen." Emma reads: "'Because he knew I was traveling, Perry liked to tease me about how I must be collecting lovers all over the world, or if not lovers, at least dick pics. "You should write a dick pic blog instead," he said. "You could probably collect ten dick pics per day, just here at the Goat, and then you could post them. Dicks from all over the world! Give me your contact info and I'll contribute." The more disgusting I found this suggestion the funnier he thought it was. And then he somehow got my email address, and . . . you can guess the rest.'"

"Oh. My. God," Yaz says, her voice a high-pitched squeak. "She has a Perry dick pic!"

I make a gagging sound, and the librarian shushes us.

"Girls really do not like dick pics, do they," Boris says, tipping his chair backward to talk to us.

"First, darling, you're missing the *entire* point," Emma says, shaking her head. "Second, those things of yours are not photogenic."

"Oh, burn," Noah says with an exaggerated moan. "Our poor manhoods."

"Third," Emma says, ignoring Noah, "if you're ever feeling like you want me to dump you, go ahead and send me one. I'll know what to do."

And then she goes back to reading the blog post, and Boris goes back to pretending his separate table is a whole other world, and that he's not listening to every word we're saying.

Of course, we're too loud and soon get kicked out of the library, Boris included. For a moment he looks like he might take off, but then Emma reaches for his hand and he gives me an apologetic look and falls into step beside her. We finally resettle on the floor at the bottom of a stairwell, since it's gone from drizzling to pouring outside, and there's nowhere else to go. Boris sits as far away from me as he can get—like three extra feet makes a difference. Although . . . maybe it does.

"So this girl, Martina," Noah says. "If she has a Perry dick pic, she probably deleted it."

"But if she didn't . . . " Yaz says. "And she was willing to share it—"

"Eww," I say, hugging my knees to my chest and cringing.

"Can you sue someone for that?" Emma says. "Or get them charged?"

"Should be, if you didn't ask for it," Yaz says. "What's the difference between that and whipping it out on the street, which is indecent exposure, right? Ooh, maybe we can get Perry arrested!"

"Ideally before Monday night," I say pointedly.

"If you can't get him charged," Yaz says, "maybe you could just get her to post it as proof."

"That would be subjecting others to the thing we're saying should be illegal," Emma says.

"Perry might actually like having his dick pic posted on the internet," I say.

"Maybe not," says Emma, scanning the rest of the article. "Because Martina says her grandmother insisted on seeing the pic, and when she did . . . she *laughed*, and said, 'That's what he was so eager to show you? That pathetic thing?'"

Yaz and I do the exact same thing at the exact same time—clap our hands to our mouths and then howl with laughter, while Boris and Noah both look quietly appalled.

"Oh, and look at the comments!" Emma says, practically leaping out of her cross-legged position. "How did I miss them? Holy cow, a new one just popped up . . . Libby!"

"What?"

"Comments!"

"I got that part. What?"

"There's a ton, okay wow. This one's anonymous. 'I work at the Goat and every girl there knows you got to watch yourself with Perry. There's always guys that get flirty and make stupid jokes but Perry's a whole other thing. Much worse. Martina's got it right and for sure Libby didn't flip out for no reason. Every single one of us has to put up with Perry and nobody does anything to stop it.' Wow, finally! And there's another one, similar, with a story about hugging with hip thrusting—eww—and a pat on the butt . . . Someone else says he joked about how he'd like to buy her for the night for his friend who was going through a divorce—the friend that was *with* him—ugh! . . . Okay, and next is a misogynist troll whose words I will not utter aloud, then a defender of Perry's honor saying none of these people can be believed because they're posting anonymously, then another anonymous waitress from some other restaurant in town, chiming in with a story, but saying she thinks it's just part of the job and the way of the world and everyone has to suck it up . . . and there's one saying all waitresses dress sexy in order to get better tips so what do they expect . . . and someone else shooting this person down . . ."

"Lemme check the Facebook group again while you're reading that," Yaz says.

"Okay," Emma says, "but still, remember—no repeating any negative stuff about Libby out loud, if there is any."

"I'm fine!" I protest.

"We want you to remain fine. People are still idiots."

Everyone is on their phones now, furiously scrolling, while mine stays turned off and in my bag. I grab a textbook and try to read, then put it down, and glance back up to see Noah looking at me.

"Want to walk to the water fountain or something?" he asks.

Be still, my heart—a walk to the water fountain with Noah.

"Sure," I say, and we both get up, push through the doors and head slowly down the quiet hallway toward the fountain.

"So," I say, "how are things with you?"

And Ava????

"Well," he says, turning to walk backward so he's facing me. "Ava and I had a talk last night."

"Oh?"

"It was civilized. The only drama is the lack of drama. Like, I brought up the breakup subject and I guess I expected her to be more upset. So we had a little bit of an argument about that, which is . . . just my stupid ego. I didn't want to hurt her or be a jerk, but then I guess I was a bit of a jerk after all, just a different kind of jerk."

"Where'd you leave it?" I say in my best just-interested-as-your-friend voice. "Are you a single man now?"

"I'm not quite sure," Noah says, turning now to fall into step beside me. "We got over the argument and then we were both kinda sad, so we said we'd sleep on it. I mean, I think she's already decided, and I've already decided, but we didn't make it official. And breakups are supposed to happen in person, right? Like, are we going to break up on FaceTime? That seems cold. So I guess I'm single-adjacent."

"Well, condolences," I say. "Or . . . pre-condolences?"

"I'm all right. Once it was clear in my head, the heartache part sorta disappeared. Now I just want it done and official. I'm having this weird worry, like, what if she changes her mind?"

"Would that make you change yours?"

"No." He stops as we reach the fountain, and glances sideways at me. "I want to be free."

"For your gap year," I say, and lean against the wall.

"No. I mean, yes. But also," he says, standing awkwardly in the middle of the hallway, hands shoved into his pockets, those eyes of his on mine, "I want to be free *now*."

"Oh," I say, unable to come up with anything more because even though he hasn't said anything encouraging whatsoever, there's something heart-stopping about the way he's looking at me, and about the way he looked at me while saying the word "now."

"Just in case," he adds.

"Of what?" I manage to ask.

"In case—actually, no," he says, interrupting himself, "I'm not going to do that."

"Do what?"

"The thing I'm not going to do."

"Okay, but what is it?"

"If I told you what it is, I'd be doing it," he says, nodding to himself like he's just decided something.

"I'm confused. Telling me what it is would be doing it?"

"Yes," he says, and gives me a really, really sweet grin.

"All right," I say.

"Put it this way," he says. "When you build something, when you build a house, even before that, when you design it, you have to do things in a certain order, or it won't work. There's a right order. You can't start with the roof, for example."

"I see."

"There's a right order, and a wrong order, or maybe a few possible right and wrong orders, but the point is if you start it the wrong way then you might screw it up and never manage to get the thing built. You see what I mean?"

"Sure . . . ?"

"Great. Thank you for helping me clear that up."

"You're welcome."

"So . . ." he says. "Are you . . . are you going to have some water?"

"What?"

"Water," he says, and then gestures at the fountain.

"Oh. No, I never drink from it. You?"

"Nah, I'll pass," he says, and we just stand there, looking and then not looking at one another.

"Should we go back, then?" I say, finally.

"Okay."

We walk back to the stairwell faster than we came, maybe

trying to outpace the many unanswered questions brought up by this conversation. When we get there he immediately grabs his stuff, says, "I have to go," and leaves.

"Where's he going?" Emma says, staring after him.

"He's going to build a house," I say. "Or something. Actually, I have no idea."

I sit down again and they go back to reading, then suddenly Yaz goes, "Ooooooh!" and we all jump.

"What? What?" Emma says.

"Holy . . ." Yaz says, not looking up.

"What is it? Show me first," Emma says, reaching for Yaz's phone.

"Oh, come on," I say, "I'm not that fragile."

To my annoyance, Yaz waits for Emma to give her a thumbs-up, then says, "This guy Jason—oh, it's Jason from the hardware store, I think—he was there, Libby. On Sunday, with his kids in your section. Do you remember?"

"Think so. Family of six? They were near the service station."

"Ooooh," Yaz says, fanning herself and practically jumping up and down with excitement. "Someone posted a link to Martina's blog this morning on Complainers, and then obviously a bunch of people read it, and then Hardware Store Jason has come on and posted because he's got, like, eight pictures of his kids doing something dorky, but *you're there in the background, and so is Perry*, and . . . Jason says he only checked his pictures yesterday after he heard about the big fuss, and . . . the background is pretty blurry in most of them, but you can see that Perry's got his hand on you in every. Single. Photo. On your waist, over to the side of your hip, onto your lower back, almost on your butt . . . then *on your butt ahhhhh*! Four photos in a row with his hand on your butt!"

"Let me see."

Yaz hands me the phone and Emma and I swipe through. As she's said, the photos are blurry, but on the upside, there are a lot of them, and they all show Perry touching me inappropriately.

The bell rings then, and I head to my next class feeling more hopeful than I have in days.

17

@RICKSNOTROLLING

I've just walked into my room after school that Thursday when Emma calls.

"Do you remember that guy on Complainers—he hasn't posted in a while, but he's one of those guys people try to bait on purpose. Roland Rickland?"

"Y-yeah . . ." I say, starting to get a bad feeling. "I remember Roland."

"Okay. So it might be nothing . . ."

"But . . . ?"

"But he's back. And very much on your side, as are others since Jason posted the pics. I just . . . I never thought of it before, but Roland Rickland . . ."

"Uh-oh . . ."

"Listen, I could be way off, but he . . ."

"Sounds a lot like my dad?" I say, pacing from the door to my desk as this horrible possibilty comes together in my mind.

"I mean, it might not be," Emma says. "But the other thing is, I can't match every name on there to an actual person in Pine Ridge, but I know or have heard most of them, and I've never heard of a Roland Rickland. So I did a quick 411 check, and there is no Roland Rickland with a phone number in Pine Ridge. Not that there would have to be. But then there's also . . . your dad's name is Rick . . ."

"It's him. I know it is. Shit."

"What are you going to do?"

"Good question."

———

I need to see what this Roland person is saying online for myself before approaching my dad. So, for the first time in days I go to Facebook and check Complainers. I try to skip directly to Roland Rickland's comments there, and mostly succeed in not reading anything else. Then I go over to Martina's blog, where Mr. Rickland has written a lengthy comment. It reads exactly like my dad.

Still, I decide to do a quick search, just to make certain Roland Rickland isn't real and from somewhere nearby.

I type the name into Google, not expecting much.

And that's when things get interesting.

Which is to say, worse.

So much worse.

———

Twenty minutes later, heart pounding, having taken screenshots and saved links and backed everything up on a thumb drive just in case, I look at the time. It's just after four p.m., which means Mom won't be home for an hour or so.

I take a few bracing breaths, review my plan, if you can call it that, and then launch myself out of my room before I can chicken out.

"Dad," I call out, as I march down the stairs to the basement. There I find everything in chaos. Dad's files are on the floor outside his office/Jack's room; his computer, printer, a mess of cables, and an ancient lamp are set up on the bar. There are paint cans sitting at the bottom of the stairs, and all of Jack's trophies are piled haphazardly on the coffee table.

Dad, meanwhile, is perched behind the bar on the creaky vintage stool, hunched forward and bashing at the keyboard of his laptop like a man possessed.

"Dad," I say.

He looks up, blinking like he's having trouble coming back to earth.

"Libby!"

Easy, I think. *Go easy.*

"What . . . ah, what are you going to do with Jack's stuff?"

A heartbroken expression crosses Dad's face and then disappears so fast I'm not sure I really saw it, then his mouth twists like he's tasted something sour and he says, "Throw it out. Or he can send me his address and I'll ship it to him, at his expense."

"Isn't that . . . a little harsh?"

"Jack . . . is a disappointment," he says, then zeroes in on me. "You, however . . ."

Here we go.

"I just found out about your takedown of Perry Ackerman," he says, puffing up with pride. "That was heroic!"

"No, Dad, it was dumb. It got me fired."

"Bah! You don't need that job anyway."

"Yes, I do," I say, still trying to figure out how best to deal with this, and with the other thing, because the plan I had when I came down here (make a grand speech that will completely change my dad's mind about everything and magically turn him into a totally reasonable person) doesn't look promising.

"Well, you can get another one!"

Right, I think but do not say. *How's that going for you?*

"You should have told us Perry was harassing you," Dad continues, clearly in the zone where no input is needed from me to continue the conversation. "I shouldn't have to hear about this at the hardware store."

And I shouldn't have to be trying to hang on to a job where I'm being sexually harassed, but here we are.

"Sorry about that," I say.

"I would have liked the chance to be there for you," Dad says, looking disconcertingly concerned all of a sudden.

"Listen, Dad, you wanted me to be independent, so that's what I'm trying to do."

Yes, that has to be the strategy—convince him I'm doing what he's wanted me to do all along, and get him to back off.

"You were right," I continue, trying to channel my mother and her work-around skills. "About how the job, and all of this, would help me build character. It really has. I've learned so much. And I take things so much less for granted. That's why I'm hoping that you'll . . . continue with your very wise hands-off . . . uh . . . parenting, and let me handle this."

"But Libby, I want to help. You can't ask me to do nothing."

"That is what I'm asking. Please, Dad, stay out of it. That's how you can help."

"Okay, sure," he says. "Fine."

Sure.

I see his furtive glance toward the laptop and know for certain that Roland Rickland/@RicksNotRolling will be back posting the second I leave.

I squeeze my eyes shut, trying to sort through my rampaging thoughts and emotions, and then open them again with new determination. I'm not going to be able to distract him, or do a crafty work-around like Mom would. Gentle reasoning isn't going to work and staying silent isn't an option anymore. I have to speak—really speak—not fling silent words against the walls of my mind, not submerge myself so deep that I don't even have words. I have to channel Jack, and cut to the chase.

"I want you to get off of Facebook, Dad," I say, feeling like I've hurled myself off a cliff.

"Facebook?" he blusters. "I hate that place. Why would I even be there?"

"I know you are."

"Oh, really? What am I doing, then?" he says, chin up and arms crossed.

"You're on the residents group, for one thing."

"No, you can look. I'm not there."

"Yes you are, *Roland.*"

"Who?" he says, voice cracking, but widening his eyes with almost convincing innocence.

"I know it's you, Dad," I say, keeping my tone level while inwardly quaking at being so direct with him. "I'm asking you, begging you, not to post anything else. Not on the Pine Ridge group, not on Martina's blog. And I would love it if you would delete what you've already posted."

"I have no idea what you're talking about," he says, obviously pleased with himself for managing to do his shit disturbing in such a way that no one can pin it on him, or so he thinks.

"Dad," I say, edging closer to the other problem, "if I can tell you're Roland, others will figure it out, too."

"Well, so what if I am?"

"Because," I push on, "let's say someone on there wonders, 'Hmm, who is this Roland Rickland person?' At that point they are one Google search away from the rest of it."

"What rest of it," he says, holding himself very still.

"The rest of it," I say, at the edge of another cliff now, but forcing one fear to override another. "The rest of the garbage that I just discovered. @RicksNotRolling, and your lesser pen names: RickRoland, RolledOverRick, RickandRoll, OvertheRollRick. Your secret online identities with which it looks like you've been aiming to win some kind of award for being the most frequently blocked and banned. Is this what you've been doing all this time while we thought you were looking for work? Picking fights with strangers on the internet?"

"I've been very successful with my online endeavors," Dad says, pulling his usually slouching form up to full height, fire in his eyes. "Sure, I get banned and suspended once in a while, but that just shows you I'm getting to people. I'm an influencer. A writer."

"It's not writing, Dad," I say, the awfulness of everything I found on my search propelling me forward. "Arguing with people to the point that you threaten them with . . . what was that one I read? 'I'll hunt you down and smash your imbecilic head in'?"

"I didn't—"

"I took screenshots."

"But I would never follow through on any of those threats!" Dad says, having the nerve to look offended. "That's just talk."

"It's not just talk when it contains a threat of violence! You also posted some poor woman's address online and encouraged people to come after her. That's more than talk— that's an action that endangers someone."

"That woman . . ." Dad says, his face reddening, "was being a real bitch. *She* threatened *me*, in fact! She's a lobbyist—the worst kind of lobbyist! And anyway that address wasn't even her primary residence."

"Do you hear yourself?" I ask, suddenly fighting tears. "It's horrendous. And then there's all that photoshopping, putting politicians with strippers, and heads of famous people on other people's bodies. It's not even good photoshopping, Dad. It's so obvious."

"It's meant to be obvious! Did you see the one where I put all the EU leaders in thongs and Speedos? People loved that."

"It's gross, Dad. It's so ugly. If you looked at it all at once like I just did, I think you'd see that. The memes, the threats, I mean, yes, there are a few that people seem to have found funny, but they're mean-funny. And then all those essay-length arguments in comment sections, some of them even well-researched, but then you devolve into name calling and threats. It's such a waste."

"But don't you get it?" Dad says, moving out from behind the bar, totally animated and excited now because his delusions are a fortress that apparently cannot be penetrated by facts. "I can write! And I know all about Perry Ackerman. I get why you lost your cool with him. I've heard stories. Hell, I've seen him do it! I have dirt, and I'm a writer, Libby! You can tell your side of the story, and I can add what I know. The two of us—we can take him down."

"'Take him down'? No, Dad. No, no, no."

"Libby"—he takes my hands in his—"I don't mean writing something for Martina's blog or those idiots on Facebook. I'll write a real article. An exposé! I've been waiting for a chance like this my whole life. You're not impressed with RicksNotRolling, fine, I get that. But I'm trained for this situation."

"I'm sorry, but what you've been doing . . . that's not training, Dad."

"I don't mean the internet stuff. I was trained formally. In journalism, Libby."

"What?"

"Yes! I did two years of journalism school before I met your mother. I was going to travel the world following leads and covering wars and exposing atrocities and conspiracies. I was good. Top of my class, almost. I was going to be a teller of truth," he says, eyes shining suddenly. "A light in the dark. So I didn't get to do that then, but now there's the internet. I created @RicksNotRolling because I wanted to accomplish something. Open a dialogue with people who think differently, see if we could find common ground."

"Finding common ground isn't exactly your specialty, Dad."

"But I can write."

"It doesn't matter. You can't write about this. For one thing, Mom already made the big effort of going to Perry to ask him to forgive me."

At this, Dad looks aghast and then horrified.

"Whether you agree with her or not, she went to bat for me, Dad. And because of it, Perry called Dev and Dev offered me my job back."

"But you can't just let that bastard get away with—"

"Just stop!" I burst out. "If I'm going to fight, it's my fight. If I'm not going to fight, that's my choice too. But this is not your fight."

"I have a right to help my daughter."

"Please, Dad," I say, trying to dial it back. "Please. I

believe you want to help, but I think your help might make things worse, no matter how good your intentions."

"You can say whatever you want, Libby," he says with building fury, and I realize I'm losing whatever control I had of the situation. "If I want to go to bat for you, or if I want to say any damned thing I want, I have that ability!"

He starts stomping back toward his office, then remembers he's moved it to the bar and changes direction.

"You don't even know my side of the story, Dad. You don't have the facts. And I'm not going to give them to you!"

"I don't need them!"

"Do you hear yourself? You don't need the facts? That can't be what they taught you in journalism school."

"I don't need them because I have enough of my own! I was going to give you the chance to be part of this, but guess what?" he says, all ablaze now. "I don't need you. There's years' worth of stories about Perry. And some of those anonymous posts about him on the blog of your friend? Those people are being chicken-shits, but I know who they are. I know who some of them are, for sure, because I know the stories. I'll figure out who the others are and then I'm going to publicize their names, drive them out from under their little rocks and make them denounce him publicly."

"Dad . . ." I'm practically choking with horror at this. "You can't do that!"

"I can't? You don't get to tell me!" he says, suddenly yelling right in my face. "No one tells me what I can or can't do, do you understand? NO ONE TELLS ME WHAT TO DO."

His face is twisted with fury, his spittle landing on my face, and I shrink back.

Then he breaks away, snarling, and heads back to his desk, hauling himself up onto the stool and spinning deliber-

ately away from me as he starts whacking at maximum ve-
locity on his keyboard.

I stand there, staring at his back, my heart racing, and try
not to spiral into despair.

There will be no getting through to him now. I failed.
And yet I have to stop him. Somehow I have to stop him, but
what can I do—rip the laptop from his hands? He'd just use
his phone, or Mom's laptop, or he'd go to the library, or
worse—he might run into the streets and start shouting at
passersby.

My eye snags on the modem, plugged into the wall just
around the corner, and Dad's phone, parked at the end of
the bar.

I can't stop him from writing, but . . . maybe I can slow
him down?

Yes.

I grab the phone, then tiptoe over to the modem, tug its
wires free, clutch it to my chest, and then take the stairs up,
two at a time.

At the top of the stairs I take the U-turn into the back
hallway, zoom past my room on the right, and then into the
bathroom where I lock the door, put the modem and the
phone in the tub, and close the drain.

I stare into the tub, hand on the faucet.

Holy crap. This is what my life has come to—I'm about to
drown our modem and my father's cell phone. In the bathtub.

I'm going to commit technocide.

Ridiculous.

And what if soaking the technology causes some kind of
toxic leak?

No, this isn't the answer. I just need to get myself, and the
technology, out of the house.

I snatch the phone and modem from the jaws of death-by-drowning, sticking the former in my pocket and shoving the latter awkwardly into the back waist of my jeans before yanking my hoodie down over it.

Less than a minute later I've grabbed my backpack, shoes, and keys, jumped in the car, buckled up, and am pulling out of the driveway.

I guess that makes it technapping . . . ha ha haaaaaa . . .

I may be having a psychotic break.

18

FULL OF CRAZIES

I drive past Ackerman Park (grabbing butts since 1967!), then pull off the road half a mile later at a spot that overlooks the river, turn off the car, and dial Jack.

He surprises me by answering after just two rings.

"Libby!" he shouts over the background noise. "Hang on, I'm going outside."

There's some rustling and I hear Jack asking someone to cover him, and within a few seconds the din recedes.

"Hey, sis, what's up?"

"You're going to think I'm crazy but I have to stop Dad. So I stole the modem and the—"

"Whoa, slow down. Stop Dad from what?"

"Jack, he's a troll!"

"Well, he is a bit—"

"No, an internet troll—and not the awesome, funny kind, either. I found all this . . . here, wait a sec . . . I'm sending you some pics. They'll explain better than I can," I say, and take a few seconds to message him a bunch of screenshots. It's only a few moments before I hear his notifications beeping.

"Okay, lemme look," he says. "Oh, man, okay . . . oh jeez, what the hell. You sure this is him?"

"He admitted it. He's proud of it."

"Damn. Okay. What were you saying about the modem?"

"Right," I say, my thoughts tumbling as I try to catch him up. "So he's been up to no good online, and in the meantime he's found out about Perry, and now he wants to write an exposé, and it's bad enough if he does that but if people also—"

"Wait, wait, what about Perry? You mean Ackerman?"

"Oh," I say, remembering that Jack knows nothing about that part of the story. "Yes."

"My man, Perry!" Jack says. "What's going on with him?"

I close my eyes and suppress a groan as I remember that Perry was (and still is) a big supporter of the high school football team when Jack was on it. He bought their jerseys, hosted postgame parties, came to every game.

"Ever notice anything about how *your man Perry* was with . . . females?" I ask, and then hold my breath, hoping Jack isn't about to disappoint me.

"Uh-oh, what'd he do?" Jack says, but he says it with a mix of dread and affection, the way you might ask a dog you love if he ate your shoe.

"I don't think I can talk to you about this," I say.

"What? Of course you can."

"All right, *your man* Perry was sexually harassing a teenage girl. Groping her, making comments and gross jokes, and she freaked on him, and now the town is in an uproar."

"Shitty but not surprising," Jack says. "Dude needs to learn to keep his hands to himself. But this girl—why didn't she just leave? I've seen Perry trying to hit on people, but usually they just laugh at him, maybe give him a swat, and walk away. But instead she freaked on him? Sounds like this girl's just looking for attention. Anyway, what's this got to do with Dad?"

My brain is exploding in fifty directions and I want to smash something.

"Lib?"

I really should just hang up. But instead I grip the phone and start speaking with barely controlled fury.

"*This girl*," I say, "was most assuredly not looking for attention. *This girl* couldn't walk away because Perry was her customer. At a restaurant. Called the Goat. And *this girl* needed the money she was making so she could pay for rent and college tuition because she is fucking broke."

"Whoa, whoa, wait, Libby . . ."

"*This girl* didn't have the option of walking away from the hug-with-pelvic-thrust, or the boob grope or the butt grab, or millionth sexist joke or implied sexual threat. *This girl* just wanted to make her money and go home and she is not enjoying the attention from the video that's gone viral of her screaming like a psycho at Perry Ackerman, or the attention of the accompanying viral video that depicts her with a tail, and barking like a dog, or even the attention of the photos someone posted that show Perry's hands on her ass for all the world to see," I spit. "Newsflash: no one wants that kind of attention. Fuck you, Jack."

And then I do hang up.

I expect him to call right back, but he doesn't. Which is probably better. Too upset to drive, I leave my phone on the seat and get out of the car to stare at the river, feeling like its rushing torrent matches my current vibe perfectly.

I don't know what I thought Jack could do, why I thought he could help. He's the one who ran away and refuses to come back. And maybe I overreacted to what he said, but the fact remains that he's clueless about Perry, and about being female, apparently. At least with Mom, even though I disagree with her methods, she got it.

Crap!

Mom.

I head back toward the car at a run, hop in, start the engine, then dial.

"Libby?" she says, her voice coming on the overhead speakers after only one ring.

"Mom!" I say, trying to sound casual. "Have you talked to Dad recently?"

"No, I'm still at work—just finishing."

"Great. How about I come get you?"

When I'm halfway to the Inn, Jack finally calls back but I ignore it, and then, just as I'm pulling into the parking lot, it rings again. No thanks. I turn on Do Not Disturb just as Mom's approaching, and banish Jack from my thoughts. He's not here, and I don't have time to worry about him right now. Once Mom is in the passenger side, I drive a few yards away to the far side of the parking lot.

"What's going on?" Mom says, her own spidey senses alert.

"Remember how it's been nice that Dad hadn't found out about the Perry situation?"

"Uh huh . . . ?"

"Well, now he has," I say, and then explain.

"That's certainly inconvenient," she says when I'm finished, "but if he's posting with a fake name, no one will know it's him. And I hate to say it, but so what if someone figures it out? Your father arguing with people is nothing new."

"It's not just that, Mom," I say, trying to stay calm enough to ease her into the RicksNotRolling situation. "Do you know what he's doing down there in the basement all day? He's being a troll. On the internet."

"You mean . . . he's playing some kind of computer game? With trolls?" The confusion and consternation on her face would be hilarious if the situation wasn't so awful.

"If only. But no, Mom. A troll is . . . You really don't know what a troll is?"

"Small, wrinkly faced creature with crazy neon hair," she says, crossing her arms. "Alternately, massive brutish creatures who eat hobbits and turn to stone in the sunlight. Your father, despite his many shortcomings, is neither of those."

"No, Mom. I mean, yes, but no. Let me try to . . . You get newspapers online, right? Do you ever scroll down to the very end and read people's comments?"

"Oh!" she says. "No, those comments sections are full of crazies. What type of a person wants to spend their time having pointless arguments with complete strangers?"

I just look at her.

"Oh," she breathes, and then wrinkles her nose as if she smells something rotten. "Oh, how awful. And yet predictable."

"If you want evidence, I have screenshots. Um, those are pictures you take with your computer of things on the internet."

"I know what a screenshot is," she mutters. "Don't be rude."

I pull up the screenshots, hand her my phone, and watch her pale as she swipes through them.

"Good lord," she says finally.

"Something is wrong with him, Mom."

"Obviously."

"No, I mean really wrong. But the main issue right now is

he's using one of his troll names on the residents group, and as soon as he posts this big 'exposé' and starts outing people who want to be anonymous—"

"Oh no," she flaps her hands in front of her face, trying to fan herself. "No, no."

"Someone will figure out it's him, and then if they Google the troll name . . ."

"They'll find the rest of it, and at that point we may as well move. Not to mention it'll undo everything I accomplished when I went to see Perry."

"Exactly."

"Damn it," she says, using up her full yearly quota of swearing. "All right. Take me home, and then you go somewhere else for a couple of hours while I handle this."

"What are you going to do?"

"I'm going to use my feminine wiles."

Eww, I think but do not say.

"Not to underestimate your . . . wiles," I say, looking at her doubtfully, "but are you sure they're equal to this situation?"

"Quite," she says, and I decide not to ask any more questions.

19

THE STOMP

I've had three more calls and five texts from Jack, but I'm driving around Pine Ridge while Mom works her "wiles" and ignoring him. I've got stolen technology in the trunk of the car, there's nowhere I can show my face in town without causing a ruckus, Yaz visits her grandparents on Thursday nights, and I feel like I've already taken up enough of Emma's time today with my problems.

Which leaves Noah.

Admittedly, this business with my dad did drive him out of my mind temporarily, but now I'm thinking about his offer for me to come over and "stomp around."

But I'm also thinking about how he took off early from school, and how he may be in the middle of dealing with this Ava thing, and how the fact that I want to know what's happening so badly, even in the midst of a family crisis, is exactly the reason I should stay away. If there's anything possibly going to happen between us, which could be entirely my imagination, I should stay away. For a day, at the very least.

But if he is my friend, which he is, and I need somewhere

to hide out for a while, which I do, there's nothing wrong with that, right?

He may not even be home.

I'll just . . . drive by and see.

Noah's house and his dad's snow removal/landscaping business is on an acreage just on the other side of the river at the far edge of town, which is still only a three-minute drive, and maybe a fifteen-minute walk, from Main Street.

When I get there, I pull onto the shoulder, trying to determine whether he's there, though short of actually seeing him, that's going to be difficult. And what if he sees me out here on the road, staring at his house?

Stalker vibes. Not good.

I'm about to leave when I hear honking, and suddenly I see him, pulling up in his stepmother Jen's car, right behind me.

Busted.

He jumps out and comes toward me, and I open my window.

"Hey!" he says.

"Hey," I say, casual, like I'm not having one of the most messed-up days ever, and like even in the middle of that messed-up day I'm not still dying to know whether he's finally single and . . . "I was just . . . going to text to see if you were home. Didn't want to bug Jen or your dad."

"You okay?" he says, those brown eyes of his all too perceptive.

"Ish?"

"You're not." He states it as a fact.

"Well," I say, with a tense shrug, "I thought I'd take you up on that . . . stomping thing. And also I might need you to harbor some runaway technology."

"Runaway technology?" he says, looking intrigued.

"Long story."

"You know my Plan B if architecture doesn't work out is to be a spy, right? Come on," he says, and gestures toward his house.

We both drive in, and meet a minute later on the cobblestone path to the front door. Noah lives in one of those gorgeous old redbrick farmhouses, with antique trim and a big, many-windowed addition at the back.

"So, runaway technology?" he says. "Is that code for 'stolen'?"

"Kind of."

His eyes widen. He looks so worried I almost laugh.

"Oh, it's nothing illegal—it's my dad's phone and our modem. It was a . . . preventative robbery," I say, trying to keep my tone light. "Dad's on a tear about Perry and I'm trying to keep him contained. You could think of it like holding on to someone's car keys when they've had too much to drink—my dad shouldn't have internet access when he's upset."

Or at all.

"It's way more spy-like if I hide it," Noah says. "I could bury it behind the barn."

"If that makes you happy," I say. "But let's wait till I hear from my mom, because it may not even be necessary. She was going to try to talk to him. Or something."

"Sounds like you've had a day," he says, his angular face going serious again.

"Yeah, things are a little intense." I glance down at my phone, insides roiling. Jack has stopped calling and texting, and there's nothing from my mom yet. "I'm . . . not trying to come here in a crisis and then refuse to talk about it, but . . ."

"But you don't want to talk about it."

"For a bit. If that's okay."

"This is exactly what the Stomp is for," he says. "Shall we?"

I nod.

"Unless you need to stomp alone. That's cool too."

"No, let's go," I say.

———

The Stomp goes through the copse of trees that separates the yard of the house from the landscape yard. It winds around the old barn where the snowplows are parked, involves some optional and nonoptional climbing over rolls of sod, giant boulders, and a small hill of quarry stone, and then rolls out onto the surrounding fields, over a tiny creek, around fallen branches, and so on.

It's hard at first. My body feels like a boulder I'm having to drag uphill. My shoulders are tense, my chest and back feel tight, and there's a thrum of panic, barely under control just beneath the surface of everything. Basically I just want to crumple into a fetal position and rock back and forth until this is all somehow over.

But I'm with Noah and he's sharing this very cool thing with me. He sets a good pace, checking back over his shoulder frequently to make sure I'm all right, and I'm far too stubborn to lag behind. Before long my breath is coming faster, and soon I'm warm enough, even in the crisp spring air, to have to take my sweatshirt off and tie it around my waist. I have my phone in my pocket and I'm on alert for my mom to call or text, but the tightness in my chest is loosening and my thoughts have stopped racing. I'm still super emotional, maybe even more emotional, but I can actually take a full breath.

"I feel better already," I tell Noah, coming up close behind him.

"Told you so." The trail is wider here, and he slows down just enough that I catch up and walk beside him.

"When I was younger and my parents were getting divorced, I had a couple years where I was just pissed off all the time. It was my dad who sent me outside to burn it off. 'Go stomp it off, son.' He used to let me kick the pile of pea gravel to wear myself out."

"I remember your angry phase."

"You do?"

"Of course," I say, with a sideways glance to make sure I'm not digging into something I shouldn't be, but Noah's expression is peaceful.

"Hope I wasn't too obnoxious."

"Nah, just gloomy and a little edgy. All that gravel kicking must've purged the worst of it."

"It's very satisfying. It's dusty, but it doesn't do any damage. Anyway, that's when we made the trail, and I still use it."

We walk for a few more minutes then head up a hill where a beam of the day's last sunlight hits us, and pause there. The view is stunning, with rays of light streaking golden across the field.

"Painters wait all day to capture this kind of light," I say, slightly awestruck.

"Yeah, it's nice," Noah says. "One of those things that's almost easier to paint than capture with a photo."

"Easier for you, maybe."

"No, anyone I think. Either way you gotta grab it fast."

I nod.

"In September and October you can go out into the

middle of that field," Noah points off to our left, "and fall straight backward into the grass without hurting yourself. It catches you. I like to just lie there looking up at the sky, totally alone in the world."

"That sounds really good right about now."

"Best to wear pants and long sleeves, or it gets itchy, though," he says with a rueful chuckle. "Which I learned the hard way. But the grass, after you fall in it, forms a kind of nest with circular walls. I'm always trying to imagine how to design a building that would feel like that inside."

"With a domed roof, maybe," I suggest.

"Yeah," he says, "sky-colored, or made of glass, with light-colored wood."

"I can picture Yaz making it into a yoga thing."

"Ha. There's already Goat Yoga, Paddle Board Yoga. This could be . . . Field of Tall Grass Yoga? The slogan needs work," he says with a grin. "But wow, I could host my own Burning Man."

"Except yogis aren't known for pants and long sleeves, so it would be more like Itching Man," I say, and he cracks up. "Or Itching *Person*. To be inclusive it has to be 'person.'"

"Yes! 'Itching Person Yoga Festival'!" he says, raising a fist toward the sky. "It's going to be huge."

We laugh, and it hurts like it's shaking sharp things loose inside me, but it also feels good.

Then I turn my face to the sun and close my eyes and pretend I can stay here forever.

"Libby . . . ?" Noah says after a couple of minutes.

"Mm?" I say, keeping my eyes closed.

"I went to see Ava this afternoon."

Whoa. Back to reality. I open my eyes and try to study his expression, but he's shifted to look at me, resulting in the sun being behind him, which means I can only see him in silhouette.

"Oh?" I say in a desperate effort to sound neutral.

"Yeah. I drove the two hours, and got there in time to pick her up from school. That's where I just got back from."

"Maybe this wasn't the right day for me to stomp."

"What? Why not?"

"Well," I say with an awkward shrug, "would you rather be alone?"

"No, this is good. It's perfect. I needed to see her. But I'm fine. It's all good."

"Good meaning . . . ?" I shift to try to see his face better just as he turns back toward the sunset. Argh.

"I mean good," he says, and though I can normally read him, this time I can't—not from his tone, and definitely not by staring at the back of his head.

What the heck does "good" mean? It could mean once they saw one another in person they realized they were madly in love after all. And they've hashed it out and decided she's going to go on the gap year with him. Or he's going to give up his gap year to be with her. Or they're going to spend a bittersweet/tragic last few months together before he leaves. Or it could mean they had an entirely pleasant breakup and he's already remembering her fondly.

All I know is I'm not in the mood for guessing games.

"All right, cool," I say, and then turn abruptly and step out of the shaft of sun and start down the hill, following the path. I'm annoyed, but more with myself than with him, because I don't need this. And anyway I should not be hoping for declarations from a boy who just broke up with his girlfriend *today.*

If he broke up with her.

"That's great," I add, over my shoulder, then focus on finding my footing on the narrowing, now-shadowy path.

I get about five strides down before he says, "What . . . ? Libby, wait . . ."

I school my face into neutral before stopping and turning back to him. "What?"

"What just happened?" he says, lifting his arms to the side in obvious confusion.

"Happened?" I'm attempting to channel my mother and her "everything is perfect" tone while being flooded with a wave of hurt and fury that I know are unreasonable.

"Yeah," he says, brow furrowed, "*happened.*"

"Nothing happened. We're stomping. We should probably finish the loop before it starts getting dark."

"But . . ." He stands there, all bewilderment, and asks, "Don't you want to know how it turned out with me and Ava?"

"Only if you want to tell me. Maybe you need to have your own . . . processing time and if so, great. No problem." Yikes. I feel like I might cry. Or start screaming at him. Trying to forestall both of these possibilities, I turn and start down the trail again.

"I just had two hours in the car to process," he says, following me. "And I'd already done most of the processing I needed to do."

"Great," I say over my shoulder.

"Why do you keep saying that?"

"What?"

"'Great.'"

"I don't," I say, determined to stay focusing forward, and moving forward.

"Yes, you do."

"I've said it twice."

"Three times."

"Okay, three." I stop and face him, hands on my hips. "So what?"

"So you're acting weird all of a sudden. You look . . . mad, or . . ."

"I'm fine. I'm just . . ." I look down and busy myself untying my sweatshirt from my waist, trying to shove down my freak-show overreaction. "I'm just getting cold, that's all." I pull the sweatshirt over my head, grateful for the few brief moments he can't see me. Maybe I'll just stay here.

"We broke up," he says, just as my head is emerging from the collar.

"Oh," I say, freezing for a moment before adjusting my sleeves and yanking the hem down around my waist. "Really?"

"Really."

"Great," I say, then nearly collapse with chagrin to have used the word for the fourth time. "I mean . . ."

Noah raises his eyebrows.

"Not great, uh . . ." Yikes, I am not equipped for this today. "I mean, I'm sorry, because Ava is a nice person and you're a nice person, so . . . that's . . . sad. At the same time it's good because . . . that's what you wanted, right? And because it's resolved now? So, gr—uh, yay for that."

He nods slowly, eyes on mine.

I hug my arms to my chest, a ball of mortified, mixed-up emotion, but still trying to brazen it out.

"Libby . . ."

"Yes. What?"

"Are you okay?"

"Sure. Fantastic. Why wouldn't I be?" Ha ha ha ha haaaaaa.

"Well, lots of reasons, actually," he points out.

This elicits a semi-hysterical bark of laughter from me.

"Seriously," I say, ironically relieved to be reminded of my myriad other problems. "Pick one."

"Sorry."

"It's fine."

"But earlier . . . we were talking and . . . I . . ." He trails off, suddenly looking almost as much at a loss as me. "It's really been a crazy day. And week. But . . . I was extremely happy to see you parked in front of my house."

"I wasn't parked, I was just pulled over."

He frowns.

"There's a difference," I say.

"Okay."

"I'd just pulled over, I hadn't put the car in park."

"I'm not arguing."

"Me neither," I say, blushing and mad and in pain but also secretly a tiny bit hopeful.

"Pulled over or parked, I was happy because you were actually the person I most wanted to see right then, Libby."

"Yes, but . . . oh." I stop as the words land. "Really?"

"Yeah."

"Well. That's good, right? Good, um, timing?"

He just stands there, and so I start babbling. "And it makes sense that it would be me you wanted to see, because I happen to be the one you had confided in about this, and, well, that's the thing about friendship—there are things I go to Emma about, or Yaz, but then there are things I would come to you about instead because—"

"No, it's not that," he says.

"Oh," I say, intensely relieved to have been cut off.

"Well, it is that, but also," he says, and takes a step closer to me until we're parallel on the hill with the trail between us. "Remember earlier, by the water fountain? I started rambling about how you can't start a building with a roof, and . . . all that stuff . . . ?"

I nod.

"I don't want you to think I'm a jerk," he says, eyes searching mine with that super direct gaze of his.

"Why would I?"

"Well, last year, last spring . . . after you and Boris broke up . . . and I sorta . . . expressed a romantic interest in you . . . ?"

"Uh huh . . . ?" I say, trying to stand still despite the elephants that are suddenly stampeding through my insides.

"Well, at the time you seemed to have strong ideas about . . . uh . . ." He looks at the ground and shifts from one foot to another.

"About how long a person should wait to be with someone new after a breakup?"

"Yeah," Noah says, lifting his eyes.

"I had this idea that I should go through some kind of . . . respectful mourning period."

"Yes, that," he says.

"Which I now realize was ridiculous, because I was so over Boris already. I just didn't want to hurt his feelings by moving on too fast. Obviously I shouldn't have worried," I say with a grim smirk.

"Nope, ol' Boris recovered pretty quick."

"And then you went off and fell for Ava."

"I wouldn't have," he says defensively, "but I thought it was just your nice way of telling me you weren't interested."

"Well," I say, taking the plunge, "you were wrong."

"Okay," he says, "so what about now?"

"Now?"

"Yeah. Does this mean you're no longer a believer in the 'respectful mourning period'?"

"I think it depends on the situation," I manage to say.

"What if the situation was that I wanted to be with you?"

All the breath goes out of me in an audible gasp.

"I'm not saying right now *today*," he rushes to clarify.

Why not?!

"That *would* be a little speedy," he says. "I'm just saying . . . what would you think about that?"

What I think is that if he so much as touches me I will catch fire.

"Take your time," he says. "I'm only dying five hundred times per breath here while I wait."

"I want to," I say. "I really want to. You have no idea."

"But . . . ?"

"My life is a mess and you're leaving."

"Succinct analysis," he says, shoulders dropping in seeming discouragement for a moment before he regroups. "I do see your point. Both points. But look, the mess part I can handle."

"You don't know that. It's not just Perry, my family is a lot to handle—they're . . . it's really . . . worse and weirder and more dysfunctional than I even knew."

"That doesn't scare me," he says, leaning forward, all problem-solving earnestness now. "We had some very messy times around here during the divorce. I get it. And I've known you a long time, so even if I don't know the inner sanctum stuff, I know the players. I know you. I won't run screaming."

"You don't understand, my dad is . . . there's something really wrong with him. More than I realized."

"What I said still stands," Noah says. "People go through

stuff, are going through stuff all the time and it's not the . . . that's not the exception, you know? Like, it's not that 'real life' is only when nothing is going wrong. It's all real life."

It's killing me to keep raising these objections when all I really want to do is throw myself at him, but I have to. For the sake of my heart and our long friendship, I have to. For the sake of not jumping into this without clear expectations on both sides, I have to. For the sake of not bursting into flames and then becoming needy and clingy and desperate, I have to.

"What about the you leaving part?" I persist. "You just went through this with Ava—you don't want a long-distance relationship during your gap year, and I can't go to Europe with you, not that you're asking. But I mean, is this a fling you're suggesting? That ends when you go?"

"I don't know," he says, hands shoved in his pockets now. "My feelings aren't really fling-ish. They've been around too long. But I guess if a fling is all the stars are aligned for, I'd take it."

I know what he means. There's a big part of me that wants him under any circumstances—a day, a week, three months. I already let one chance pass me by and lived to regret it. But I am scared, too—of entering into this when everything is so crazy in my life, of getting hurt, of being so bad at relationships/screwed up about sex that I ruin it, and most of all because I'm not sure I can be with Noah in a halfway measure.

"I don't know if I'd be good at having a fling, Noah. But of course, we could be totally sick of each other by August, and then it would be great to say, 'hey, that was a nice fling,' and then off you go to Europe."

"Or we could be madly in love and impossible to separate

by then," he says. "And in that case we'd figure it out. We won't know unless we give it a shot. I mean, we haven't even kissed. Maybe all this is premature. Maybe we'll kiss and it'll be bad and all the chemistry will fizzle."

"Yeah, right," I say, trying to keep my eyes from dropping to his lips, and not succeeding.

"Well, probably not," he says, and gives me a smile that says he noticed.

"Are you trying to get me to kiss you?" I say, and for a few moments all my worries and objections fly out of my brain.

"I honestly wasn't, at this exact moment," he says, his voice husky, "but I find myself suddenly not picky about the timeline."

I swallow a thousand butterflies and feel myself taking a step toward him just as he does the same, and yes there are reasons not to but I don't remember them at the moment and I don't care, I want to kiss Noah and he wants to kiss me, and . . .

Ping!

My phone pings and also vibrates with a text, and we both stop in our tracks.

If it's Jack I will kill him.

"Ignore it," I say.

"Agreed," he says.

But. It could be Mom.

"Actually . . ." I say.

"You should check it," he says, stepping back, the nearness of him leaving me in a whoosh.

"Right." I pull the phone out of my back pocket, look at the text, flush, and then swear under my breath.

"What's up?" Noah says, looking concerned.

It isn't from my mom or Jack. It's from Kyle, and even

though there's nothing problematic in it, suddenly I feel physically ill.

"It's nothing. Just. Someone from work. Uh. Checking on me."

"Are you okay? You look weird all of a sudden."

Kyle. Stupid Kyle. He's just trying to be nice but he picked the worst moment and now I want to throttle him—not just for the interruption, but for making me think about him at all. Because Kyle and Noah shouldn't ever exist in the same moment—in the world or in my head. What happened with Kyle makes me feel so gross that it threatens to taint everything. Even this. Especially this.

"I'm all right. But actually, I should probably be ready to get back in case my mom . . ."

"Hey, it's fine, no rush," he says, and reaches out to touch my cheek. "Let's finish stomping."

—

A few minutes later my mom does text, telling me the coast is clear and that I should come home now. Back at the house I give Noah our modem but decide to keep Dad's phone since that's easy enough to hide.

And then we're under the giant maple tree on his driveway, standing unnaturally far apart, with everything uncertain and undecided between us.

"You'd have thought I was a jerk if I kissed you today anyway," Noah says finally, shifting the modem from under one arm to under the other. "Not as much of a jerk as if it'd happened before I broke up with Ava, but still."

He looks so unsure of himself all of a sudden, and yet so adorable and beautiful, standing there framed by the cedars that line the drive, and the ice-and-navy sky behind him.

"You're not a jerk, Noah. You're one of the best people I know."

"Well, thanks, but I know you have a lot going on, as your phone was so kind as to remind us. So maybe it's not even fair for me to have brought it up. I just didn't want to wait, in case . . ." He's been looking at me, but now his gaze drops.

"In case . . . ?"

"In there's a chance it could work."

"I think there's a chance," I say, feeling a smile sneaking onto my face. "I just want to be careful."

He looks back up, smiles.

All this goofy smiling, even in the middle of a crisis.

"How about this," he says. "Could we agree to think about it?"

"I'm going to be thinking about it anyway," I admit. "So, sure. Let's agree to officially think about it."

"Excellent." He lets out a breath I didn't know he was holding, and his goofy little smile breaks into the biggest, most heartbreakingly gorgeous smile, and I barely manage to stop my hands from coming up to clutch at the place over my heart.

We stand there grinning again, like cupid-slain dorks (or maybe that's just me), and then he says, "How long do you think the thinking part should last?"

I start laughing, and he shifts the modem from one arm to the other again.

"I don't know."

"Are there rules?" he asks, and I detect mischief in his tone.

"Rules?"

"Like, am I allowed to try to influence your thinking?"

"In what way?"

"Well, some combination of rational argument, charm, chocolate, maybe some hand-holding?"

"You want to hold my hand?"

"Maybe. If you'll let me."

Hand-holding has never sounded so hot.

"When would this hand-holding occur?"

"Randomly?"

"Okay," I say, knowing full well that if we start holding hands in public that it's as good as posting relationship status. "Surprise me."

"I will."

"I really should go," I say, glancing toward the car, but not going. "Wish me luck."

"Okay. Good luck," he says, and then he comes forward to give me a hug made quite awkward (but still sweet) by the modem, and then I somehow manage not to stumble on my way to the car, and not to take out any shrubbery as I back out of the driveway.

20

STOWE FAMILY UTOPIA

Not quite sure what a "clear coast" could mean when it comes to my dad, I approach the house with caution. My caution turns to concern when I see a pile of furniture—from Jack's room if I'm not mistaken—at the edge of the yard, like it's been put out as trash.

I let myself in on tiptoe, half expecting to have to duck flying objects, but right away I realize there's no need for quiet. There's an '80s metal ballad blasting in the basement and my dad is down there somewhere, singing along.

What on earth.

"Hello?" I call out, and Mom appears from the family room in a threadbare shirt and paint-spattered overalls that I sincerely hope are not her wile-working clothes. "What's going on?"

"What's going on is I saved our bacon," she says in a low voice, though she still looks worried. "At least for now."

I inhale. "It smells like paint."

"Your father has had to drop everything for an urgent project," she says at normal volume. "He's painting Jack's room."

"Now?"

"Yes, now," she says. "Because we have our first renters coming next week!"

"What? Really?"

"Yes!" she says in a loud, excited voice, while simultaneously shaking her head.

"You made up fictional renters?" I whisper to her.

"They're not fictional," she whispers back. "I've had some people inquire, because the Inn fills up. And I did tell someone we could be ready as early as next week, and that I would send them photos. But . . . I may have *implied* to your father that they're coming on Monday."

"Wow."

"He already had the paint, and he'd taken half of his stuff out of there, I just . . . moved up the timeline. Hopefully this will keep him busy long enough for you to resolve your work situation."

"Yes, but what about the *other* situation?"

"What other situation?"

"That he's . . ." I drag her by the elbow into the family room. "Mom, we can't go on like this. The troll thing is so much worse than all his petty arguments. He was already prone to picking fights with people, but maybe the social consequences held him back a bit. On the internet, though, there are no visible social consequences, plus it's addictive."

"He just needs to be distracted from it, honey," Mom says. "Not to worry."

"Oh, I'm worried."

"One thing at a time," Mom says, patting my arm like this is going to help. "The room down there will need a few coats of paint because the paneling is dark. That should take most of tonight and tomorrow, and maybe even part of Saturday.

Plus I helped him pull the furniture out of there, and lo and behold the bed frame broke, and there are stains on the dresser, so I helped him haul all of that up and out to the front. Then I went online and ordered a bunch of furniture—a bedframe, a side table, and an eight-drawer dresser, all the kind you have to assemble yourself. It's being delivered tomorrow, and putting it together should keep him occupied through the weekend."

"You're insane," I say, moving to the front window and looking out at the curbed furniture.

"If not, I'm thinking we could do a garage sale," she says, coming up beside me. "A garage sale would help pay for the new furniture at least."

"Wow. Okay."

"I said I'd handle it, and I'm handling it. What do you think I do all day at the Inn?"

"I'm really starting to wonder!"

"I handle things. Come up with creative solutions, deal with unreasonable people, find quick fixes."

"Okay, but . . ."

"By the way, I'm going to pack his office stuff in boxes and put them in the garage, supposedly just for the short term because we're crunched for time, but that can be his next project—finding everything and sorting through it. Of course he'll be mad, but that's survivable."

"He'll still have his computer, though. Has he noticed the internet isn't working? Or that the modem is gone?"

"Not yet. I was thinking now that you're home I could go down and help him, and block him from leaving Jack's room if necessary, while you go on the computer and delete whatever it is he's managed to write about Perry."

"Good plan."

"Great," she says.

"What about when no renters show up?"

"I'll deal with that when it happens," she says with a brief freaky-cheery smile. "Or maybe I'll actually find us some renters."

I want to tell her that this is unnecessary. I want to be able to have a reasonable conversation with Dad, or, given that I already tried that, I want to her to find some way to put her foot down, to get through to him in a normal way. But the truth is that given how things went between him and me earlier, it might not be possible.

"This is really screwed up, Mom."

"I know."

"And a bit . . . sneaky."

She lifts her eyebrows.

"But . . . I think the phrase I'm looking for is . . . thank you?"

"Yes," she says, and beams. "That's the one. You're welcome."

Five minutes later Mom is running interference with Dad while I get behind the bar and onto his laptop.

He has no password protection, and the article is right there. To his credit, it's four thousand words long already. I feel a twinge of guilt, but this has to be done. Still, I'm curious enough that I take photos of each page before deleting the words on the document, trashing the document itself, and then emptying the trash.

Then, keeping an eye on Jack's closed door, I quickly open my hotspot, tether to my phone, then open the browser, which Dad has conveniently open to Complainers already. I scroll through as quickly as I can, finding his posts and deleting them.

I'm doing one last check through, skimming only, but stop in my digital tracks when I see a post from Kyle.

"I work at the Goat as a host, and though I might get in trouble for posting this, Perry Ackerman was way out of line Sunday night. It's not just the hand on the butt, he was all over Libby, touching her waist, her back, her sides, and making inappropriate comments. He does it to all the female servers and they all just try to laugh it off, but I've come to realize they don't actually find it funny. I feel bad that I haven't done anything to try to stop it and haven't spoken up until now. Something is wrong with a system where so much focus is on tips, and being friendly and not simply on doing your job as a professional. The customer is not always right and this customer was every kind of wrong."

Holy cow.

I take a photo of Kyle's post, then quickly go to Dad's settings and change his password so he can't get back on Facebook at all. It's an invasion of his privacy, but desperate times call for desperate measures, and again I rationalize that it's for his own good.

I disconnect from the hotspot and close the laptop just as Jack's door opens a crack, and then Mom emerges, looking for another roller.

I come out from behind the bar and give her a discreet thumbs-up.

———

Up in my room I can still hear the music, and Dad's voice, and then Mom's, warbling alongside his. They sound so happy. Like if someone just walked into our house right now, they'd have no idea.

The only person who would get this situation is Jack.

Jack, whom I told to fuck off earlier.

I feel sorry about that now. I don't want to fight with Jack. And so much has happened that I'm not even sure what exactly he said—just that it felt like he was going to take Perry's side, and he assumed this unnamed girl was looking for attention. Right—that last part was what really set me off. Of course he wouldn't have said that if he'd known it was me we were talking about. But even if he wouldn't have, isn't that just as bad? Worse?

Now I'm mad all over again, and also mad that he's stopped texting and trying to call me. He was supposed to keep trying—to not give up.

When the phone pings a minute later, I expect it to be him.

Instead, it's Kyle. Again.

Things have kinda blown up and you're
pretty quiet. You okay?

I'm so annoyed, and on the verge of telling him to go away. And yet, having just read his post, I can't. He has stood up for me more than anyone else has. And he's been checking on me daily since Sunday and, I think, sincerely trying to be supportive. (Possibly while also hoping to get laid again, but still.)

I hesitate, my finger over the keypad, but I'm spared having to make any decisions for the moment, because another text is coming in from him.

Don't know if you saw but I wrote some
posts, telling the truth about Perry.

Feeling grateful to Kyle continues to be the height of irony. Still, I wrinkle my nose and text back, Thank you. Hope you're not in trouble for it. I'm fine.

Now please just go away.

The phone pings again and I nearly throw it against the wall. It's good that I don't, though, because the new text is from Noah.

I found it, it says, and then another text comes right after, and it's the drawing of the bird in flight that he said he'd give me—the more polished version of the one I have on my wall.

Nice, I text back.

You want?

You have no idea, I think but do not say.

Is this part of your campaign of influence? I say instead.

Are you influenced?

Yes.

Then yes.

21

WIN-WIN

Friday morning my mom calls in sick and she and Dad are already back working on Jack's room before I leave for the day.

After first period I find the drawing of the bird in a plastic sleeve in my locker, obviously slid in there by Noah, and stand there looking at it and blushing. Only Noah could make me blush over a bird. Then at lunch he sits on the bench next to me and takes my hand under the table, causing me to lose all logical thought of any kind.

I'm still holding on to that blissed-out feeling two periods later when I find out some of my fellow students have started a petition demanding Perry apologize to me (as if) and that the Goat give me my job back, and that all the restaurants in town enforce anti-harassment policies or face being boycotted.

That's a pretty big wish list, but apparently it already has hundreds of signatures.

Of course having a bunch of teenagers boycott isn't going to make much of a difference to any of the businesses—half of them don't want us anyway—but it's still impressive, not to mention heartening.

It also makes me feel absolutely terrible.

Because what will all these people who've signed it think if/when I go back to work on Monday, and make the apology?

Maybe worse is that I can feel a mounting expectation from Emma and the others that I'm going to do something now—make a public statement, refuse to apologize. Admittedly, when I agreed to it I was just buying time, hoping things would change. And they have changed, but not enough. Everything still feels so precarious, and there's no way forward that'll make everyone happy. I don't know what'll make me happy either. I have to survive. I have to be able to live with myself. I don't know how to do both, and I don't feel brave enough for any of it.

And so now, along with everything else swirling around inside me, there's this noise, a repeating question: *What do I do? What do I do? What do I do?*

———

After school I go straight home, anxious to check on my parents.

When I get there they're in the basement, starting to unpack the boxes of to-be-assembled furniture that have been delivered, and debating where to put things. I'm about to go down to start helping them when my phone rings. Private caller. It's probably either a spammer or a scammer, and I'm briefly tempted to give the phone to Dad, who loves baiting them.

But Dad's occupied, so I answer.

"Hello?"

"Libbbyyyyyyyy!"

My heart stops and I actually stagger backward, bumping into the front hall closet doors.

"Y-yes?"

"It's Perry."

"Ackerman?" I ask, as if there's any question.

"Hi there," he says, and I hear the reptilian leer in his voice, and imagine the glittering slash of his eyes. "I thought we might have a chat."

"Um . . . just a sec . . ." I glance down the staircase and then walk briskly down the hall to the bathroom, go inside, close and lock the door, and turn on the fan to eliminate the possibility of anyone overhearing the conversation. Then I sit on the edge of the mint-green tub, and say, "How can I help you, Perry?"

"I talked to your lovely mother the other day, and to your boss."

"Yes," I swallow. "Thank you . . . for that."

"You're very welcome," he says smoothly.

This is freaky, but he doesn't sound angry. Maybe I can get the apology over with now. It's worth a try.

"Perry, about what happened, I—"

"That's not what I'm calling about," he says, his voice booming over mine. "Here's the thing: you're a sweet girl. And your mom explained your situation—you're trying to save for college, family finances are not good, you're stressed out. And then, it's been a crazy week in the world, and on the interwebs, you know?"

"Uh huh . . . ?"

"But I don't look at a crisis the way other people do. I look at a crisis and see opportunity. That's what's got me where I am today."

I have no idea where he's going with this, so I just wait,

staring at the tidy stack of twenty-year-old hotel soaps on the window ledge.

"I thought a lot about this, and the fact is, Libby, you're a hard worker. I've seen it and Dev said so too. And we've always gotten along, you and me. So how do we turn this into a win-win situation?"

"I have no idea."

"Aha! But I do. I have a great idea. You come work for me, doing brewery tours. You're perfect for it. You're personable, articulate, good with people. You give each group some history of Pine Ridge, talk about the origins of the building, sing my praises for saving it, and then walk them through the process of the beer making. Then you leave that group in the store after encouraging them to buy lots of beer, and go back and get the next one."

"I—"

"Now," he says, rolling along like this is a fait accompli, "you won't make quite as much money as you're used to at the Goat, but we'll get you up to full time as soon as possible and then you'll be eligible for benefits, which would, I think, make up for the difference."

"But—"

"It's brilliant. It gives you a job, and me a good employee. And it'll have the added benefit of quieting down all the ridiculous gossip. I mean, people are vicious, aren't they?"

"Yes," I say, since it seems the only viable response, and since my head is still spinning.

"I've been shocked by the vitriol," he says. "Anyway, there'd be no public apology needed—you simply start working for me, we present a united front, everyone sees there's nothing to see, and we all live happily ever after."

Ohhhh. I get it. And suddenly I feel like a fish about to be hooked.

"Perry, I don't think—"

"And you haven't even heard the best part. Your mom told me your grades are fantastic, you've applied to six schools, and you've already been accepted to half of them. She's very proud of you, you know. But like any mother, she's also worried."

"Her and me both," I mutter.

"Exactly. That's another way I might be able to help. Have you heard of the Ackerman College Fund?"

"No."

"I set it up a few years ago. It's a fund that subsidizes up to seventy-five percent of college tuition, for four years of school, decided on a case-by-case basis and taking both merit and need into consideration. Anyone who works for me is eligible to apply, and the odds of you getting approved by the committee, Libby, would be very high."

"Really?"

"Yes. Because the committee is me."

And there's the hook, its tip aimed at my throat.

I have to reject this now, right now, before my brain starts doing the math, and counting the money, and trying to estimate how many hours and incidences of Perry—eyes, words, hands—I could handle for the sake of my future before I lost my temper, lost myself, or both.

"Perry, I don't—"

"Come onnnnn," Perry says. "This is an offer you can't refuse."

"Well, I'm not sure," I say, trying to keep my voice from shaking, trying to shove aside the illusion of freedom he's dangling in front of me, and remember it's not freedom. Because those pictures are out there, and the stories, too. So he wants to bribe me, and use me for damage control, and keep me under his thumb. Not to mention, what further, worse kinds of harassment might Perry think he can get away with at his own brewery? With someone he's managed to bribe and discredit? And who's hoping like crazy to be approved for college funding by his *committee of one*?

Right. No. No way.

"That's quite an offer, Perry," I say, carefully keeping my fast-building fury in check, because more than ever, I need my job at the Goat. And would rather have my job at the Goat, where I'll only be harassed occasionally by Perry, as opposed to every single day. And so I force myself to sound reasonable. "But I really like my job at the Goat. And I wouldn't want to disappoint Dev a second time, you know? Especially after you went to the effort of convincing him to give me this second chance. But thank you. It's a very generous offer."

"I'm not taking that as your final answer, Lib," he says.

Shocker.

I'm starting to think "don't take no for an answer" is the first directive in some How to Be a Man manual that guys are given when they hit puberty. *Some* guys, I correct myself.

"Take some time to think about it. The offer's open until, let's say, Monday. You decide on Monday before your shift that you'd rather not go in there again, and rather not deal with the whole circus of apologizing, plus be part of a great organization, with benefits, and get help paying for college, you call me, and we'll be golden, doll."

"Thanks, but—"

But nothing. Because he's hung up already.

22

POWERPOINT

Noah texts an hour later.

Hey.

Hey, I say back, happy to be distracted from thinking about Perry, and how I'm going to handle things at the Goat on Monday.

You busy?

Like, in general, or . . . ?

Tonight . . . ? Now-ish? We could talk about
how the thinking is going.

My heart does a little flipping, skipping thing.
Let me check something, I say.

Okay.

I go downstairs to see what's going on with my parents. Jack's room is fully painted, Dad is in the bathroom adding a fresh coat of white there, and Mom is in the middle of the rec room floor, staring at the pieces of the furniture she's planning for them to assemble, and surrounded by boxes.

"Everything all right?" I ask.

She looks up, eyes wild. "We may have bitten off more than we can chew."

"Don't panic," I say. "I have a couple of things to do, but then I'll come back down and we'll figure this out."

Back upstairs I grab my phone and text, I have to help my parents put furniture together but possibly free after that?

I'll help. I love that stuff, Noah says.

Hm. Noah coming over and watching movies with me in my room is one thing, but direct, intentional interaction with my parents is quite another. I really try to insulate my family from my friends, and vice versa, to everyone's benefit. Boris came over maybe three times the entire time we were dating, and even Emma doesn't hang out here much anymore. Still, Noah said he could handle my messy life. Maybe it's time to find out if that's true.

Come on over, I tell him.

I regret this immediately, but I don't take it back. I run down to the basement, wondering whether I should make my parents change clothes, or beg them not to be weird, or if that would defeat the purpose. Not to mention asking them not to be weird is pointless.

"Help is on the way," I announce. "You remember my friend Noah?"

"Of course."

"He's really good at putting this stuff together, apparently. And he's coming over. To help. For a bit."

"Does he paint?" Dad says, peeking his head out of the

bathroom. "Because I'm starting to get high from the fumes."

"It's latex, Rick," Mom says, her tone crabby. "You can't get high from latex."

I zoom back upstairs, with time to either bathe or beautify, not both, and I decide to go with clean versus fancy.

I take the fastest shower ever, throw on some nice-smelling body lotion plus clean jeans and T-shirt, then brush my teeth, whip a comb through my dripping hair, and manage to get to the door just in time to open it before Noah rings the bell.

"Whoa," he says, stepping back in surprise.

"Sorry," I say, coming out onto the porch in my bare feet, and closing the door behind me. "I was just trying to prevent you from ringing the doorbell."

"Oh," he says, and frowns, and then raises a hand as if to touch my hair, but drops it. "Your hair . . ."

My hair is dripping all over my shoulders.

"I showered."

"I figured."

"And you changed," I say, pointing at his chest, which is now covered by a lightweight button-down with abstract palm trees, instead of the plaid shirt over T-shirt he was wearing earlier.

"Yes," he says.

"This little . . . potential romance we're thinking about is turning us into terrible conversationalists," I say, and that seems to break the tension.

"I dunno," he says, "maybe it's cute, both of us acting like huge dorks."

"Speak for yourself."

"Oh, burn."

I grin.

"But I like how you're calling it a 'little romance,'" he says.

"Potential little romance."

"Yes, potential. And 'little' is just the right amount of disparaging to keep me on my toes."

I laugh.

"But maybe it won't be a little romance," he says. "Maybe it'll be a big romance."

I don't even have a response for this. Just a crashing feeling in my chest.

"So what if I'd rung the doorbell," he says, switching topics smoothly. "Does something bad happen?"

"Demons, rabid dogs, my parents coming up and staring at us."

"Oh," he says, "okay."

"It's them I'm jumpy about, not you."

"You don't have to feel jumpy."

"Okay," I say, making no move to go inside yet. "But, for example, you should probably know that although they need *some* help with the furniture, it can't all get done tonight. Ideally we leave them with enough to keep them occupied through the weekend. Also you should probably know about the fictional renters."

"Fictional renters?"

"My dad thinks they're getting ready for some renters. And there might be renters at some point—they're not entirely fictional—but he thinks they're coming on Monday, which they definitely are not. I'm really throwing you into the fire."

"I'm ready," he says. "Confused, but ready."

Then he comes up beside me and takes my hand, once again causing me to feel like I might keel over, and pulls me toward the door.

Within five minutes Noah has taken charge. He sets my mom and dad on the task of putting the bedframe together while he and I tackle a side table, and goes back and forth, helping and cajoling them along.

Miraculously both my parents are on their best behavior—which is to say actual good behavior from my mom, and a not-small amount of talking from my dad about the "gold mine" Jack's and my rooms are going to be, and the occasional rant about hotels and the evils of big corporations. He's obviously energized to have a brand-new, captive listener, but Noah deals with good humor. I even feel safe enough to go to the kitchen to make sandwiches at one point, and Mom grabs a bottle of wine for her and Dad.

After the sandwiches and a final pep talk from Noah, we take the empty plates back upstairs and leave them to it.

He follows me into the kitchen, which is dimly lit by the stove light, and therefore looking its best—the metal, harvest gold cupboards, matching appliances, and coordinating plaid wallpaper softening, the colors giving off their warmest vibe.

We set the plates in the sink.

"That was impressive," I say.

"It's just building stuff," he says with a modest shrug. "And don't worry, there's lots for them to finish up tomorrow and Sunday."

"Thank you."

"I didn't realize your dad was so set on booting you from the house, though," he says, his expression serious.

"Well, it's not like I want to stay here," I say, the brewery tour job suddenly flashing through my mind and causing me to inwardly shudder.

"But I'd think it'd be weird, not having it to come back to," he says, "at least to visit."

"Yep."

"Should we do these?" he says, then gestures toward the dishes.

"Sure."

"You know what?" He stoppers the sink and turns on the water. "It's actually a good idea, how we're thinking about things, and not rushing."

"It's only been a day—not sure we can really claim the 'not rushing' thing yet," I say, and pass him the soap.

"My point is, high school is almost over, and that comes with a lot of change. Neither of us wants to hurt the other, or be hurt, and it's worth taking time, figuring things out. Last night I would have just jumped in."

"And now you wouldn't?" I say, seized with sudden fear, but trying to sound calm anyway.

"No, I just mean I had time to think about the stuff you said," he says, and puts the sponge in the water and starts to wash the first dish. "We talked about whether it would be a fling, and right away I thought no. And having slept on it, I know it for sure. It wouldn't be a fling—for me anyway. Even if it didn't end up lasting past the summer, it wouldn't be casual on my part. Not that there's anything wrong with casual."

"So . . ."

"So you were right to ask questions. Because I think if we do this, and if we fall in love . . ." He hands me a dish to rinse.

"Jeez, Noah," I breathe, taking it.

"What?"

"I always knew you were blunt, but I never thought about how that would be in a situation like this."

"Too much? Talking about love and stuff? Am I not supposed to do that?"

"No, it's . . . great, just . . . a bit shocking. Anyway, sorry, go on—you were saying, if we . . ." I swallow. "If we were to do this, and fall in love . . ."

"Then it's going to suck come August."

I exhale, and nod. This is the weirdest, most intense conversation to be having while standing side by side doing dishes. And yet I'm very happy to have something to look at, something to do with my hands.

"If we decide to do long-distance, it'll suck, if we decide not to, it'll suck," he says. "I mean, basically the better it is, the worse it is. Like we could end up spending the whole summer crying."

"Wow, you make it sound so appealing," I say, laughing.

"Hey, I am *that guy*. Hard sell, all the time."

"Ha."

"The question we both have to answer for ourselves is: are we up for a big emotional risk—for everything sucking in August? Or is it better to stay friends?"

"What about if we just . . . decided without deciding?" I suggest. "Like, not rush, as you said, but also not have to come to some big decision—just . . . see."

"Libby, I'm a very definite person. Not rushing makes sense but at some point I want to be past thinking, 'Does she like me?' and 'Will she still want to be with me tomorrow?' At some point I want to feel like, if I'm going to jump in, you're coming in with me."

"You mean emotionally, or . . ."

"Or what . . . ?"

"Or do you mean . . . sexually?" I say, embarrassed, but

determined to have better communication about all possible sex in my life going forward.

"Oh, shit, no," he says. "I meant emotional risk."

"Oh. Okay." I grab a dish towel and start drying and placing everything on the counter beside me. Even though this is everything I've wanted to hear from Noah for over a year now, my brain is really full, and my feelings are all over the place, and I'm scared. Finally I turn toward him, and say, "I like everything you're saying, but I just need to get through the next few days and this thing at the Goat before I can give this my full attention, you know?"

"I'm cool with that," he says, and pulls the stopper out of the sink while I take the small stack of dishes across the room and put them in the cupboard. "I'll take partial attention."

I turn and lean on the opposite counter and look at him. My attention is more than partial. And already just staying on the opposite side of the room is challenging. It's like there's an elastic band stretched tight between us, pulling me back.

"What about kissing?" he says, gazing at me with singular focus. "Could that be added to the thinking phase?"

"Wouldn't that be cheating?"

"It's more like . . . helping. Gathering information."

"I think . . ." I say, as the elastic pull draws me back across the kitchen toward him. "I think yes."

And then I'm reaching my hand up to touch his face, and he's catching it in his, and holding it there, and then, super slowly, we move closer, and I go up on my toes as he leans down, and then we pause there, just a couple of inches apart.

Finally our lips meet, and brush, and meet again, and it's like lightning, but if lightning moved like molasses. It's slow and sizzling and perfect, and I start to lose track of time, of everything . . .

And then the bad thing happens.

And it happens fast.

We're kissing, and it's perfect, and then it's more intense and still perfect, and then, wham—a flood of images and sensations slices through reality, slices between Noah and me, and my brain is flashing like some kind of malfunctioning PowerPoint presentation, with visions of Kyle/Boris/Kyle/Perry/Boris/Perry/Kyle, and it's not real but it feels real. They feel more real than Noah, who's right here with me.

I cry out, and then hurl myself backward from Noah, and stand, gasping, against the cupboards on the other side of the room.

"What's wrong?" Noah says, looking panicked. "What is it?"

"I'm sorry, I'm sorry! I'm fine!" I say.

But I'm not.

He starts coming toward me and I hold a hand up.

"Don't," I say.

"Okay," he says, backing up. "What did I do wrong?"

"You didn't do anything." I hug myself and shake my head, and can't stop shaking it, trying to get those images out.

"Are you having a panic attack?" he says. "Like Emma?"

"I don't know. I'm sorry. I have to—"

I break off, and bolt from the kitchen, past the dining room, and down the hallway to my room, where I throw open the door, dive underneath the ghastly duvet, and curl up there with my entire body, including my head, covered.

I huddle there, squeezing my eyes shut and willing myself not to cry, willing so hard.

It's not long before I hear careful footsteps in the hall, and then Noah's voice from the open doorway.

"Can I come in?"

"No," I say from under the covers.

"Can I . . . talk to you from here?" he asks, voice incredibly gentle.

"Maybe," I say, making my hands into fists.

"Could I . . . would it be okay if I just come in far enough to close the door? Since . . . your parents . . ."

"Fine."

I hear the door closing and then for a few long moments nothing happens. I'm under the covers, and Noah must just be standing there. And feeling . . . what?

I whip the duvet off abruptly and sit up.

Noah's leaning against the door, very still, watching me, looking worried.

"You might want to rethink your thinking," I say.

"About what?"

"Me. I'm . . . I don't know what just happened, but I'm . . . I guess I'm a bit damaged. You might not want that."

"Maybe we just moved a little too fast."

"It's not that."

"What is it, then? Has it happened before?"

I shake my head.

"Talk to me," he says, taking a step toward me, then thinking better of it and reversing. "Please."

"I can't, Noah. I need to . . . I can't talk right now."

"Okay. Puppy videos?"

"I think I need to be alone," I say, the tears finally spilling onto my cheeks.

"All right. Should I call Emma to come be with you? Or . . . ?"

"No, I'll be fine."

"You don't look fine," he says, and the worry on his face pierces me.

"I am," I say, swiping at the tears and getting up and coming partway toward him. "I had a great time tonight, but I have to sort this out . . . by myself before I can talk about it with you."

"Okay," he says, and drops his head. "I'll go."

"It was a good kiss, Noah."

"Yeah, it was," he says.

And right then, when he lifts his eyes back up to mine and I see the confusion in them, I feel the unspoken fact there between us:

Yes, it was a good kiss, until it wasn't.

23

BREAKING

The first thing I do Saturday morning is email Dahlia Brennan.

I remind her who I am, ask for an appointment, and give her my cell number, because damned if I'm going to let this Kyle/Boris/Perry stuff ruin my ability to make out with Noah. Assuming he's willing to make out with me and hasn't decided after sleeping on it that I'm too much of a head case.

I don't know if I'm even equipped to talk to this almost-stranger, and the idea makes me nervous, but I figure the earliest I'll hear back from her is Monday, so I have time to think about what to say, and how to say it.

But then my phone rings, and it's her.

"Hello?"

"Hi, Libby," she says, her voice just as simultaneously commanding and calming as it was in person. "I got your email."

"Wow, that was fast."

"I know it can take a lot of courage to make that first move in reaching out," she says. "I don't like to leave people hanging once they have."

"Oh, well, thank you."

"We can meet sometime next week, but I've got a few minutes now, too. Is it a good time?"

"Just a sec." I get up from my desk, cross the room, and pop my head into the hallway. Seeing and hearing no sign of my parents, I pull back in and close the door.

"Yes. I can talk," I say, and then perch tensely on the end of my bed.

"So," she says, "how are you?"

"Fine," I say, although that's not true. And why did I contact her to talk if all I'm going to do is lie? "Sorry, no. I'm having trouble, but I'm crap at talking about it. I just mean, I'm not, as I said when we met, in an emergency situation."

"What would you consider an emergency situation?"

"An emergency situation would be where I should be going to the hospital or the police. I'm not in danger, not physically injured, or even hurt, and never was. It's not that kind of situation. But, well, actually it's two situations. Oh, wait, no," I say, remembering Perry, "technically it's three."

"Three! Wow, I did not see that coming."

For some reason this makes me laugh—a slightly embittered snort, but still a laugh.

"So, three situations . . . ?" she prompts.

"Yeah. One pretty clear . . . you might have heard . . . ah, about a recent . . . thing with Perry Ackerman?"

"Oh!" she catches her breath. "That's you. I'm so sorry. What a nightmare."

"A bit."

"A bit, huh? I'm starting to see you're a master of understatement."

"Maybe a little," I say, a grin in my voice despite the fact that I haven't got much to smile about. This woman seems to get me. And she's being so normal and real.

"So that's what you call a nonemergency?" she presses.

"Oh, no, I guess that *is* a bit of an emergency. Sorry to confuse you—I've got some mid-level family emergencies going on too. Life goes on all boring and uneventful for so long and then—whammo—ten kinds of shit hit the fan. I can barely keep track at this point."

"All right, so . . ."

"But that's not the main thing I contacted you about. It's the two other situations that are messing with my head. Each totally different but with the common theme of . . . that the consent was . . . murky."

"Ahh," she says. "Go on."

"I freaked out in the middle of kissing someone last night—someone I really wanted to kiss. He didn't do anything wrong but suddenly I felt sort of . . . well I can't even explain it in words."

"Can you try? Take a couple of long breaths," she suggests, "and just see if anything occurs to you. Any words or feelings."

I realize that even though I haven't been able to stop thinking about what happened with Noah, I've been pushing the actual moment away every time it starts to replay. And now my stomach is clenching and I'm gripping the ruffle of the duvet.

"Or not," Dahlia says. "It's up to you."

"No, I can do it," I say, and take a couple of the suggested breaths. "I guess it was . . . well it was so good, because I'm into this guy and finally we kissed and it was amazing . . . and then I guess . . . we've been waiting a long time so it got intense really fast, and then it was like, boom. There they were. Kyle and Boris. The two other—situations. And a bit of Perry, too. Suddenly it was like they were there too. Almost . . . between us.

Noah and me. And then I just felt so gross and embarrassed, and I stopped and kind of shoved myself away from him."

"And what did he do?"

"He was—we were both totally shocked. He thought he'd done something wrong and I didn't know what had happened. He was good about it, but I didn't even know what to tell him. I mean, what the hell was that?"

"I suspect you had what's called an intrusive memory," Dahlia says. "Which is exactly what it sounds like—a memory, usually of something difficult, negative, or traumatic, which intrudes, comes when you don't want it, didn't expect it, and when you can't necessarily control it. It's very common in situations of sexual assault. You may be experiencing some post-traumatic stress disorder."

"No."

"No?"

"I should not be traumatized. I refuse to be traumatized—that's ridiculous."

"Well, I like your determination," she says in a wry tone.

"Why?"

"Because it means you'll be strong enough to face this situation and deal with it. Traumatized doesn't mean broken," she adds. "But we don't have to put a label on it if you'd rather not. Or . . . let me put it differently—you may have unprocessed trauma."

"Okay . . ."

"It seems like part of what you're struggling with is whether you have the right to be upset. Or . . . if you are indeed traumatized, whether you've earned your trauma. Normally I would wait until we were talking in person," Dahlia says. "But do you want to tell me what happened with these two boys? Boris, you said, and Kyle? Even just a short version?"

I stand up, walk to the window. Our backyard is a neglected mess, but still beautiful in that wild, new spring way. And then there's me, looking out at it from behind glass. Like I could end up looking out at my possible relationship with Noah from behind glass—seeing it but separated from it. I roll my shoulders, exhale, then say, "Yes."

Dahlia and I talk for almost an hour. Mostly she listens, and asks smart, deep questions, and she confirms what I already know—that I did not give enthusiastic consent.

"You didn't consent to sex with Kyle at all," she says. "And with Boris, I can see how he may have been confused, but deep down he must have known something wasn't right."

"Yeah, and I mean, like I told you, he and I talked about it."

"It's positive that you had that conversation with him," she says, "but I'm troubled that he's so much in your life still."

"He's trying to keep his distance."

"Is it enough?"

"You don't understand," I say. "I hate conflict, and I have so much to deal with right now, and if suddenly I drive Boris completely away, one of us would have to explain why, and then I'd have to talk about this with everyone, and it would become such a huge thing and take so much energy. The thought of all that makes me just want to collapse. It would be much worse, in my mind, than having to cope with him being around for the next couple of months. Not to mention, he is my friend and . . . "

"Okay, I hear you," she says. "Just keep an eye on how you're feeling around him."

"Better, generally speaking," I say. "Which makes me wonder if I should confront Kyle? If I could get the courage up I think, well, I think he should know."

"Everything in this process is up to you—keep that in mind," Dahlia says, her tone thoughtful. "Studies definitely show that avoidance has the effect of making things worse, and that facing things and talking them through, as we're starting to do, will make recovery faster. But you might consider waiting on talking to Kyle until you've had more time working through it on your own. Then you and I could sort of plan it in advance—how, where, what you want to say to him, what you're hoping to accomplish with the conversation. And we can plan how you might do that at a time and in a place that's safe for you—physically and emotionally."

"That makes sense." Though this means that I have to keep fending him off in the meantime.

"Something I want to emphasize," she says, "is that the things you're experiencing—the intrusive memories, and other sudden, bad feelings," she continues, "even in severe cases, as long as a person gets help, these symptoms fade. They may even start to fade within a couple of weeks. I have some strategies I can give you when we meet, but the biggest thing is talking it through, facing it. And you're doing that, so hang in there."

———

We make an appointment for Wednesday afternoon, and I hang up feeling wrung out, but also a million times better.

But then I start to worry about Noah, and whether he's going to text or call me today after what happened last night. I sit there in my bed staring at the phone for a few long minutes before finally deciding I'm being stupid. After all, I'm the one who freaked out and then sent him away.

Morning, I text. You still there?

Are you???

Yes.

In response, he sends me an extremely cute, smiley picture of him, his head on his pillow, and his hair a wild mess.

Is that a yes?

Yes. You okay?

Much better. I'm really sorry.

Don't be. Clearly not your fault.
Still wondering if it was mine.

No. Really not. And now I'm scared
I've scared you away and also thinking
I wouldn't blame you.

What kind of wuss do you think I am?

Are there a bunch of varieties of wusses?

Ha. I am not scared that easily.

Okay, I . . .

???

Yikes, my dad is hollering. I have to go.
Talk later?

Sure.

And then the shit hits the fan.
"Goddammit, Andrea! Where the hell is all my stuff?"

I almost collide with my mom in the hallway as we both head toward the top of the basement stairs.

"Andrea! Libby!"

Mom and I pause, looking at one another.

"What do we do?"

"I'm so tired," she says, completely devoid of her usual everything-is-fine attitude. "I don't know."

"Well, don't you still have the rest of the furniture to build? And then you can get the room set up and fuss around with it."

"If I can get him back on that project," she says, "but listen to him down there."

I listen. Dad is grumbling, swearing, and shuffling around, probably behind the bar from the sounds of it.

"Not good," I agree.

"I wish I could just lock him in the bathroom for a couple of days," she says.

"Seriously," I say.

The swearing and slamming around downstairs is intensifying, which means we're on a countdown to Dad exploding, unless Mom can perform some miracle and get him calmed down and/or distracted.

"Andrea! What the hell?" Dad shouts.

"Coming, dear," she calls out, then whispers, "Maybe I could just whack him over the head?"

"Mom!"

"Just to knock him out," she says. "Not kill him."

"Oh, well then," I say with an eye roll. "That's much better."

"Andrea!"

"Yes, dear," she says in a singsong voice, and starts down the stairs with me following. "What's the matter?"

"You cleaned me up!"

"Well, yes, just temporarily," she says, while I observe the carnage of the eight-drawer dresser, which they obviously, and unwisely, started putting together while under the influence last night.

"Guys, what happened?" I say. "It looks like Ikea barfed all over our floor."

"You and your friend abandoned us—that's what happened," Dad says, striding over to the mess and glowering at it.

"We can fix it," Mom says, hustling after him. "Come—we're very smart people, you and I."

"I need my computer! My papers! And where the hell did I leave my phone?"

"Here," Mom says, putting a piece of pressboard that might be the side of a drawer in his hand. "Let's get this done so that we're ready for the renters—"

"You said they're not coming until next week."

"But they wanted to see photos, remember?" she says in a calming voice. "So let's finish this, and then set the room up, and then we'll find your things."

It's quite amazing that Mom has managed to distract Dad for this long—almost a day and a half—but I'm not sure she's going to be able to reel him back in now.

"No!" Dad says. "This furniture is garbage. It's impossible to figure out, and so flimsy!"

"But—"

"Watch this," he says, and then takes the piece he's holding, and breaks it in half. "See? Total garbage."

And then as we watch in horror, he picks up one piece after another, breaks them, and chucks them back on the floor.

We know him better than to try to stop him. If we do he'll only get more worked up, whereas this way hopefully he'll get his frustrations out and then go back to normal. Or should

I say, "normal." Usually these things tire him out, at least.

And so we stand and watch while Dad breaks literally every single piece of the dresser.

When it's done, he stands up tall, hands on his hips, and says, "There. Those boneheads should give you your money back."

"Someone should," I mutter.

"You're welcome to call them," Mom says, a glint of steel in her eyes.

"Damn right I will," Dad says, proving he's still got some fighting mojo left.

"Let me get the customer service number," she says with freakish agreeableness.

She takes the stairs at a run and returns with the landline phone and a shipping receipt a minute later, and hands them to Dad.

"Here, darling. There's the number."

Dad dials, a gleam of anticipation in his eyes, and settles in for the call.

"Ha!" he says after a few seconds. "On hold!"

Here we go.

He will count the minutes he's on hold, and when he finally gets some poor hapless customer service person on the line he'll report the number of minutes with his very special brand of outraged relish. Then he'll tell a very lengthy story about the furniture, in which he is the aggrieved hero (though what he'll tell them this time, given that he's the one who deliberately broke every single piece of it, I can't imagine). He'll tell them, then, how the furniture is flimsy and the company that made it is evidence of corruption, greed, and the downfall of humanity, and by the way they damned well better give him his money back. At this point he'll be put on hold to talk to some other department, which will fill him with more gleeful outrage, and he will count the minutes he's on hold again, and add it to the original minutes, and report all to the next person put forth to talk to him, and start demanding that he also be compensated for his time. This next person will likely have to hear the entire story again, and will not be able to help, or not be able to help to my father's satisfaction, and Dad will demand to speak to a manager, and try to get the employee numbers of the people who have refused him so far, which they will refuse to give, and then he'll be put on hold again, and count the time, prowling and feeling aggrieved but also somehow enjoying every minute of it.

It could take hours.

And I take back everything bad I've ever said or thought about my mom—she's a genius.

Back up in the kitchen, we close the pocket door and make a pot of coffee in silence. It's been a while since Dad's had this kind of meltdown, but it's familiar territory.

"Maybe it's better for him to just keep doing his fighting online," I say finally. "I feel like we stop him in one venue, and he just moves to another. Like a super un-fun game of whack-a-mole with no giant stuffed bear at the end if by some chance you manage to win."

"No prize whatsoever," Mom says in a sad, flat voice.

"Except coffee," I say, pouring one and passing the mug to her.

"Except coffee," Mom says, raising her mug to her mouth and sipping with her eyes closed.

"At least the online stuff is anonymous," I say.

"It's terrible, though," Mom says. "I looked at some of it last night after he went to sleep. Awful. And more far-reaching than any of his Pine Ridge vendettas. Here, at least, he's contained."

"Yeah, but we're contained with him."

She sighs.

"Mom, I really think he needs help."

"We just have to get through this and he'll settle back down."

"But he was never actually settled. We just thought he was because he shut up about it and kept all his activities secret. He needs therapy, medication."

"Honey," Mom says, pulling her robe tighter around her waist, "he'd never agree to any of that."

"Well . . . can't we force him? Like into some kind of re-hab? I mean, I don't think troll rehab exists, but if they look at it as an addiction, or . . . symptom of depression or some-thing . . . ? I'm really worried. Like, beyond worried for my-self and whether he sticks his nose into this Perry issue."

"I know, I am too. But somehow we'll muddle through. Speaking of Perry . . ."

"What about him?" I say, tensing up.

"Have you planned what you're going to say to him on Monday?"

"Oh. 'I was wrong, forgive me, yada yada, I'm just a poor, overly emotional girl who really needs her job, blah, blah, blah . . .'"

"What are you going to wear?"

"Clothing."

"But you need to look your best."

"It's a uniform, Mom," I say. "A Goat T-shirt, and matching pants or skirt in black. There aren't a lot of variations."

"Hmm," she says, starting to pace the kitchen, "the skirt is more appealing to someone like Perry, obviously, but at the same time could be seen as encouraging . . . but you still want to look attractive . . . so I'd say the pants—your stretchy ones—and just a little extra makeup."

Ugh.

"I'm not putting on extra makeup for Perry Ackerman. In fact it's probably better for me to wear less makeup, because then I look younger, and that will hopefully remind him it's a teenager he's been harassing."

"Oh, that's quite strategic," she says, looking far too excited, considering. "Yes, go for dewy—some of that shimmery lotion, a light shade of gloss . . ."

"I have homework," I say, and leave the kitchen before my head explodes.

Back in my room I have a text from Kyle.

Do you want to have coffee today?
Or tomorrow?

Damn it, Kyle is everywhere. I turn the notifications off on my phone, but then turn them back on because if Noah texts, or Emma, I don't want to miss it. Kyle is driving me nuts. Why won't he just go away?

Possibly because I haven't told him to.

Because I don't 100 percent want him to, because he's an ally. An occasionally drunken raping ally. But he's on my side, and I need people on my side. I even like him most of the time. And I don't want to go back into the Goat on Monday and be in an argument with him.

I guess I would just rather be secretly mad.

And plagued by flashbacks of him whenever I try to kiss someone else.

And hope that I'll eventually forget what happened between us.

'Cause all of that is working so well for me.

24

MANSLAUGHTER

Dahlia would probably disagree with this course of action, but I'm feeling so much stronger and braver since I talked to her this morning, so I text Kyle back, accepting his offer to go for coffee, but explaining that there's nowhere I can go right now without attracting a lot of attention. He says he has an easy solution, and half an hour later we're parked in a nice shady spot behind the gas station—the same place Emma and I left him that memorable, horrible morning—and Kyle is returning to the truck with a box of doughnuts and two coffees from the kiosk.

I curl my hands into fists, then release them, trying to stay calm.

Time to process some trauma.

I'm pretty sure at this point that he doesn't even know what he did. Or he knows he pushed things but thinks it turned out for the best. Or maybe he was drunk enough that the memory is too fuzzy for him to clue in. Or he knows and he's going to apologize. I never would have expected it from Boris, and yet it happened.

Kyle does look awfully grim and determined as he strides toward the truck.

"Hey," he says, once he's set the stuff on the roof and opened the door. "Nobody's around. You want to sit in the back?"

This reminds me of his more suggestive offer of climbing into the bed of this same truck with my duvet last Sunday, but this doesn't feel like the same type of invitation, so I agree.

We climb up into the back and sit facing one another, the doughnuts and coffees between us. Kyle seems keyed up, so I decide to wait and see what he has to say before I advance my own agenda.

"I have something I wanted to give you," he says, looking solemn.

Then he grabs the backpack he brought from the cab of the truck, unzips it, pulls out a binder, and hands it to me.

"What's this?"

"Remember how I said my mom's a lawyer?" he says, leaning forward eagerly now. "I talked to her, like I said I would, about whether you have a case against Perry, or against Dev. I didn't know everything that happened, but I told her what I observed, and some of the stuff I've seen him doing to other servers. My mom is so pissed on your behalf, and on everyone's. And by the way she's pissed at me, too, because I stood by and didn't do anything. I got three 'I brought you up better than this' lectures this week."

"Poor you."

"Nah," he says, missing my sarcasm. "I can handle it."

I take a bite of a chocolate-glazed doughnut and try to mentally regroup, since this obviously isn't going to be an apology.

"Anyway, my mom gave me a ton of info and helped me compile some facts and resources for you, and summed up your options. Of course it's also your option to do nothing. But you do have just cause to sue, or to go to the police and try to get charges laid. It's all in here, with pros and cons and possible outcomes and timelines and stuff. And my mom—all her contact info is there too."

"Thank you," I say, chewing a bit too violently, and studying Kyle.

Yet again, I don't want to feel grateful to him, but I am.

I don't want to think of him as a good person, but based on most of his actions, all but the one, he is.

And he also isn't.

People are full of contradictions. Someone whose politics you hate might spend their spare time rescuing puppies, or knitting sweaters for orphans. Someone who sexually harassed you might have saved a ton of people from poverty and losing their homes. Someone who assaulted you might get you free legal advice from their mother.

Contradictions, yes, but at the same time, I made a plan to confront him, and just because he's done something nice doesn't mean I shouldn't follow through. Even if the thought of it makes me feel like I swallowed a bowling ball.

"You all right?" Kyle asks with a concerned frown. "You seem a little . . ."

"Look," I take a breath and then let it all out in a rush. "I'm messed up."

Kyle looks at me with questioning sympathy, and waits.

"I don't know how to say it diplomatically, and it's off topic, but I've been really . . . upset . . . about the night we spent together."

"Upset?"

"Yeah, upset."

"Look," he says, "I get it—it was a one-off for you. That's fine."

"No, that's not it."

Kyle frowns, definitely clueless.

"It's because I said I didn't want to have sex," I say. "I said it clearly and more than once. I said 'no' and you just . . . pushed ahead and did it anyway."

Kyle's mouth opens, then closes again, and he gives a sharp shake of his head.

"I realize I went along with it," I continue. The bowling ball is dread, and it feels like it's rising through me, up from my gut to my chest and toward my throat, where I feel like it might choke the life out of me. Still, I'm committed, and Kyle is waiting, wide-eyed and looking truly horror-stricken, for me to continue.

"I went along with it," I repeat, "and I know we were both drinking and so maybe things were fuzzy. But I know I said no, and that you heard me say it, because you responded. I don't think I gave you any indication that I'd changed my mind, either."

Kyle's face is morphing into an expression of shock and disbelief.

"What—"

"Just listen!" I say, my voice like a knife to pin him in place and shut him up. "I've thought about this a lot and read up on the definitions of what is consent and what isn't. I'm fully aware of the many factors that look bad on me in this situation—all the reasons people wouldn't think you were at fault and three-quarters of the world would just call me a lying slut and dismiss everything I'm saying. So you don't have to say any of that."

"I wasn't, but—"

"I let you sleep over, I made out with you and got naked with you in my bed and did a lot of sexual things with you— things that often lead to having sex. And when it happened I didn't fight. I only stopped you to get a condom. And from then on I participated."

"You didn't just participate," Kyle bursts in, "you had a good time! I mean I was drunk, but I clearly remember you enjoying it."

"Yes," I say, cheeks burning, but holding firm. "All of that is also true."

"So . . . ? I don't get it. We had a great time. Both of us had a great time."

"But I said 'no sex' and you said 'okay' and then later when it looked like sex was about to happen, I said 'wait, no, wait,' and you said 'okay, relax,' or something to that effect, and then when I had relaxed because I was trusting that you understood the boundary, you just went shoving on past it like I hadn't said anything. It shouldn't matter what happened after that. It matters that I said no."

Kyle's jaw is clenched so hard I can see the muscle twitching, and I realize that I should have had backup in place for this situation, or someone with me.

"You're saying I raped you."

"I'm saying I didn't consent to having sex with you. Which . . ." I exhale forcefully, "yeah, that's what they call it."

"I'm not—I don't . . . honestly I don't even . . . okay, I do remember you saying 'no sex' at the beginning, but I don't remember . . . I just remember having fun and things getting pretty wild, and being so into it. I am *not* a rapist, Libby."

"Maybe not usually."

Kyle slams his hands down on the truck bed and makes a

short, but anguished, howling sound that's more pained than scary.

"Settle down, Kyle!" I snap. "I'm not saying you're the guy who comes jumping out of the bushes to attack someone. And I don't think you're a guy who'd violate a passed-out girl beside a dumpster, or roofie someone's drink. You're not that."

"Gee, thanks."

"In a way it feels like . . . you know how with murder, there's a hierarchy: first degree, second degree, manslaughter? This would be more like . . . manslaughter. The manslaughter of rape."

"But you *let* me."

"Because I wasn't expecting it!"

"You wanted me, though. I know when a girl wants me."

"I wanted you . . . the way someone might want a piece of cake, but decides it's not the best thing for them at that moment," I say, quickly adapting some of the material from Dahlia's presentation, substituting cake for tea. "My mouth might be watering over a piece of cake but if I *make the choice not to eat it*, or if I just swipe some of the icing with my finger, should someone then shove an entire piece of cake in my mouth? And if they do, even if it tastes good and I end up swallowing it, is that okay?"

"No, but . . . but you could spit the cake out, and nobody's forcing you to eat the *whole rest of the cake* after that," Kyle says, gesturing to himself as he says "rest of the cake."

"True, but the point is—"

"Also!" he interrupts. "If the cake, once it's in your mouth, is so good that you go ahead and eat the rest of it, then maybe the person who snuck you that first piece was right—you needed that cake."

"Oh!" I sit up tall, now furious. "So they've done me a favor?"

"Well . . ."

"Why does that person think they have the right to take the choice away from me?"

"Arghhhh." Kyle presses his hands to his head for a moment and squeezes. "This is so messed up."

"Very."

"I really liked you," he says. "I still like you. And the funny thing is—or maybe it's not that funny—but I felt so used waking up in this parking lot in my truck."

"*You* felt used?"

"But I tried to shake it off. Then I thought it was weird that you were so cold to me at work, after. Now at least I know why. But I showed up the other night and again today because I felt bad about what happened to you with Perry, and about all the garbage online that's happened since then. And I gotta be honest—on Sunday? Watching Perry and how all over you he was, I wanted to beat the crap out of him."

"Are you sure you weren't just jealous of someone besides you doing things to me without my permission?"

"What the hell!" Kyle shouts.

"Quiet," I hiss, eyes darting around the parking lot and back of the plaza.

This . . . is not going quite as well as it did with Boris.

"What do you want from me?" Kyle hisses back.

"I want you, and every other clued-out person of the male species, to understand. And not do it again—to me or anyone else."

"Oh, so this is for my own good."

"It *is* for your own good because guess what? You'll have a better chance of getting to have sex with someone more than once if you don't start out by raping them. And a better chance at not being accused of rape—a circumstance many people might consider inconvenient, and is entirely avoidable via *getting people to agree to have sex with you.*"

"Fine," he says.

"And not constantly trying to push past their boundaries."

"Fine, fine, I get it," Kyle says, almost shouting again. Then he scrambles off of the flatbed and backs away from me like I'm a bomb about to go off.

"And it's also for my own good, because I'm not okay about it. I haven't been okay since it happened, and I needed to tell you. It wasn't without consequence."

"Okay, okay. But. Just. I need . . . a break . . . from this conversation."

"I'm not enjoying it either," I say, and hop out too, keeping as much distance as possible between us.

"So I'm gonna go," he says, hands in fists by his sides and looking like he's either going to punch something, burst into tears, or both. "Is that *allowed*?"

"Don't be an ass," I snap.

Then he blows past me, throws himself into the driver's seat, slams the door, and revs the truck engine like every idiot macho boy ever. Moments later he's roaring out of the parking lot, and away down the street toward the highway, the rear gate still open, and leaving a stream of spilling coffee and doughnuts behind him.

That was fun.

I stand there a minute, trying to slow my too-fast breathing and pull myself together.

Maybe I shouldn't have used the words "rape" and "rapist." Maybe I did it all wrong.

But . . . is there a right way to confront someone about

sexually assaulting you? One in which they *don't* get upset?
Doubtful.

I really should have had someone there to support me or
keep me safe in case he flipped out, though. That was not the
smartest. My gut instinct about Kyle is that he's not a violent
person, and we are somewhere somewhat public, but if I'm
ever in this situation again (please let me not be!) I won't do
it solo.

Still, I spoke up. I stopped avoiding it, and confronted it.
Hopefully this will go some way toward the processing I
need to do to get over it, and help me get back to kissing Noah
without having creepy flashbacks.

And Kyle's reaction, just like Boris's, isn't my problem.
It's not my job to make him feel better about this, no matter
how supportive he's been over the Perry thing.

I start to walk. The air is fresh, it's spring, I will look for
crocuses and tulips pushing up out of the earth in people's
gardens on my way home, and calm the hell down.

I've just reached the front of the other side of the gas station and stepped onto the sidewalk when I hear the sound of
an engine and look up to see Kyle's truck driving back in my
direction, now at a more judicious speed.

He pulls up beside me, window down, and an apple crul-
ler falls out the back onto the pavement.

"I'm sorry," he says, stiff-faced.

"Sorry for what?"

"For not making sure you . . . wanted . . . er . . . were
agreeing . . . to have sex. I never meant to be forcing you.
That's not me. Or it shouldn't have been. And man, my mom
would castrate me if she ever found out I did that. Anyway,
I'm just trying to wrap my head around this. I remember it

differently, but mostly I *don't* remember, and you do, so . . . I'm really sorry."

"Okay."

"You don't have to forgive me or anything."

"That's true."

"Right." He grips the window ledge and stares forward. "Right, okay. This is unbelievable. Because, as you know, I've been reading all about this stuff, never thinking it would apply to me, or to anything I've done. And all along . . . I'm basically no better. But, okay. You don't owe me anything."

"Thank you for apologizing, though," I relent. "And not trying to make me out to be a liar. That helps."

"Good."

"Good."

We stay like that for a few long, awkward moments, then he says, "Also, um, your purse is still in here," and gestures toward the front seat. "And . . . I still want you to take the binder."

"If it didn't fall out," I say, glancing rearward, "and isn't soaked in coffee."

Kyle's eyes widen in realization, then he curses, turns off the truck, and gets out to check the back.

I follow.

One coffee cup is still lolling there on its side, milky coffee trickling out. The doughnut box is there too, but empty, and the binder's right at the edge of the open gate, and likely would have fallen out at the next turn.

Kyle picks it up and inspects it, still swearing under his breath, and then wipes the bit of coffee that spilled on the cover off onto his shirt, leaving a brown mark across his chest.

"Bit of coffee, but it'll dry and it's all still legible," he says, then passes it to me, grabs the coffee cup and doughnut box, and slams the gate up.

"Thank you."

"I'll get your purse," he says, taking the garbage, opening the passenger door, and settling it on the floor, before taking my purse off the seat and handing it to me.

"Hey, I can take you home," he says. "That was a dick move to drive off and leave you here."

"It was, but I'm fine. It'll only take five minutes to walk."

"I see how maybe you don't want to be alone with me," he says, and hangs his head.

"I *came* here alone with you, Kyle. And depending what happens we'll be back working together at the Goat, so . . . I mean we've cleared the air and hopefully we can be professionals about this. Can we try that?"

"Fine. Fair."

This time when he leaves he does it with deliberate calmness, closing the truck door carefully, not revving the engine like a testosterone addict, and driving away like a fairly reasonable person.

Huh.

25

SHINING ARMOR

Dad's still on the phone when I get back, and Mom is in a barely controlled frenzy. She's cleaned up the broken dresser pieces, vacuumed, bought flowers (??), and is huffing back and forth, and up and down the stairs like there's some kind of urgency. I finally corner her in the garage, where she's trying to arrange the bins.

"What's going on? I thought you were trying to drag all of this stuff out through tomorrow and ideally even Monday, and now you're zooming around like it all has to be done right this second. What are you going to do with Dad tomorrow? And in general?"

"It's all under control," Mom says, swiping hair out of her face with her forearm.

"Sure," I say.

Then, for hours it seems, she's cooking. A lot. Like maybe her next plan is to feed Dad into a food coma. Speaking of which, there are loud snores coming from the basement, where he has conked out, finally exhausted from all his shit disturbing.

I seek refuge on the porch, in a chair with a book, and am

just starting the second chapter when a car pulls into the driveway, and then someone is getting out of it.

Someone I recognize and can hardly believe is real.

Jack.

Jack!

Jack, whom I have not laid eyes on in over two years and have missed so much and begged to come home so many times and was so furious with the last time I talked to him.

I surge up out of the chair, the book falling onto the porch floor, and two seconds later I'm tackling him, nearly knocking him over, and he's laughing, arms around me.

"I'm so mad at you," I say, still squeezing him.

"I know," he says, squeezing me back and lifting me off my feet.

Finally he puts me down and we stand there, studying one another.

"You've changed," he says.

"Yes, I'm ancient and jaded now," I say, and he grins. "And you're a . . . really grizzled beach bum who doesn't use enough sunscreen."

"Ouch!"

"Seriously, you're still in the doghouse," I say, trying to glare at him.

"Even after coming all this way?"

"Well . . ."

Jack in person is hard to stay mad at. There's something grounding and calming about him. He has a warmth, a twinkle, a way of listening that makes you feel heard.

"What are you doing here?"

"You asked me to come."

"I've been asking you that for two and a half years. Was it just that you were waiting for me to say the magic words?"

"You mean 'fuck off, Jack?'" he says with a glint of amusement in his hazel eyes.

"Yeah, those ones," I say with an unwilling smirk.

"Listen, Libby, I'm so sorry," he says with sudden urgency. "I went online right after we talked and I saw . . . well, later I read up on Dad's . . . activities, which are extremely worrisome, but first I saw all the stuff about you and Perry. The videos, the blog post, the photos. Why didn't you tell me?"

"I *was* telling you."

"But you didn't say it was you! I would have had a totally different reaction if you'd told me that."

"That's not actually a point in your favor, Jack."

"What? Why not?"

"It means that if it were just some girl, you wouldn't— never mind that right now. You were saying?"

"Just . . . I'm just so sorry that happened to you in the first place, and about all the mess that's come since then, and that I didn't give you the benefit of the doubt. And as for the rest of it—Mom and Dad—you've been telling me things are bad, and I didn't really get it. But for you to be that upset, and hang up on me, it shocked me. And then when I realized the full extent—"

"You still don't realize the full extent," I say, cutting in.

"Regardless, I haven't wanted to come home since I left— have not been tempted at all. But I just suddenly knew I needed to be here. So I got on a boat and then a plane, and I'm here to help. If I can."

Part of me wants to tell him that Mom and I have things under control, but you would have to have a pretty broad definition of "under control" to consider that true.

"What is it you think you can help with?"

"Dad," he says. "I hope. Seems like he's circling the drain, you know? To be spending his time that way. It's screwed up. And maybe I can talk him out of booting you from the house in July."

"Ha. Good luck with that."

"And . . . Libby, I haven't seen Perry in a really long time, but we were buds."

"Oh, barf."

"No, but . . . maybe I could talk to him. Sometimes guys are just dumb, and they don't realize their attentions are unwelcome. I see it in the bar all the time. Not only that, sometimes their attentions *are* welcome, and people hook up, fall in love, live happily ever after. So it's tricky. But I think if I just explained it to Perry, he'd feel bad about it."

"Oh, you naive man-child," I say, shaking my head. "Perry knows his attentions are unwelcome. He doesn't care. Trust me. How about you focus on Mom and Dad."

"All right."

"Are you ready to go in?"

Suddenly Jack is shifting his weight from one foot to the other, and looking anxious.

"Don't worry, Dad's asleep," I say. "He spent half his day on the phone haranguing a series of customer service representatives trying to get them to replace something he broke himself, on purpose. If only he'd been a lawyer, he'd have been literally paid to argue, and we would be so rich by now."

Jack's broad chest rumbles with a laugh that's like a warm blanket.

"Anyway, he conked out on the couch downstairs after all that, and we're just waiting for him to wake up revived and remember about Perry, and start wreaking havoc again. Because that's the pattern when he's like this: get up, wreak havoc, sleep, repeat."

"Fun."

"Yeah," I say, and sigh. "Anyway we can probably sneak you in to see Mom first. Don't be scared—I'm not sure she's even really that mad at you anymore. And if she is, I'll bet she forgives you the second she sees you."

He shrugs, and something in his expression triggers a realization.

"She knew you were coming, didn't she! You told her and not me?"

"Well you weren't answering my calls or texts," he says, hands up defensively. "And I thought she might want some . . . emotional preparation. I'm sorry!"

"It's fine," I say, shaking my head. "Explains a few things."

Then I take his arm, and he hefts his overnight bag over his shoulder and follows me inside.

When we walk into the kitchen, Mom gasps in the general direction of Jack's beard and the wild straggle of hair curling just past his shoulders, clutches at her chest, and then says, "You're so hairy!"

Jack and I both burst out laughing.

"You didn't warn her about the facial hair?" he asks me. "I know you saw photos."

"It's not something you just drop into conversation."

"It's still me, Ma," Jack says, and holds out his arms.

She bursts into tears, throws herself at him, and clings for a good five minutes while he pats her back and says nice, calming things. Meanwhile, I keep a lookout for signs of Dad emerging from the basement.

"Dinner," Mom finally gasps, and pulls away. "We should have dinner. I've almost got everything ready."

"How can I help?" Jack asks.

She's already set the dining room table with all the fancy

things we never use, just like she did in January for the dinner where they announced that my education money was gone and they were kicking me out. I can't help feeling that the more effort my mom makes for a meal, the worse it's going to go.

"You two start putting the food on the table and I'll go . . . ah . . . get your father. Just . . . don't stand near the top of the stairs, Jack, or you might give him a fright."

"Roger that," Jack says.

"And try not to upset him," she adds.

I snort.

"No guarantees there, Ma," he says with a nervous glance at me.

"At least until after dinner?"

"I'll try."

Two minutes later Jack and I are standing anxiously behind our customary chairs in the dining room, listening to Mom chivying Dad up the stairs, and Dad grumbling and groggy and saying something and not being hungry.

"But I told you, I have a surprise," she's saying as they reach the top.

And then they round the corner and Dad stops in his tracks.

"Surprise," Mom says in her cake-with-tragedy voice.

"Here we go," I say under my breath to Jack.

Dad's expression goes from irritation to confusion to shock to joy to pain to something that might be fear, and then finally settles (predictably) on flinty.

"We taking in strays?" he says to Mom.

"No, Rick, it's—"

"I know who it is," he barks. "What's he doing here?"

"He . . . Jack . . ." Mom casts me a wild look as though this reaction is a surprise, then says, "Jack came for dinner! He's here for dinner."

"Yes, dinner," I say. "All the way from Greece."

"Isn't that nice?" Mom chirps.

"Hi, Pops," Jack says without a trace of his usual bemusement.

"They don't serve dinner in Greece?" Dad says.

Jack is gazing at Dad like he's thrown—not, I think, by Dad's rude reception of him, but from how Dad has changed. He's aged kind of suddenly over the past couple of years, but it's not just that. Some essential spark is gone from him. It's happened right in front of me, in increments, but I imagine it must be a shock for Jack.

"Food's great in Greece," Jack says. "I came to see you."

"Me!"

"All of you."

Mom gestures for us to sit down, and three out of the four of us move to pull out our chairs. Dad, though, stays where he is.

"If you're here to say something," Dad declares, pulling himself up, "then say it."

Jack glances from Mom, to me, then back to Dad, and the two of them share a long, loaded look. Then Jack backs abruptly away from the table and says, "How 'bout you and me go for a drive, Dad? I'm not hungry yet anyway."

"Oh, so now you want the car," Dad says.

"No," Jack replies, refusing to rise to the bait. "I rented one. Smells new and it's got a big engine—you'll like it."

Jack starts toward Dad, slowly as though not to spook him.

"Come," he says, voice gentle.

"But . . ." my mom practically wails, "dinner! And you just got here . . ."

"I'll be back, Ma," Jack says as Dad lets him take him by

the arm and propel him toward the front door. "Dad and I just need to have a talk first."

"But . . ."

"You two go ahead and eat while everything's still hot."

"Well," I say as we listen to them drive off. "What do you think—did that go better or worse than the last meal we had in here?"

Mom doesn't respond.

"I'm thinking worse," I say, "since the dinner didn't actually even occur."

"This isn't a joking matter," Mom says, her tone flatlining.

"Oh, come on—what did you think was going to happen? That we were going to pretend the last few years didn't exist?"

"Yes!"

"That never works, Mom."

"It always worked in my family," she says, drifting back toward the dining room table and staring wistfully at it. "Things happen, you can't fix them, so you simply step over it and carry on."

"And how close is your side of the family these days? How often do you all hang out?"

The answer, as she well knows, is never.

"That's beside the point," she says.

"You know what they do at Emma's? They debate. For fun. They even argue sometimes—not just one person ranting and everyone else having to listen—everybody gets a turn. They have rules, and people jump in to referee if needed. It used to freak me out. But they work things through. They listen to each other, and by the end of it they sometimes agree to disagree, or if it's something they have to make a decision about, they take a vote—very democratic—or her parents use veto power. But they usually resolve things, and half the time they end up laughing. Can you imagine?"

"No," she says, and sinks into her chair. "Sounds exhausting."

"And this isn't?"

"Oh, this is, too."

"You know what?" I say, looking at the table. "I'm lighting these candles. What the hell are we saving them for anyway?"

Mom's perfect posture collapses—a sign of how disappointed she is, and I get matches from the kitchen and light the candles that have never been lit.

"And I'm starving," I say, "so I'm going to eat."

"May as well," she says with a gloomy expression on her tired face.

"And," I add, ready to press my luck, "I'm having a glass of wine."

"Pour me one, too."

So I pour for us and we pick at our food, a now-sad meal of Jack's favorite foods—macaroni casserole, ribs arranged in a fancy, upright circle on a bed of greens, mini pizzas, plus vegetable skewers with cucumber, olive, tomato, and feta that are clearly meant to invoke Greece. We sip the wine and listen for the car returning and don't even bother trying to make conversation. As the sky outside sinks to full dark we pack dinner up and put it in the fridge. Then Mom produces a chocolate cake, sets it in front of her, sticks a fork straight into it, and starts eating.

"All right, then," I say, and then I grab my own fork and we sit there eating cake by candlelight, and waiting.

And waiting more.

Dad and Jack finally arrive back after eleven, to find Mom and me sitting in the dark living room.

"Jesus Murphy!" Dad exclaims when Mom snaps on the one light that has a good bulb in it, and then Jack laughs like he's a drunken, busted teenager coming in after curfew. They're both in one piece and the tension between them seems less, but Jack looks sad and Dad looks weary and diminished.

"You could have texted," I say, sounding exactly like the busted teen's parent.

"Sorry, Lib," Jack says, "I left my phone in my pack and it's probably on silent."

"We ate the cake," Mom says, all of her fake cheer gone. "And if you want dinner, you'll have to get it yourselves."

"We're good," Jack says. "Uh, sorry, Ma."

"I'm going to bed," Dad announces, and without further ado, he leaves.

The three of us stand for a few quiet moments, listening to Dad's footsteps as he heads down the back hall to his and Mom's bedroom, and then to the door closing.

"Well . . . ?" I say in a soft voice to Jack.

"It's taken care of," he says.

Mom gives a gasp of relief and goes to hug him, but I'm not satisfied.

"What, exactly, is taken care of?"

"All of it," Jack says over Mom's shoulder. "Well, not your problem with Perry. But Dad's not going to write or post anything, and he promised to stop with RicksNotRolling, and take down all his accounts."

"You're kidding."

"Nope," he says, seeming to puff up a bit. "I handled it."

"Huh," I say.

"What?" he says.

"It's just . . . you have one conversation and, boom, everything's fixed?"

"Just the old Jack magic," Jack says with a grin I don't quite believe.

"This is not a matter for jokes and charm, Jack," I say. "Seriously."

"Are you even happy I'm home? Cause you're being pretty hard on me."

"Being easy on people hasn't been getting me anywhere."

"Libby, shhh," Mom says, wringing her hands.

"Look, of course I'm happy you're here," I say, lowering my voice but not stopping. "But you've been gone a long time. Things are different. Worse. And some of the things that are different and worse are because of you. So, like, if you cause a problem, I'm not sure you get to win a prize for coming back to solve it. But I also doubt that you have solved it."

"Libby!" Mom says again.

I turn to her. "Come on, Mom, Dad's not well. You know that. The stuff he does—the arguments, the troll stuff, systematically destroying an entire dresser this morning—that's not normal. But they're also not the problem, they're symptoms of whatever the problem is. So whatever it is you said or did to get him to stop, Jack, maybe he will stop those particular things, but he'll just find something else."

"I think my being here is going to help, though," Jack says. "At least to heal our relationships. I hope."

Mom is nodding and looking at Jack like he's a hero.

"How are we supposed to heal when you just go off in the car for a secret conversation, though?" I ask. "When Mom and I are literally shut out of the entire process? That's bullshit."

"Please, Libby, I'm tired."

"*You're* tired!"

Mom shushes me.

"Yes, I'm tired. We can talk more tomorrow, I promise,"

Jack says, his eyes pleading. "I've been awake for almost twenty-four hours."

I exhale, and try to let it go. "Fine."

"All right, Jack, you poor boy," Mom says, coming alive with purpose. "I've got your room ready. In fact it's been re-done! Unfortunately there's, ah, no dresser because your old stuff got taken from the curb and the new one . . . but it doesn't look like you have much luggage anyway. Let's get you settled. You're staying for a few days, aren't you?"

"Yeah, Ma, don't worry."

"So, we'll have time to talk tomorrow. Bedtime for everyone," Mom says, and then wags a finger at me, "and you let your brother sleep."

Jack gives me a semi-reassuring wink, then yawns.

And with that, she hustles him downstairs, leaving me standing there, wondering why I don't feel any better.

26

A BIT OF BLACKMAIL

I'm still in the front room, sitting in the dark again texting with Noah, when Jack comes tiptoeing back upstairs fifteen minutes later.

I put the phone facedown and whisper "Hey" as he makes his way toward the front door, and have the satisfaction of making him jump yet again.

"When did you get so lurky and sneaky?"

"You're the one sneaking, I'm just sitting here."

"Yeah, lurking!"

"No, texting." I hold up my phone. "Not the same."

"If you're not too furious at me, wanna come outside? Turns out I . . . need some air."

"I'm not furious. Just frustrated. I'll come."

"Okay, but . . . truce?"

"Truce."

I let Noah know, then leave my phone at the door, and Jack and I slip quietly into our shoes and duck out.

In the middle of our front yard under the red maple tree is one of those bench swings of the everlasting-plastic-with-canopy variety. It sits tilted on an angle, facing both the driveway and the street, and far back enough to have a view of the front door as well.

It's almost always too buggy, too hot, or too cold to sit out there, but tonight is just right—too early in the season for bugs, but warm enough if you have a sweater on, which we both do.

"You think this thing'll still hold us?" Jack says as we approach the swing.

"Live dangerously and sit on a count of three?" I suggest.

He takes my hand and we back our butts toward the bench.

"One, two, three," he says, and then instead of sitting down slowly and gingerly as I planned to do, he drops down hard and fast, dragging me with him, and then kicks back hard like he's daring the swing to either crack or tip over. The plastic seats moan ominously as we rock backward, and the whole thing sways, but holds together.

"You idiot," I say with a gasp.

Jack pushes us off again, and we swing in a more reasonable arc this time.

"Remember when you tried to do an underdog with this?" I say.

He winces at the memory. "Worst crash ever. What parents get this as a swing for their kids, though? What's wrong with a tire swing? Or a good old-fashioned wood plank?"

"I think Mom imagined she was going to sit out here and read or something. It wasn't really for us."

"Huh."

"So . . . what'd you say to Dad?"

"Whoa, I thought we had a truce."

"We do. What did you say?"

"Man, you're stubborn," he says with a sideways glance at me.

"Family trait."

"Ha."

"So?"

"I just said . . . what I told you before. That he should stay out of this Perry thing and let you handle it your own way, that I knew about the online stuff and it has to stop. And he agreed."

"Just like that? You were gone a long time."

"Well, it did take some . . . discussion."

"I think you're keeping something from me. I'm not twelve anymore, and frankly that was too easy."

"Easy!"

"Yes, easy. He's had one negative consequence after another—no career, no job, no friends left, no family who'll tolerate him except us. We're knocking ourselves out here doing damage control, and damage prevention, and we are getting damaged ourselves in the process. And then you—someone he's furious with—come home and spend a couple of hours talking to him and he agrees to everything you say. What am I missing?"

Jack puts his foot out to stop the swing and looks at me.

"You're right, you're not twelve. So maybe you're old enough to understand that I can't tell you," he says, and then looks away and starts pushing the swing again.

"So there *is* something. Some way you had to convince Dad."

"I'm not saying anything more."

"Something you agreed to do . . . ?"

Jack chuckles, but shakes his head.

"Or . . . something you can hold over him—a bit of black-mail?"

"No," he says a little too quickly.

"That's it."

"Let it go, Libby."

"But if you know something, I should know it too. I'm the one who's had to live here, Jack, all the time. If you would just tell me—I won't use it, I'll only hold it in reserve."

"It's not like that. Come on, I came to help, I am helping, can you just let me do it the way I need to? And trust me?"

I don't want to drive him away, so I back off. "Fine."

"Now can we talk about something else?"

"Sure."

The swing goes back and forth, back and forth, and the crickets are chirping, and I hear a car door slam somewhere down the street.

And then I say, "How come you dropped out of college?"

And Jack says, "You said we could talk about something else."

"That *is* something else," I say with a frown, and I'm readying a follow-up question when he gets to his feet. "Where're you going?"

"Are you hungry?" he asks. "Because I'm starving. Let's go raid the fridge."

"There's a ton of food left from dinner, but tell me—"

"Nope," he says, "no more heavy stuff tonight. I'm done talking."

"Fine."

"Fridge?"

"Okay, okay," I shake my head, grumbling, and get up off of the swing. "Mom just about killed herself making all that food for you so we may as well."

"Great," he says with the old Jack grin. "Let's go."

27

LOW-KEY MISERABLE

Sunday morning I wake to the smells of breakfast food, the sound of Mom singing along to the radio in the kitchen, and *"You said we could talk about something else." "That is something else"* on a repeating loop in my mind.

I roll over, desperate to get back to sleep, but then decide to check my phone, and find a text from Emma with the latest news.

Martina's blog piece about Perry now has over four hundred comments, most of them server nightmare stories. The conversation has been noticed and linked to by a couple of bigger news sites. And thirteen anonymous women have posted claiming Perry has sent them dick pics.

Meanwhile, the moderator of the Crotchety Complainers has closed comments on the post about me, and taken down the video, but left up the photos from Jason. And a total of forty people have shared stories about Perry harassing them, or someone they know, on Martina's blog. But very few have chosen to do so non-anonymously, and none of those are from the brewery, the Goat, or the Inn—no one he could fire, in other words.

Best part of weekend so far? Emma texts. Apparently
Perry showed up for karaoke at the legion last night and
sang the drunkest version ever of I Will Survive and then
So What by Pink.

> ???? That one about still being a rock star
> and having rock moves?

Yep.

> OMG.

With hip thrusting, and. . . . then
supposedly he thrust so hard one
time that he fell right over.

> NOOOOO.

Probably traumatized the seniors.

> !!!!!!

He's cracking, Lib.

> We lock our doors don't worry.

Conversation about sexual assault and
harassment in restaurants and bars is
blowing up. People are talking about the
tipping system and wages and everything.
But besides that I think Perry goes down.

> And if he does? And the brewery and inn
> go out of business?

We'll be gone from here.

                                              Ooh. Cold.

YOU ARE NOT RESPONSIBLE FOR
THE WHOLE TOWN LIBBY.

                                          So loud Em.

You're not.

Five minutes later I'm perched on a chair beside Jack's bed, a steaming coffee in hand, and another on a coaster on the new bedside table.

"Hey, Jack," I say in a soft voice, "wake up."

He moans, then rolls over onto his back.

"Jack."

"Whoa," he says groggily, eyes opening to slits. "Jeez, Libby."

"I brought coffee," I say, gesturing toward it. "I figured you might want to fortify yourself with caffeine before having to face Mom and Dad. You still drink coffee?"

"Of course," he says. "Coffee is a serious thing in Greece."

We sit, each drinking our coffee in the dim light, and I try to calculate what might be the optimum number of sips for him to have before I ask my question. I have this idea emerging, of taking the best from each of my parents and making a new me. This me will not be a batshit reactionary, or a frozen coward, and is not submerged in numbness. She is deliberate, wily, and calm-seeming like Mom, and singularly determined like Dad. She is smart, patient, relentless, and brave, and she can also cut to the chase just like Jack does when needed.

Plus Jack is the perfect person to practice on, and I have the perfect subject to practice on him with.

"So Dad's the reason you quit school," I say, a little scared, but pouncing when the moment feels right.

"Y-no, what?" Jack sputters, nearly spilling his coffee. "I never said that."

"'*How come you dropped out of college?*' '*You said we could talk about something else*,'" I say, putting one hand up with quotation marks. "I've been thinking about that part of our conversation. That was intended as something else. It was a change of subject. Except apparently in your mind it wasn't."

"Whoa, Sherlock," he says, squinting warily at me. "You're way off."

"Okay, then why did you drop out of college?"

"I didn't want to be a doctor, okay? I get faint at the sight of blood."

"Seriously?" I do a quick inventory of my memories, looking for one in which Jack faints at the sight of blood, but all I've got are images of him groaning over this or that injury, or wincing as Mom or Dad bandage him. But I was young, and in my own world.

"Always have," Jack says, "but my math and science grades were high and Dad badly wanted a doctor in the family. I figured I'd grow out of it. But it isn't just the blood. I don't want to look inside bodies, cut things open, any of it."

"You could have switched majors. You didn't have to take off to another continent."

"Maybe I just needed some space, Lib."

"From what?" I say, keeping my gaze trained on him and my purpose steady. "And what do you mean, 'maybe'?"

"I just mean . . . I didn't know what I wanted to do, and I didn't want to just . . . switch majors randomly and waste more money. I'd been kind of low-key miserable for I don't know how long. I needed to get away and take some time to figure out what I wanted."

"So you ran off to 'find yourself.' "

He chuckles, then shrugs.

"And have you?"

"Found myself?"

"And figured out what you want to do?"

"For now I just want to do what I'm doing."

"But that's temporary, Jack. It's not building toward anything."

"I got news for you, little sister, everything is temporary. Life is temporary." He lifts his mug toward me as if in a toast. "This coffee . . . is temporary."

I roll my eyes.

"No, really. And sometimes all you can do is build, like, one not-shitty day on top of another not-shitty day. And then maybe one good day on top of a not-shitty day, and then finally one good day on another good day. That's building something."

"Wait—are you depressed?" I ask.

"No," he says, but his eyes slide away from my gaze.

"Were you?"

"It's not that exactly, Libby. I was unhappy, but it was situational. And of course it's been hard to move so far away, leave everything behind, and to have such a rift with Mom and Dad. I get restless, too. I'm like Dad that way. I'm . . . trying not to be like Dad in other ways. I know you think everything is so much worse since I left, but Dad was . . . Dad before that, too."

"But he was crazy about you. So proud of you. There at all your practices and talking about you all the time. I tried, like,

a million other things—track, soccer, tap dancing, music—
hoping to find something I was that good at, so he'd be as into
me as he was into you. Nothing worked."

"Because you weren't good at them, or because Dad wasn't
interested?"

"Maybe both." I shrug.

"If you weren't doing it for you," Jack points out, "that
might be why nothing stuck. But all that attention from Dad
wasn't so great, Libby. He'd take it really hard when we lost,
or if I didn't play enough in a game. He'd get obnoxious with
other parents, coaches, refs. Even back then, Mom was constantly having to show up with baked goods to smooth the
waters. And it took me a while to disentangle from that, and
recover, and understand. Now I'm trying to just be steady,
and do my thing. Work hard, swim in the ocean . . ."

"Build good days?"

"Yeah."

"What about the money, Jack?"

"Money?"

"You said that you didn't want to waste money switching
to a random major, but instead you spent it."

"I didn't spend the money. I dropped my courses that fall
just early enough to get refunded, and I sublet my place, and
so, yes, I used some of that money to get to Greece. But since
then I've been supporting myself."

"Where's the rest of your education money, then?" I press
on. "Mom and Dad's goal was to have the same amount saved
up for each of us when we went to college. I saw what was in
mine as of last August, so if you had the same amount in
yours . . ."

"Yes, well—"

"That was a lot of money, Jack. Plus didn't you have

scholarships? If you didn't spend it, where is it—sitting in the bank somewhere waiting for you to decide what to do?"

Jack is very still in the bed suddenly, watching me like I'm a wild animal he doesn't want to scare off.

"You know I would give you the money if I could," he says.

I do *not* know that. I'm not sure what I know anymore.

"I'd give it to you, or I'd loan it to you," he continues, looking pained.

"So . . . what . . . you have it invested or something?"

"Yeah. Exactly. It's invested."

I cock my head, trying to read his expression in the dim light and trying to interpret the gut feeling that's just overtaken me.

"There," I say, more to myself than to him. "'Invested.'"

"Huh?"

"What you just said about the money being invested," I say with growing conviction, "you're lying."

"I am not," he says, blustering. "You're imagining—"

"Do you not have it?"

"I . . ."

"Did Dad take it? Is that why you quit school?"

"I already told you why I quit school."

"Just tell me," I say, getting up from the chair and standing over him. "I'm in the middle of making decisions that will affect the course of my entire life, without knowing all the facts. I have a right to know."

He slumps forward, head in his hands.

I'm waiting, and feeling he's on the brink, when suddenly Mom is calling, "Brunch, darlings!" from the top of the stairs.

"I have to get dressed," Jack says, getting out on the far side of the bed.

"Please, Jack . . ."

"Okay," he says, facing me across the unmade bed and suddenly talking in a whisper. "But you have to promise . . ."

"Sure, sure," I say, waving him along.

"Dad told you he turned the whole fund over to me, right? Because I was old enough to handle the money myself?"

"Yes."

"So, what if that wasn't true? Hypothetically?"

"That would mean . . . you never had the money?"

"Hypothetically."

"Then where—"

"Brunch!" Mom calls.

"We've gotta go up," he says, then goes to his pack, pulls out a sweater, and puts it on over his T-shirt and pajama pants. "We'll talk about this later."

"Promise?"

"Promise."

28

SHITSTORM

Two minutes later my family is gathered around the table for yet another attempt at a normal family meal like the slow learners we obviously are.

Jack, across from me, is rumpled but alert, Dad, at the far end, looks like his usual self, and Mom, opposite Dad and nearest to the kitchen, is chirpy in a way that isn't even fake. Her insistence on pretending everything is fine is in full force, but she's also so happy to have Jack home that it's coming off her in waves.

She's even, I suspect, prepared a mental list of subjects that are suitable for conversation, and these she dishes out alongside the food—for example, the hole in the backyard fence, hurricane statistics, deep sea archeology, a bit of gossip from the Inn (only about out-of-towners—no talk about locals), fun facts about nocturnal mammals, and a recent trip to the dentist.

Jack and I do our best to run with these conversational gambits, and, in fact, so does Dad. But each subject only lasts so long, and then we're back to the clinking of cutlery on plates and the many subjects we cannot discuss—e.g., school, my job, Jack's job, Dad's lack of job, Greece, travel in general, Perry, politics (local, national, international), anyone from Pine Ridge, anything to do with relationships of any kind, anything to do with world events of any kind.

I even jump in to regale them about the horrors of my first day of apartment searching—the fish place, Sarah the drone-shooting nudist, woebegone Trevor with the creepy, cave-like basement he thought I could have parties in. I am taking a risk mentioning anyone local, but it gets us through another few minutes.

When Mom manages to somehow connect her teeth-cleaning story to one about her coworker's deceased pet rabbit, I don't know whether to scream from the tension, or stand up and applaud her virtuosity.

To have our family together and peaceful around a table is an amazing feat. There's something so reassuringly normal about it, and something so painful and beautiful about how everybody's trying.

But it's also awful. Fake and fraught and never going to get better. Jack's laughing at Mom's description of the pet rabbit's obituary, and Dad's nodding along, and Mom is gathering herself for another anecdote, and suddenly I'm thinking about everything that's been going on, and the secrets people are keeping, and how I'm sitting here with the people who are supposed to love me most, and we can't talk about any of it.

Suddenly I want to cry all over my pancakes, or throw something.

Because this is not the goal—this is not the solution *or* the goal.

And so I decide to throw a firework into the conversation.

"Where did all the education money go?" I ask, determined

to stay calm no matter what happens next.

The effect is instantaneous. Jack stares at me wide-eyed, Mom looks like she'd retract her head into a shell like a turtle if she could, and Dad has paused, a forkful of eggs halfway to his mouth.

"I understand that there's nothing we can do about it," I add, fighting a panicked instinct to walk this back before it turns into a shitstorm. "But I'd like to know where it went."

There's a super silent silence and then Mom bursts in with, "How about another pancake, dear! I think your blood sugar is low."

"No, come on," I insist. "We have to be able to talk about things *as a family*. Otherwise we're going to end up not being a family. Everything is too fragile, like we're all going to break if anybody says anything difficult."

Mom makes a weird, flapping/calming motion with her hands and mutters something about "keeping a lid on things."

"I think we need to take the lid *off*."

"Libby, no," Mom whispers.

"Yes," I say, even though I feel like I might throw up and/or die. "Everything started going off the rails when Dad left the brokerage, and went all the way off when Jack quit school and moved to Greece. And now, if it's even possible, they're worse. My education money is gone and Dad is unemployed and unbalanced to the point that he broke over forty pieces of wood yesterday for no good reason."

"I am not unemployed, I'm self-employed!" Dad says, cutting a sausage with savage force. "And your mother is the one who ordered all that crap furniture. It wasn't even real wood, it—"

"The wood is not the point! The point is that Mom and I

are doing backflips trying to manage you and work around you all the time."

"What are you talking about, 'work around me'?" Dad says as Mom signals frantically at me to shut up and Jack watches it all. "That's bullshit."

"It's not," I say, swallowing my bone-deep fear of his rising temper and pushing on. "You go into every single situation like a wrecking ball. You were so determined to write that article about Perry, even though it would make everything worse and I begged you not to, and even though it was an almost certain path to the entire town finding out you're RicksNotRolling—maker of death threats and spreader of digital pestilence—that the only thing I could think of to do was steal your phone and rip our modem right out of the wall."

"Oh, excuse me if I wanted to stop you from having to go prostrate yourself in front of that bastard Perry Ackerman," Dad says, arms crossed like he's barely containing himself, giving me a vicious glare. "Excuse me for wanting to support my own daughter, and trying to help."

"You don't want me to have to prostrate myself in front of Perry," I press on, "but you're one of the chief reasons I have to do it. You've put me in a position where I have no choice."

"No choice, huh?" he sneers. "You're going to sell your integrity! Give up! I never imagined a daughter of mine would just lie down and let some scumbag walk all over her."

"Why not?" I say, something breaking inside me. "I let you do it all the time."

Mom gasps and Dad goes completely still for a moment, then says, "Pardon me?"

"You walk all over us all the time," I say, years of pain and held-back anger tumbling the words out. "You're doing it right now. You steamroll over us, hammer us down until we're exhausted and have nothing left. You have to be heard the most, and you have to be right all the time, and you have to be the only one with a valid opinion, with *any* opinion."

I'm crying furiously now, but nothing is going to stop me from saying the rest of it.

"So of course I let Perry Ackerman walk all over me. How would I know how to fight someone like him? I'm not allowed to fight in this house, much less win. You're the only one who gets to win. You win and win and crush the life out of the rest of us. And meanwhile, all I know how to do is roll over like a dog that's been kicked too often and smile at every shitty thing that happens to me. Or once in a blue moon, when I've been pushed too far, freak out like a psycho and ruin everything I've worked for. That's how I am. You're not happy with it? *Well, you're the one who made me this way.*"

There's an awful pause then. Jack looks devastated, Mom has shrunk back in her chair and wrapped her arms around herself, and Dad, for the moment, is staring at me, completely blank.

"Let me get this straight," Dad says after a few beats. "You're a coward and it's my fault?"

I lift my chin and say, "Yes," and wait for the explosion.

"I gotta say, Dad," Jack surprises me by breaking in, "I agree with Libby. I haven't been here long, but there's a lot of yelling. A lot of you yelling, and a lot of Libby and Mom being really messed up by it."

"How dare you?" Dad says, throwing his fork down on his plate and clenching his fists.

"Just look at yourself!" I say, still crying but bolstered by Jack's support. "You're so angry all the time, Dad. You're not well."

"I'm angry because the world is shitty and full of injustice, and somebody needs to fight it."

"I don't think the fighting is getting you anywhere," Jack says. "If you were actually correcting injustices, I think you'd feel better. You'd have a sense of accomplishment. Be happier. But you don't seem happy."

"Of course I'm not happy," Dad says, less volcanic for the moment, but more despairing. "I wanted to *do* something. *Be* something. And instead I'm nothing. Nothing in a nothing town that's sucking the life out of me. I don't need you to tell me what's wrong with me, I know what's wrong with me. The world is a shithole, and I'm miserable in this place."

Mom makes a sound of distress, and Jack puts a hand on her arm.

"We did it for you," Dad continues, "for you two kids. Moved here to give you good childhoods in a place we could save money for your futures. So you could make something of yourselves. But then Jack pissed it all away, and—"

"Whoa, wait," Jack says. "I'm not taking that on."

"What on?" Dad says.

"That whole 'I sacrificed everything for my ungrateful children' crap," Jack says. "You and Mom chose to have us— that's not our fault. And it doesn't mean you get to control who we become or what we do with our lives, or that you get to blame us for the fact that you're unhappy, or don't like where you live. I think you'd be unhappy anywhere you went because it's like Libby says—you're not well. You're depressed."

"I have good reason to be depressed!"

"And you're taking it out on all of us, and have been for years," Jack says, his own temper frayed now. "As for me supposedly pissing everything away—you never even asked if I wanted to go into medicine. You just started telling me that was what I wanted. And I let you."

"Medicine is an incredible career! A meaningful career."

"But it wasn't my dream, Dad. I never even got to have a dream—I was too busy trying to live up to yours."

"And that's why you went to Greece? Is that your dream?" Dad says, disdainful but also asking for real. "Bartending?"

"I went to Greece to get away from you."

"Well that's great," Dad says, then picks up his fork, looks down at the food on his plate. "Congratulations, you succeeded."

"I didn't do it to hurt you," Jack says, like it's being wrenched out of him. "And it wasn't because I don't love you. I do love you."

"Could have fooled me!"

"I love you. And Mom. Of course I do," Jack says, looking from Dad to Mom, who's shrunken into a kind of lockdown position in her chair and only stares at him. "But you're a lot to handle, Dad. You dominated my life. I see you meant well by it but I needed to get some separation from your opinions, and your expectations—to figure out who I am, what I want. Libby thinks I got all this amazing attention that she never got, and it was a lot of attention you gave me, but it wasn't all amazing, Dad."

"That's perfect," Dad says, his head practically buried in his plate now, like maybe he doesn't want us to see his face. "That's what you can put on my gravestone, 'It wasn't always amazing.'"

"Don't talk like that!" Mom says, voice pleading and face panicked.

"Oh, I'm not going to off myself, Andrea," Dad says, fi-

nally looking up, eyes haunted but jaw set. "Not going to give
these two ingrates the satisfaction."

"Dad, listen," I say. "We're trying to talk to you. The other
day you were freaking out so much you were spitting in my
face. You were trying to shut me up so you wouldn't have to
hear my opinion, and to distract me from what I was trying
to do. And it works, Dad. Even now, although this stuff is important too, you've got us totally distracted from the question
I asked in the first place—about the money."

"Oh for God's sake, I'm not—"

"No. What happened to the money, Dad?" I say, refusing
to let him get me off track. "My money, and Jack's money?"

Dad's glare fastens on Jack, furious again. "You told her?"

"No!" Jack says.

"What did you tell her?"

"Nothing!"

"Jack didn't tell me anything! But guess what?" I say.
"*You just did.*"

"I—I . . ." Dad sputters.

"Where's the money, Dad?" I say, getting to my feet, insides clenching. "What happened to it?"

"What is she talking about," my mom says, starting to
come out of her lockdown pose. "Rick?"

"Nothing," Dad says, ramping up to full blaze again. "She's
lying! But! If I'd needed that money it was mine to spend. I
earned it and I don't have to answer to her, or Jack, about
anything. I'm the parent, the adult! And I've had just about
enough of being blamed for everything and interrogated in
my own damned house. I don't have to put up with this shit!"

He gets up and shoulders by me, then starts marching
out of the dining room.

Which means it's over.

It's over and I failed and nothing will change.

Except all of a sudden Mom is on her feet with a large serving spoon in hand, blocking Dad's exit, and practically knocking him backward with the word, "No."

"Damn it, Andrea, let me go!"

"No, no, no," she says in a voice that's high and tight and like a knife. "This is not happening again. I will not have this happen two meals in a row, people walking out when I've worked so hard."

"What?"

I get out of the way fast as she stalks toward Dad, and he, seemingly surprised right out of his anger, backs up and keeps backing up, all the way to his chair.

"Sit," she hisses.

He sits with a grunt and I sit too.

"Second helpings!" Mom says, and then reaches for the platter of scrambled eggs and dishes a large spoonful onto his plate, then does the same to Jack's plate, and mine. Then she goes through each platter, dishing out pancakes, berries, and sausages, piling them onto all our plates with barely contained violence until each plate is a heaping mess.

Dad tracks her every movement, totally gobsmacked as she finishes by discharging massive dollops of whipped cream onto the center of each plate, regardless of whether it lands on sausage, pancake, or egg.

Jack and I exchange a glance that says, *Holy shit, she's lost it.*

"Eat," she says, standing over Dad.

Dad stabs at his plate without even looking down, and then lifts the fork to his mouth and takes a bite, chews it, swallows. He has never seen her like this. None of us has.

"Now," she says in a tone that could bring on the next ice age, "I thought all this time that it was just Libby's money, and only because of the credit cards, and living above our means since you stopped working. But did you take Jack's education money as well, Rick?"

"I . . ."

"*Did you?*"

"I didn't take it, I borrowed it. I was going to pay it back," Dad says—seeming to crumble and at the same time already trying to scramble for a defense. "Jack told me he had enough to get through the year! I never told him to quit scho—"

"Stop trying to make this about Jack," Mom snaps. "Why did you need to borrow the money?"

"Why does it matter? It's gone."

"It matters because it's not just *your* life! It's not just *your* house, *you* being the parent and the adult. I have been in mourning," Mom says, with a hundred tons of grief in her voice. "I lost my son for over two years over a lie. A lie *you* told me."

"He quit school, left the country. Didn't tell us, didn't consult us, never respected us enough to tell us why!"

"What on earth would you have needed so much money for?" Mom says with terrifying focus. "Did you spend it on your political garbage, or—"

"It's not garbage, it's—"

"Dad got sued," Jack says, loud enough to cut through.

Dad freezes. Mom swivels to look at Jack.

"Sued?" Mom says. "For what?"

"Just tell her, Dad," Jack says.

"Why don't you tell her, since you're so eager to throw me under the bus."

"*Me* throw *you*?" Jack says with a bitter bark of a laugh.

"You have one chance to tell me the truth, Rick," Mom says, white-hot and pulling the conversation back on track. "And that chance is right now. I suggest you take it."

For a moment it looks like he's going to bolt, but something in her eyes must convince him that bolting would be worse than talking.

"Fine, yes, I got sued," he mumbles, staring straight down at his still-heaping plate. "Some clients—the basement of the house I helped them buy flooded . . . long story, but they sued me, the brokerage, the home inspector, the other agent, and the previous owners."

"But you have insurance for that," Mom says.

"Y-yeah . . . usually. But . . ." He takes a deep breath. "I'd just been ousted by those assholes at the brokerage, and they were sending my mail in these big packets, and I just . . . I was so mad, and . . . I wasn't opening them."

"Oh no," Mom says, putting a hand to her chest.

"I didn't open the insurance company's letters," Dad continues, still unable to look at any of us. "Which means I then failed to provide them with the information they asked me for. I also didn't show up in court because I didn't know I was supposed to. So . . . because I didn't cooperate with them on legal matters, they didn't have to cover me. Everybody else got sued and was covered, and I got sued and wasn't. And I was left with a massive bill."

"Oh no," Mom says again.

"I didn't want you to know," Dad says, finally glancing at Mom, then looking away, shamefaced. "I'd already lost my job, and I didn't want to cause you more stress. So I went to see Jack near the start of his third year and he said he could get through on his scholarships and summer job money, or even get a loan. I was going to repay the fund. I hired a lawyer with some of Jack's money, to fight the insurance company. It was a long process, and there was an appeal, but finally last fall it was over, and . . . we lost. So then I owed the original money, plus the lawyer fees, and . . . it was a large amount. More than we'd saved up in both of the kids' funds."

Mom takes this hit with a stifled whimper.

I feel sick—as much for her as for myself at the moment.

"I was going to try to pay it off in installments. I put a bit on one credit card, more on another, then I got a third card I never told you about. But it wasn't long before I could see I wouldn't be able to keep up with the payments, and the interest was going to drown us. So then I knew we were going to need Libby's money, too."

"Rick," Mom says, "damn it."

"I know," he says.

I look from one family member to another. We've gone quiet in a just-hit-by-a-truck-and-rolled-to-the-side-of-the-road-to-recover-or-die-in-peace sort of way. Mom's face is ravaged and streaked with silent-falling tears, Dad's looks hollowed out, Jack is shell-shocked, and I feel like my insides have been pulled out, thrown around, and put back in.

It's Mom who starts moving first, slowly picking up a couple of dishes and walking them to the kitchen. Jack does the same, then so does Dad. I get up, grab some glassware, and follow. It's the eeriest table-clearing ever—the only sounds the clinking of plates, cutlery, glass, until everything is in the kitchen and we start the next part—scraping the insane mounds of food off our plates, Dad not even complaining about the waste of food. It's funny how we somehow still know how to do this as a unit, even without any eye contact at all.

Still, I realize, we're not quite done. I don't want to kick

Dad when he's down, but this is the most undefended I've ever seen him, which means I might get through.

Jack is filling the sink with water to wash the serving platters while Dad loads the dishwasher and Mom starts transferring leftovers into smaller containers.

I position myself near the doorway, take a couple of breaths, and say, gently but firmly, "Dad, I think you need help."

"No, I'm good," he says, placing some forks into the dishwasher.

"No, I mean . . . help. Someone to talk to."

He glances up at me, and I see my mom's shoulders tense.

"Just listen," I say, before he can start objecting. "Everything that happened with the lawsuit, the insurance company . . . it happened because you weren't well. Weren't functioning."

"I made a couple of mistakes in a system that's stacked against me, that doesn't mean—"

"You admitted you're depressed."

"I'm not gonna talk to some stranger about my feelings."

"Listen," Jack jumps in to help, "you could have something as straightforward as a dopamine imbalance, or it could be serotonin-related. Chemical, in other words. And that's something you can get tested, and then treated medically. I'm talking about a simple blood test, Dad."

"But you should also go talk to someone," I urge.

Dad, as exhausted as he looks and must be, is drawing himself up again, getting ready to fight when Mom looks at him, her expression bruised and her eyes filled with bleak determination, and says, "He'll go. Or he won't have us."

Dad makes a sound like he's been punched in the gut.

"We can't live like this anymore," she says.

"Fine," Dad says, suddenly looking as scared as I've ever seen him. "I'll do it. I'll do all of it."

"And your troll activities end immediately," she says.

"Yes."

"And we make a plan *together* to start paying that money back, even if it does require renting out the kids' rooms."

"Okay."

"And you promise not to speak or write *one word to any-one* about Libby or her job or her situation with Perry Ackerman."

"But—"

"Not one word."

"Fine," Dad says, and I release a breath I didn't know I was holding.

"Good," she says, and then turns away just as Dad takes a limping step toward her, and leaves the kitchen.

Dad looks at Jack, and then me, and I can tell that he wants to say he's sorry, and also that he won't. Not yet, anyway.

29

KISS AND MAKE UP

Jack disappears into the basement, Dad goes off after Mom, and suddenly I need air. I grab shoes and sunglasses and practically stumble out into the sunlight.

I'm sort of a mess, let's be honest. The light spring breeze feels like it could knock me over and I'm looking at the outside world with a sense of unreality, like I'm seeing it all through a wall of thick, slightly blurred glass. But I'm also okay. Or will be. Already I feel lighter, and I can tell I'm going to feel better, *be* better in a substantial and hopefully permanent way, once I recover.

My steps lead, inevitably, to Emma's, where Vivian studies me for a moment in the foyer, then gives me a big hug. Emma's family talks about (almost) everything, so there's no doubt Vivian knows what's been happening, at least in regards to Perry. Still, she doesn't say anything—just gives me one final squeeze then ushers me down to the basement rec room. Emma's there, pacing and muttering to herself, and Yaz is on the floor in downward dog with Ben, an actual dog, lying beneath her.

"Hey, guys," I say. They both turn. The walk over restored

me somewhat, and I feel like I'm presenting as normal, but Yaz stands right up, says, "Whoa," and rushes over, as does Ben, who gives me a friendly slobber on the hand.

"Hi, Ben," I say, and give him a fast pat on the head, then discretely wipe my hand on the back of my pants, like he might be insulted if he saw.

Emma nudges Ben away, eyes on me, while Yaz pulls me over to the couch. She pushes me down gently onto it, and stares into my eyes until it makes me feel squirmy.

"What happened?" Emma says.

"Uh . . . family stuff," I say, unable to fathom how I would find the words to sum it all up for them.

"Shhh," Yaz says to us both. "Just wait. Don't talk."

I've been through this with Yaz before, and it's best to just let her do her thing. She gazes at me and then says, "May I?" When I nod, she lays her head on my chest, above my heart, and wraps her arms around me.

Yaz has top marks in science, is a killer basketball player, and is also a little bit woo-woo, in the sense that she believes she's reading my aura and/or beaming some kind of moon energy into me right now. What cannot be denied, though, is that sometimes Yaz knows what a person needs, even when they themselves don't. I don't need more talking, and I do, apparently, need a really good, long hug.

For a few moments I'm fighting tears, but then warmth steals through me and I begin to relax.

Yaz sits up after a minute or so, and carefully disentangles herself from me.

"Thanks, Yaz."

She smiles.

"So," I say, turning to Em and looking for something normal to discuss, "what are you studying for?"

"European History test, but I can barely read my notes."

"I made really good ones for that," I say. "You want them?"

"How on earth did you have time?"

"It was a couple days ago," I explain. "Besides, you gotta do something while you're waiting for the sky to fall. I'll scan them and send them to you later."

"You rock," she says, perching on the arm of the couch. "Did you hear that Perry posted on Complainers?"

"No," I say, barely able to drag my attention to Perry after the day I've had. "Uh, what did he say?"

"Just a big spiel thanking people for their support, and saying the situation's been blown out of proportion. And . . ."

"And . . . ?"

"Then he brags about what a nice guy he is that he actually got you rehired . . ."

I groan.

"And about how he'll be going to the Goat tomorrow night to 'kiss and make up' with you."

"He said that? Kiss and make up?"

"Yep. People should be able to tell just from that phrase that he's a harasser."

"Honestly it's like breathing to him," Yaz says.

"So . . . ?" Emma tilts her head and stares at me as though trying to read my mind. "Is that enough to convince you?"

"Convince me of what?"

"To speak up! Now is the time to tell your story. I could record it on my phone and then send it to Martina, who has got a gazillion new followers over the past few days, and it'll be huge."

"Em, no."

"Why not?"

"Look, despite all the online stuff, the fact is I don't have

enough concrete, real-world support to go up against him—
not without putting my entire future at stake. You might
think I'm being melodramatic, but I'm talking about facts.
Math. Money. About how, trying to change the world, I might
not just fail, but also screw myself over to the point that I'm
stuck here in Pine Ridge with Perry Ackerman forever and
will never achieve anything."

"But—"

"You want me to fight, Em, but you're in a much more
secure position than I am. Both of you are. And I'm happy
you are. But as of last Monday there are no other jobs for me
in this town, unless you include the one Perry offered me at
Ackerman, and I need to work."

"Wait," Yaz says, just as Em says, "What?"

I tell them about Perry's phone call.

"That is biblical-scale temptation," Yaz says, sounding
awed. "Wow."

"And proof that he's scared!" Emma says. "The photos are
clear evidence he was harassing you—"

"But half the people who've seen them probably think it's
funny, or that I'm just uptight, or that I encouraged him. Or
they believe what Perry's been saying—that they're photo-
shopped. You've been reading the comments, tell me I'm
wrong."

"There are people who're anti-Perry. Lots," Emma insists.
"And even if no one from the restaurant besides Martina and
your friend Kyle have come forward, behind closed doors
people are talking, things are changing."

"Yes. And I'm not saying I don't have faith in things changing, or that I don't want to do something. I do. And there
might be a way. But I don't want to be stupid about it, and
whatever I do, it won't be before tomorrow night. Tomorrow

night, although it sucks, I have to go in there and apologize."

"But you're planning something?" Emma asks.

"Not planning," I admit. "Thinking."

"Thinking isn't—"

"Hey, Em," Yaz says in her most soothing voice. "Ease up. She's going through a lot."

"Fine," Emma says, but she doesn't look happy.

"Hey, I heard a bit of news too," Yaz says. "My uncle drove by the Goat the last two mornings, and both times the owner was outside, painting."

"Painting?" I say.

"Over graffiti," Yaz clarifies.

"Uh-oh. What did it say?"

"That's the really bad part," Yaz says, letting Ben climb all the way onto her lap, even though he's far too big for it, and causing me to have to stand up. "Today it was already painted over when he saw it, but yesterday it was, 'Go Back Where You Came From' or something like that."

"Oh no," Emma says, and she's gone rigid.

"Where they came from is the suburbs," I say, incredulous. "Forty minutes away."

"They don't mean the suburbs, trust me," Emma says, looking grim.

"Obviously," Yaz says.

"You think it's because of . . . what's been happening?" I ask.

"No, it's because people are racist," Emma says. "My family's been here for three generations and people still say racist stuff to us."

"Seriously?" Yaz says, looking as surprised as I feel.

"Yep," Emma says. "Never anything as harsh as that graffiti, and usually just insensitive jokes, stereotypes, that kind of thing. But if you think about it—if that still happens to us, when we've been here for three generations, and are well off, and when half of the babies in town were delivered by my mom, imagine how it is for Dev and Maya's family—being brand new and trying to make a go of it in a small town that for years barely had any non-white people."

"Why don't they set up cameras? Get whoever's doing the graffiti arrested?" Yaz suggests.

"You'd have to ask them," Emma says. "But they probably don't have a lot of confidence that the cops would care, much less help."

"Well, okay," Yaz says, clearly struggling. "Maybe they could . . . try to raise awareness then. Talk to people about how hurtful it is."

"It's *meant* to be hurtful, Yaz," Emma says, looking more irritated by the second. "And they're running a restaurant. They don't have time to give people anti-racism lessons, and they can't afford to, either. Nor should they have to."

"Right," Yaz says, "I see your point. Sorry."

"Yeah, I'm sorry too, Em," I say, not quite sure which part I'm apologizing for, but just feeling I haven't acquitted myself as well as I could have in this conversation, and maybe in life overall in regards to these issues.

"Whatever, it's fine," she says, pacing away a few steps, then coming back. "I'm partly mad at myself that I've been urging you to make a big stink without thinking about how things might be for them. Not that I don't think you should take a stand, but . . . it should be against Perry, not them. I hate this."

"Well," I say, "as my dad would say, the world is a shithole."

Emma smirks, then Yaz gives one of her wry grins and says, "Such an inspirational guy, your dad."

Back at home I text Nita to see if she knows about the graffiti, then scan and send the study notes to Emma. Then I open the binder from Kyle and start flipping through it.

He clearly spent a lot of time and effort pulling information together. There are legal definitions, names of cases I can google, lists of types of charges, statistics, and an entire page of resources, both legal and psychological.

On the final page is a typed letter from Kyle's mom— whose name is Celia Roth—detailing her experience with sexual harassment and assault cases, and offering me free advice and/or representation.

I've just finished reading it when Nita texts back.

Dev doesn't like to talk about it but yes. It's been happening less often but he keeps a can of paint in his office and checks early each morning so he can deal with it discretely. He and Maya don't want to make a big deal, and feel it's just one or two idiots. That's what they hope anyway because they have not encountered any other problems besides this since moving here.

That's awful! I text back, and add an angry face emoji.

Yes. I think it's also why Dev didn't do anything to stop Perry and why it's good you're coming to apologize. I know it's not fair, but Perry has a lot of influence. So . . . thank you. Please don't tell Dev I told you about the graffiti or the paint can.

I won't.

I get it about harassment. I used to have
this guy who'd sit at the bar writing poetry
and then read it out loud in this huge
voice. Called my eyes "enthralling soul
daggers" and asked me, in a different
poem, to "suckle at the fingertip"
of his love.

                                        Ewwwwwww

Matt gets hit on behind the bar too, fwiw.
5 marriage proposals this year and some
very graphic suggestions.

                                        Yuck.

I think there's something wrong with how
people view servers—not just the female
ones. Big subject and not all solvable at
once but I promise I'll try to help. We'll talk
more.

                                        Okay.

See you tomorrow?

                                        Yep.

    I put down the phone and pace my room, upset. The number of unfair things in the world seems to multiply by the day, or maybe it is just my awareness of these things that's multiplying. Regardless, it's frustrating not being able to do anything about it.

    Although it's not true that I can't do anything. I've actually accomplished a lot recently in the changing-things

department, and in the being-braver-and-smarter department as well. So maybe I can figure out a way to respect
Maya and Dev's wishes, and not make things worse for them,
but still do something about Perry.

I have to try.

I go back to the binder, reread Ms. Roth's letter.

Then I go to the photos on my phone, and do a quick scan
of Dad's deleted exposé.

I may not be in a position of power at the moment, and I
may not feel as strong as I'd like to, but I am not alone, not
stupid, and not without resources.

And so I make a phone call.

A few minutes later I pop my head into the kitchen. Mom
and Dad are holed up in there, guzzling coffee and going over
bank statements. It doesn't look like fun, but Dad is docile.
Meanwhile, Jack has gone to the store and bought light bulbs,
and is going through the house replacing all the dead ones.

"Can I borrow the car?" I ask.

Mom and Dad wave me off with distracted nods, and I go
to meet with Celia Roth.

———

Later, I drive out to Noah's.

"Hey," he says when he opens the door. "I figured I might
not see you until tomorrow at school."

"Well, I don't have much time and I'm so tired I feel like
I'm going to fall on my face, but I wanted to see you."

He smiles that smile that kills me. Most of his smiles
kill me.

"You want to come in? I'm here solo."

I step into the foyer. "I've been sexually assaulted," I say
without preamble.

"I know," he says, the smile disappearing. "Perry."

"Not just Perry."

"Oh," he says, blinking. "Shit. Really?"

"Yeah. It's nothing major. Or I thought it wasn't. It wasn't anything, you know, violent. But the other night when we were . . . uh . . ."

"Kissing," he supplies.

"Yeah. I had a kind of flashback. It was so sudden and unexpected . . . and obviously I freaked out."

"Wow. Okay," he says, staring intently at me. "So . . ."

"So I'm going to get help about it. I already started. Yesterday. I talked to that woman who came to our school, the public health nurse. I'm going to go see her a few times. She called the flashback an 'intrusive memory' and says I may have unprocessed trauma. Which means I have to process it, I guess."

"Makes sense."

"She did say that this stuff—these, um, kinds of symptoms—usually fade, especially once you start to address . . . things."

"Good," Noah says, but he looks a bit at a loss.

"They could fade really fast, like a couple of weeks, even. Or not," I say, bracing myself. "You might want to take this into account."

"Take it into account how?"

"About us. Me. That it's not just my bonkers family and my financial woes and my work problems that are part of the package. It's this, too," I say, and then raise my hands in a mock cheer. "Surprise!"

"Listen," he says, expression grave, "if you don't want . . . if this changes things and you just want to be friends, I understand."

"Is that what you want?" I say, a cracking feeling beginning in my chest, even though I was prepared for this.

"If it's what you want," he says. "Or . . . need?"

"Noah!"

"What?"

"I'll handle the part about what I want and need. What I'm asking is what do *you* want? Do you want out?"

"I . . ."

"Because that's not what I meant. Unless it's what you want because I'm too complicated and messed up. If so, I get it."

"You're not too messed up."

"What if I can't even kiss you?"

"Well," he looks down, and then back up, and kind of rolls his shoulders like he's trying to shake something off. "Not gonna lie, that would suck."

"That's what I'm saying."

"But, we could do other things. We could develop some new . . . kissing alternative."

Despite the intense situation, I start laughing.

"I'm serious. Hey, for example, my little cousin, she likes to do this thing where she sticks her tongue into the inside of her cheek, you know, so her cheek sticks out." He demonstrates this. "And then she gets other people—only really special people, of which I am one—to do the same, and then touch the pushed-out part of their cheek to the pushed-out part of hers. And then, in the advanced version, if you manage to graduate to that, she moves her tongue inside her cheek, and you try to follow with yours, inside your own cheek."

"What . . . ?"

"It's harder than it looks, but a very specialized means of communication."

"And this is your plan?"

"Admittedly it's not sexy," he says with a grin, "but it is

fun. Or, like, we could do trust-building stuff where you close your eyes and fall backward and I catch you, or we could build a raft together or something . . .

"And if it sinks?"

"I think it's the building that's the point," he says. "But this woman told you the problem would fade, so maybe we just wait, stomp, hold hands, and go slow."

"Okay . . ."

"Or . . ."

"Yes?"

"I mean, we could just keep testing out the kissing," he says with a deceptively casual shrug. "Test it, pause, test again, and just be really careful. And . . . if that memory thing happens, we just stop and take a break and, like, don't freak out about it. That's, of course, if you're willing."

"How about now?"

"You sure?"

In answer, I reach for him and very carefully kiss him, then stop.

"Okay?" he says, and I nod and go back for another kiss, and then another, very slowly. And then, because I'm going to die if I don't continue, I continue. Carefully. Slowly. He kisses back, also carefully and slowly, pulling away every so often, just far enough to look into my eyes and check, before coming back. A few more kisses and he checks again. "All fine?"

I nod, more than fine except for the fact that he's stopped.

"Should we . . . maybe quit while we're ahead?" he says. "Like, maybe we could aim to . . . I don't know, build toward a streak?"

"Of kisses where nothing goes wrong?"

"Yeah . . . or not . . ."

"How do we count them," I ask. "Per kiss, or per kissing session?"

"Whatever gives us the greatest feeling of accomplishment without detracting from the . . . experience. But Libby," he says, still serious, "are we . . . have we decided?"

"About?"

"Well, we were going to give it a few more days, but I feel like we're both leaning toward . . . August sucking. Or is that just me?"

"No," I say, "it's not just you."

30

HE MUST LIKE YOU

Monday morning I get another call from Perry.

I don't pick up, but he leaves a message, reiterating his job offer, and telling me this is my last chance. He sounds a bit unhinged, which matches with Emma's reports of his behavior over the weekend.

I'm nervous all day—so much that it's actually a relief when Jack finally drives me over to the Goat for what I've come to think of as my "apology shift." The parking lot is crowded, so I have him take me to the service entrance.

"Good luck," Jack says with his warm-blanket grin.

"Thanks."

"Do you want me to come in? And just hang out in the bar? Not right this second—don't want you to look like you had to arrive with your big brother or anything." He lifts his phone. "I've got some emails to send, so I could just hang out here and then slip in a bit later."

"You don't have to do that," I say, though I'm moved that he's offering.

"What if I wanted to? Not to interfere, I promise, but just to be there."

"Okay," I say. "But behave yourself."

"Promise."

Two minutes later I'm hanging my stuff in the staff room and tying my apron around my waist. The kitchen staffers are quiet, none of them greeting me, but one waves at least, and another winks.

I'm just bracing myself to go out front when Dev comes in through the door I'm about to exit. He steps aside to let me pass, and I stand by to let him pass, and then we both try to go through at the same time again. Awkward. Finally I step right into the currently empty dish pit to my left and Dev comes along.

"You're here," he says.

"I said I would be."

"Thank you," he says, looking relieved and shamefaced at the same time. "Libby . . ."

"Yes . . . ?"

"Since we last spoke I have read the accounts of Mr. Ackerman's past behavior, and also Martina's story. I knew he was sometimes inappropriate, but I did not understand the extent or . . . ungentlemanly . . . quality of it. It's shocking. And the . . ." Dev looks like he might die of embarrassment. "The . . . photo component. Er. Have you . . . ? Did he send you . . . ?"

"Oh!" I say, realizing the source of his embarrassment. "No, Perry never sent me any photos."

"Well," he exhales. "That's lucky."

"But he has touched my butt, my waist, the sides of both of my breasts, pressed his entire body against me during multiple hugs, and made revolting sexual jokes and threats of sexual violence disguised as jokes," I say. "So the lack of a pornographic photo doesn't make me feel particularly lucky."

Yikes, I'm on a roll.

"Oh!" Dev says, backing up a step and bumping into the dish sink. "Yes, those things are . . . I'm sorry they happened. And I appreciate your coming to apologize for your part in this . . . event. I know it must be difficult."

I feel myself wanting to say it's nothing, not difficult at all, wanting to make things easier and smoother, but it's only the old me that thinks that's the only option.

The new me nods and says, "Yes."

"I will keep a closer eye on Mr. Ackerman from now on, I promise. Those things should not be happening to you, or to anyone, and I will try from now on to prevent them."

I inhale the humid, soapy-smelling dish pit air and say, "That would be helpful."

Dev gives me an anxious bob of the head that means the conversation is over, and heads toward his office.

Which means I have no further excuse to stay in the back.

I peer through the doorway into the restaurant. It's more full than usual for this time on a Monday, and it's loud with what sounds to me like the buzz of anticipation.

Maybe I'm paranoid.

Maybe it's just my imagination.

Or maybe the place is full of people who've come especially because of Perry's post, to witness the drama in person.

Regardless, it's showtime.

Stomach in knots, I head through the door and straight for the host stand, and Kyle, who has not texted me since our conversation on Saturday. Because why not pack in as many awkward moments as possible?

Heads turn as I pass, and I distinctly hear whispers containing the words "that girl" and "Perry Ackerman" and "psycho" and "apologize" and "ruin his life" and "harassment" and "ass."

Lovely.

"Hi," I say as I approach Kyle, who's got a crowd of people waiting for tables in the foyer.

"Hello," he says, all business but still sporting goat-themed apparel—a toque this time, with furry horns.

Brianna, who's there checking the seating chart, says "Hey, girl," before taking her (also gawking) customers to her section.

"Your section is the patio. Brianna's got the front half and you've got the back," Kyle says. His demeanor is stiff, but I can't tell whether it's with anger or in an effort to show professionalism. "I have a fifteen-minute wait list already, but I haven't sat you yet."

"Thanks," I say, relieved for many reasons that I'm not alone back there tonight. "I'm ready."

"I'm not going to slam you," he assures me. "I've set up the tables for Perry and his party already, and I thought we'd just leave them empty until he comes, 'cause you might not have time to turn them fast enough."

"God forbid we leave him waiting."

"Exactly."

"What time is he coming?"

"Six o'clock, party of twelve."

"Twelve!"

Kyle nods.

"Oh, joy."

"I wish you wouldn't do this," he murmurs, momentarily abandoning his overly proper attitude. "I don't get it."

"You don't have to."

"Are you . . . are you all right?"

"I'm fine, Kyle."

My first customers are "normal" ones—just there for dinner, not the promise of a spectacle. They're also immediately
distracting—a mom and dad with their adorable five- or six-
year-old, who is bawling.

Sometimes crying kids are annoying but this girl's crying
is the kind that pulls at my heartstrings. I rush over to the
booth, greet the parents, then kneel down to be at eye level
with the girl.

"Hey," I say, looking straight into her watery eyes, "I'm
Libby."

She snuffles.

"What's your name?"

"I'm . . . L-lottie."

"Cool name," I say. "Good first letter especially. L—just
like me!"

Lottie's sobs slow a little at this.

"You want to look at our kids' menu? You can color on
it." I hand her a packet of crayons from my pouch and she
takes it and clutches it to her chest like someone might try
to take it.

"You can even keep them," I say.

She tries valiantly to smile.

"Hard day?" I ask.

Lottie nods, her fast-spilling tears wrenching.

"Lottie had a social issue at school," Lottie's mom says, all
the while rubbing her hand in circles over Lottie's back.

"Jackson told me I'm not in his club," Lottie blurts out.

"What club?"

"His club. The Adam Club."

"We keep telling her she doesn't want to be in that club!"
Lottie's mom says. "It's probably a boring club anyway."

"It doesn't matter if the club is boring," Lottie insists. "If you're not in it they get to be mean to you. Because then at recess Adam and Sidney threw sand in my eyes, and I said I didn't care about their stupid club but they kept following me around, and telling me they didn't want to play with me, and then Adam stole my hat and I couldn't run fast enough to catch them and then I tripped and"—she starts to hyperventilate—"look . . . at . . . my . . . knees!"

I look. Her leggings are rolled up and she's got large bandages, with substantial blood showing through, on both of her tiny knees.

"Ow!" I say, wincing.

She regards me gravely, her little chin quivering, then asks. "Why don't they just leave me alone?"

"I don't know," I say, pained.

"They probably like you, sweetie," Lottie's dad says in a soothing tone.

"No, Dad, they hate me," she says with devastating clarity. "They told me. They laughed at me when I fell and called me a baby for crying."

"Boys are just dumb sometimes, honey," the dad says, looking desperate for some way to make her feel better. "They're not always good with communicating so they do stupid things to get your attention. I'm telling you, this Jackson fellow? He must like you."

"No," Lottie insists again, this time with a ferocious frown. "Jackson *said,* 'I don't like you, nobody likes you, you're not my friend, you're not in the club, you can't play with us'!"

Lottie's mom jumps in to support the dad's hypothesis, and Lottie looks at both her parents like they've gone insane. Meanwhile, I stand there, rooted to the spot, déjà vu and "he must like you" running hot through my brain.

My mom said the same thing to me in first grade when I told her Rod Catena and his friends—wretched cretins even back then—were spending recess throwing balls of ice at Emma and me.

"He must like you," she said, as she gently attended to the goose egg on the side of my head. "He probably has a crush on you."

I've never thought about it before, but WTF. Rod was scary. And even when my mom said he liked me, I knew he didn't. But it's hard, trying to understand someone just randomly deciding not to like you, and my mom was my mom, so I wanted to believe her.

I watched Rod after that, looking for signs. Because if he liked me, he would eventually show it. Waiting for this to happen, I became like a puppy looking for scraps, and then trying to take those scraps and thread them together into something more solid.

It got to the point that I'd be upset if he *didn't* do anything bad to me, taking it as evidence that he didn't like me anymore, didn't care about me, and I so badly wanted it to be true that he liked me. Because otherwise maybe I just wasn't likeable, which is so twisted, now that I think about it.

And here is Lottie, being told the same thing by her well-meaning parents—that these boys are bullying her because they like her.

I jump into a pause in the conversation and ask, "Why do *you* think Adam acts like that, Lottie?"

"Because he's mean," she says with certainty.

"I agree," I say. "Is that what you do when you want to be friends with someone—hurt them and act like a jerk?"

"No!"

"Right. So hopefully you can get help from a grown-up when this happens, and you can find friends who are as nice as you are. And then all of you together can tell the Adam Club to get lost."

Lottie nods gravely, and I can see her parents pondering this. Hopefully I haven't lost my tip by contradicting them.

In my peripheral vision I can see Kyle has sat more of my tables. Ideally you need to greet new customers within thirty seconds of their sitting down, so I shift gears and get Lottie's family's order, then zoom over to my two new tables to say hello and get drink orders, punch everything into the computer, and then duck behind the service station.

One of my tables is a group of women from the Inn—i.e., my mom's coworkers, and a gossipy bunch. I'm sure it's one of them who played the video for my mom last week, and they're definitely here for the show, all nudges and knowing looks. Luckily the other table is a couple on a date, with no interest in me whatsoever.

"Hey." Someone puts a hand on my shoulder, and I turn to see Brianna standing there. "You all right?"

"I'll be fine," I say, not quite hiding the tension in my voice. "Just need to get this night over with."

Kat comes around the corner and gives me a low high five.

"She posted," Brianna whispers.

"Shhh," Kat says.

"Where?" I whisper.

Kat does a head swivel to make sure no one's listening, and then says, "On Martina's blog. A few of us did. It's not fair what happened to you with that video going around and nobody knowing he's done it to literally every female who ever served him."

"Well, thank you."

"No, thank *you!* When you iced him like that . . . ?" She grins, leans in closer, and hits her chest with her palm. "I felt it. I wish I'd done it."

"Every single one of us wishes we'd done it," Brianna adds. "That was inspired."

"More insane than inspired," I say.

"Nah, inspired," Kat says.

"Heroic," Brianna says.

"And we gave you, like, a zillion points for Most Appreciated," Kat adds. "So if nothing else, you're getting dinner."

"And the prestige," Brianna jokes. "We should put that shit on our résumés."

"Get ourselves a plaque," Kat says. "Or maybe a trophy. Half of them look like dicks anyway. It's fitting."

For a few moments the three of us are hands clapped over our mouths, cackling, and I'm so happy to be back, and so relieved. But then I sag.

"What?" Brianna says.

"Nobody's going to think I'm heroic after tonight," I admit. "And you're not going to want to give me any trophies. Perry's coming in and I have to apologize. I don't want to, but I have to. I'm sorry."

"Uh-uh." Kat shakes her head. "You gotta do what you gotta do. That doesn't put you out of the running. That's what the trophy is for."

"Sometimes a girl's just going to have to bide her time, you know?" Brianna adds.

"Thanks," I say, thinking about my meeting with Kyle's mom. "Biding my time is exactly what I'm doing."

"Okay then," Kat says, starting to glance anxiously out toward her section while Brianna starts pouring waters. "We got you."

Kat gives me an encouraging whack on the back and Brianna squeezes my hand and heads out with the tray of waters.

"Annd," Kat says, standing on her toes to look over the barrier into the restaurant, "he's here."

"Awesome," I say, my insides gripping.

"Chattin' it up at the front with Kyle . . . movin' on to Nita at the bar . . . paused there, of course . . ." Kat continues to report. "Looks like he's in the middle of some big story, so you got a minute."

"Okay," I say, and decide it's better to get moving than hide here, getting more stressed by the second. I hustle out to check my section, make sure everyone has full beverages, and that Mom's coworkers' appetizers have arrived, and that Lottie and her family are okay.

And then I notice another one of my booths has been sat, and stop short when I see who's in it: Emma, Yaz, and Noah. No Boris.

"What's this?" I say as I approach.

"Just dinner," Yaz says.

"If the waitress will ever take our order," Emma says, tapping her menu.

"And we thought you might want some friendly faces in your section," Noah says. "Is that okay?"

"We're here for moral support—of you, *and* the restaurant," Emma says with a meaningful look. "We'll behave, we promise. And we can also give you our whole order now, if you want—that way you can focus on Mr. Harassy-pants."

I give a snort of laughter, then say, "Okay, sure. And thank you."

Out of the corner of my eye I see the salads for the couple arriving, and Lottie's family's entire meal. I get my friends' order and place it, then grind pepper and sprinkle cheese on the salads, remove empty glasses, double-check that I've put in everything anyone has ordered and timed it right . . . and then Perry's there, strutting onto the tile floor.

Dev and Nita are flanking him, and his horde of friends trails just behind. Nita's already got Ackerman beers for them all, and I'm grateful. It would be just like Perry to demand I make my apology while balancing a huge tray of drinks.

I hang back, trying not to hyperventilate, while Dev gets everyone settled.

Perry chooses a chair that has a command of the entire patio and both entrances, and pulls it back and a bit sideways so that there's room in front of him.

Room for me, presumably.

In front of his manspread legs.

Ugh.

Still, I just have to get it done.

I make two attempts at deep breaths, then put one foot in front of the other until I'm right back were it all started, in front of Perry.

And smiling.

What is with the smile? I hate how I can't even stop it from appearing on my face.

Perry smiles back at me, all crotch, teeth, and reptile charm.

Dev stays close, as does Nita, and even though there's music playing and people chatting and food being cooked and served, the restaurant has gone markedly quiet and I can feel people watching.

"Hi there, Lib," Perry says, faced flushed—from booze already or from being agitated about the situation, I can't tell. "I guess you didn't get my message."

"Hi . . . Perry," I say, heart thudding, all of the things I can't say combined with the things I have to say creating a logjam in my throat. "I did. And thank you, but I figured I'd just . . . see you tonight. Uh, how are you? You look . . ."

evil and smug as hell

" . . . well."

He raises his eyebrows.

"That is . . ." I clear my throat, wishing I'd written something out. Then another one of my automatic survival-with-males instincts kicks in, and I find myself cocking my head and saying, "You look a lot *cleaner* . . . than when I last saw you."

I hate going back into any kind of banter, and I'm taking a risk that this might piss him off, but on the other hand maybe we can all just have a chuckle and break the tension.

Perry's eyes narrow, and my heart thunders, but I hold his gaze.

And then he laughs, big and loud and harsh, and his entourage bursts into relieved-sounding laughter a split second later.

I exhale, grinning.

I can do this. Maybe I can do it quickly and casually with a bit of self-deprecating humor thrown in, and make it not a big deal, not an all-out prostration, and survive it with some shred of dignity while still keeping my job and not making extra trouble for Dev and Maya.

"I'm sorry about that," I say, giving him a sheepish look. "About your clothes, I mean, and the, you know, *cold shower.*"

"You thought I needed a cold shower, darlin'?" he booms, seeming to take up more space by the second.

"Seemed like a good idea at the time . . ."

Just like this conversational tactic.

"After my hot, sticky dessert?"

Gross. I'd assumed he'd be on his best behavior but instead it looks like he's half wasted and doesn't care. Like he's daring anyone to stop him, and out to prove that no one can.

Time for a pivot.

"Seriously, Perry," I say, "I'm really sorry. I should never have lost my temper with you. It was unprofessional."

"And you are normally *such* a professional," he says, and lets his eyes slide like venomous snakes down my body.

Dev takes a step forward, but Nita puts a hand on his arm to stop him, obviously hoping I'll handle this without his help.

"I try," I say, pretending to take the comment at face value.

"You sure do," Perry says.

"Anyway, I regret what I did, Perry. That's the truth. I regret it and I'm sorry."

"How sorry?"

"Sorry enough to stand here and say it in front of all these people," I manage to say, cheeks on fire and humiliated, furious tears suddenly pooling in my eyes.

"Hey, hey . . . I forgive you," Perry says, now in a soothing voice as he gets out of his chair and comes toward me, arms open. "Let's hug it out."

I knew the hugging would happen. I was planning to just let it happen—it's just a stupid hug, after all. Except with Perry, it isn't.

As he gets closer and I catch the scent of him—sickly sweet cologne, body odor, and booze—something in me just . . . refuses. *Everything* in me refuses.

I take a quick step backward and put out my hand.

"How about we shake on it?" I suggest.

Perry stops short, eyes narrowing, then says, "Aw, come on."

He takes another step toward me while I take another

step back, smiling hard and keeping my proffered hand out in front of me.

Out of the corner of my eye I can see Dev looking grim and pale. Perhaps he's recalling how he said he wouldn't "let those things happen" to me. Does he know the hugging is one of those things? Probably. But then again, there's that can of paint in his office, and his family's future, which I am potentially jeopardizing right this second. And yet I'm not doing anything wrong—just drawing a reasonable boundary for myself, offering a polite alternative, and that's after giving a perfectly good apology in front of all these people. It shouldn't damage Dev, or the Goat. I hope.

"I'll try not to be such a bad dog in the future. Okay?" Perry says.

"Thank you," I say.

"Now gimme a hug."

"I really think we should shake on it," I say. "Or how about a high five?"

"What?" Perry says, his anger rising. "Are hugs against the law all of a sudden?"

I turn in a full circle, wanting to know who's seeing this, and the answer is . . . everyone. There's Dev and Nita, Brianna, Kat, Kyle standing nearby with fists clenched, Emma, Yaz, and Noah, even Domenic and Maya have come out from the back. And then there are all the townspeople who've crowded the two entrances to the patio, a few of them with phones out. I spot a concerned-looking Jack at the back of that crowd. Plus there's Mom's group of coworkers, and tiny Lottie with her parents—all of them glued to the scene.

Even Perry's friends are looking at each other uneasily.

"That's okay, we don't have to shake if you'd rather not," I tell him. "How about we get you some *food*?"

"Food?"

"Come—all is well, we're friends again, and you look hungry," I say, taking him by the arm and turning him back toward his table.

Perry *humph*s and stumbles a bit, but lets me lead him for a couple of steps before sliding an arm around my waist as if for support. I jam my elbow close to my side to block the side boob grope that's probably coming, but I'm only fast enough to shove the hand away, not to prevent it from getting there in the first place.

I hear a couple of gasps, but Perry actually laughs.

This must finally be so far over the limit for Dev that he can't help himself, because all of a sudden he's leaping forward.

"That is quite enough, Mr. Ackerman!" he says.

"Whoa, whoa, what?" Perry says.

"Hands off of the servers, and no more dirty jokes or foul language, please. We have families here."

"Oh, come on, didn't you hear? Libby and I are friends. She doesn't mind my little games. She likes them. Right, Libby?"

I glance over at Dev, hoping for a clue about how he'd like me to respond after this big gesture of his, but get no indication.

"Riiight, Libby?" Perry repeats. "Tell your boss you like it."

Two completely opposite retorts are hurtling toward my mouth, both of them wrong. One is a lie and the other is another metaphorical pitcher of sangria, complete with more of the foul language Dev doesn't want.

I swallow them both and say, very calmly but loud enough for everyone to hear, "Actually, Perry, I'm not really a fan."

"Well, then," Dev says, a bit wild-eyed, "it's settled. She's not a fan. So let's not."

"Let's not?" Perry repeats, incredulous.

"Exactly," Dev says, and then it feels like the entire world is waiting, breathless, to see how Perry will respond.

"Fine!" Perry snarls finally. "Get me another one, then." He drops sulkily into his chair. "I'm tired of this one."

"Another . . . I'm sorry, another . . . what?" Dev says.

"*Another girl!*" Perry shouts. "One with a better sense of humor than this cow."

"Oh. Um." Dev seems to have spent all his confrontational mojo and is now looking around desperately for a solution. His eyes land on someone behind me. "Brianna! Please come serve Mr. Ackerman and his guests."

I am backing away slowly, expecting that to be it for now, when I hear Brianna saying "No, thank you."

"Pardon me?" Dev says.

"No, thank you, I got too many other tables," she says, and rolls her shoulders back and adds, "And I won't serve him."

"You won't . . . Fine! Where's Kat?"

Kat gives him a little wave.

"You serve Mr. Ackerman, please," Dev says. "Get a move on."

Another server, Tiffany, comes up beside Kat in silent solidarity, and Brianna crosses to join them.

"I won't serve him either," Kat says.

"And neither will I," says Tiffany.

"You, then," Dev sputters, pointing at Kyle. "You've learned the computer system, yes? Put the PLEASE SEAT YOURSELF sign up at the front. You're promoted."

Kyle looks from me, to Perry, to the girls, to Dev, stands up taller, and says, "Sorry, Dev, but no."

"You don't know the system?" Dev says, trying to hold onto some thread of hope.

"I do, but I won't," Kyle says.

Dev pauses, flustered, and it's clear that he doesn't know what to do. But then he notices Maya. She gives him a look that's inscrutable to the rest of us but must read loud and clear to Dev, because he nods, gathers himself, then turns back to Perry.

"Well, Mr. Ackerman," he says, voice shaky but gaining strength as he goes, "I'm sorry, but it appears that we . . . cannot serve you today."

"Cannot serve me?" Perry says.

"That's correct," Dev says.

At this, Perry bursts out of his chair, swearing, then waves his cohort to follow him, and storms toward the front door via the bar, forcing everyone in his way to either scatter or be trampled.

There's a long, long silence, with only the "contemporary mix" playlist inserting itself bizarrely into the moment as we all wait to see what's going to happen now. Regardless of what just happened, Dev might still decide to fire everyone who just defied him.

But then my friends start to clap, and suddenly all of the customers and staff follow suit, and for the umpteenth time this week I'm about to burst into tears, happy ones this time, and then Dev is shouting over the hoopla, "Okay, okay, everyone back to work!"

And that is how nobody gets fired, and the rest of the shift feels like a party, and I extract promises from every one of my customers to come back soon and support Dev and the Goat, and make a record amount of money in tips.

Emma, Yaz, and Noah leave so I can turn the table. Meanwhile, Jack has found some old friends at the bar.

In fact, Jack and his friends are still partying when I'm finished for the night, and this works out fine, because Noah is coming back to get me.

Kyle finds me out front under the blinking pink neon, waiting for Noah's truck.

"Hey," he says.

"Hi," I say.

There are a few moments of awkward silence, and then I say, "Hey, listen, I looked through that binder you put together for me over the weekend."

No need to tell him I also met with his mom—she wants me to keep everything confidential for now.

"I almost forgot about that," Kyle says. "Cool."

"You guys were very thorough. Thank you."

"Oh," he says, "hey, no problem."

"And thank you also for what you did tonight, and for posting this week. All of those things are . . . I appreciate them."

"Just the basics of being decent."

"Well, thanks for being decent, then."

"It doesn't make up for the other thing," he says with a hangdog look.

I inhale sharply.

"I won't keep bringing it up," he says, noticing. "But I just wanted to tell you that I did more reading and research about that . . . subject . . . over the weekend—"

"You're really on a roll with the research."

"I guess. Seems I've hit a point in my life where I need information. I'm really, really sorry. I wish I could take it back," he says, looking more at the ground than me. "Anyway, you did me a favor by telling me, and I will never, ever make the same mistake again. I'm planning to get really good at making sure people are enthusiastic about wanting to have sex with me. And there's not going to be as much alcohol involved."

"That's wise," I say.

"In the meantime, do you want me to ask Dev not to

schedule us together? Or . . . I could quit. Do you want me to quit?"

"No, don't quit," I say. "I don't think that's necessary."

"Okay, if you're sure," he says, visibly relaxing. "But if there's anything that you need me to do, or that I could do, to fix it or make any part of it better . . ."

"I'll let you know."

"And if you ever want to . . . you know . . ."

"If I ever want to what . . . ?"

"You know," he says, ducking his head, "not now obviously, but if you ever wanted, in the future, to give me another chance—like, for a do-over—"

At this, even though maybe I should be mad, I burst out laughing.

"Ouch," he says. "That's not promising."

"Kyle, seriously," I say. "Did half your brain fall out your ear?"

"Right. Yeah. Sorry."

"I mean, I'm willing to move past it, but this isn't a do-over situation."

"All right, all right," he says. "I get it. How about being friends someday? Do you think we might aim for that?"

"Sure," I say. "Let's aim for that."

"Want to shake on it?" he says, offering his hand.

"Yeah," I say, "that sounds perfect."

31

PLANS

When I arrive home from the Goat Monday night, Mom and Dad inform me that I can stay in the house for as long as I need to. Dad, prodded by Mom, even apologizes, and I manage to receive it without any snark whatsoever.

They look exhausted and have obviously been arguing, and have some painful stuff to work out. But everything is out in the open now, so I'm cautiously optimistic.

At the very least, we have a road map for talking about things.

Tuesday night—Jack's last night at home—he and I go back out to the swing.

"Good job the last few days," he says.

"You too."

"What are you going to do about school?" he asks. "Don't you have to send acceptances soon?"

"I do. And I don't know. It's tight. Plus I'm rethinking. I mean, I'd like to do something . . . of more importance to humanity than what I was planning before. Or, more direct and immediate importance, anyway . . . if that doesn't sound too cheesy."

"Who cares if it sounds cheesy?"

"Or overly idealistic?"

"I don't think cynicism leads anyone to a satisfying career path," he says. "Nothing wrong with having something you want to fight for."

"Yeah. Anyway, a year to think about that, not to mention save, and apply for more scholarships since now I really know I need them, might not be a bad thing."

"And you'd stay here in the meantime?"

"Have to," I say, and sigh.

"Or . . ."

"Or? There is no 'or.'"

"Well, listen," he says, looking suddenly nervous. "I have a bit of money I can spare—"

"No, Jack—"

"But I can probably give you enough to make sure you can do school in September part time at least, if you change your mind. Or if you really are going to wait a year . . . it could buy you a ticket to Greece."

"Uh, a vacation isn't exactly—"

"Not for a vacation. To work. I'm sure I can get you hired."

"As what?"

"A server," he says. "Can't promise there won't be any Perry Ackerman types, but we run a pretty tight ship, and we've got bouncers on the weekends who'll throw out anyone you ask them to. And I promise to back you up if you need it. You could save just as much money for school there as you can here because you can crash with me. I could even look for a bigger place—or you could just come and go—work, but also use my place as a launch pad, landing pad, whatever— and travel around a bit."

Travel around a bit . . .

"That's . . ." My heart is pounding all of a sudden, but I try to remain cool. "That's a very interesting prospect."

"You could come as soon as you graduate," he says. "Or whenever you're ready."

"I need to stay here for the summer," I say, trying to think this through logically, even while my mind has already leapt all the way to Noah and me on the crumbling steps of the Acropolis, eating gelato in Italy, swimming in the Aegean Sea . . . "To see the changes happen at the Goat, hang out with my friends before we all go in different directions . . ."

"Sure."

"And I might be an annoying roommate."

"Fully expected."

"And cramp your style with the ladies."

"Oh, little sister," he says, "nothing can do that."

I roll my eyes.

"But this is sounding like a yes," he says.

"You know what it's really sounding like?" I say, a grin spreading on my face. "It's sounding like August might not suck after all."

32

BUSTED

Twenty-five people recorded Perry Ackerman's Monday night visit to the Goat. Some of them post their recordings online, others take them straight to the police station, some do both.

Also at the police station, in digital files, is a significant and growing collection of Perry's unsolicited dick pics, including the one he sent Martina and three that he sent to underage girls.

That, in spite of Ackerman Brewery and the rampant cronyism and the special golfing buddy relationship Perry has with the chief of police, finally gets Perry charged, and put in jail on Wednesday afternoon. No one expects him to be in there long, but Perry's wife surprises everyone by refusing to post bail and announcing that she'll run the brewery until further notice.

I'm sure one of his friends will put up the money for him eventually, but Perry's going to be mired in legal problems and court dates for the foreseeable future.

For example, even if he were able to wriggle out of the

current charges, there's still the detailed statement I gave to Ms. Roth (my lawyer!) on Sunday afternoon, and my option to press charges, which I plan to. I'm also going to start quietly helping her connect with women all over town who've been harassed, or may have been harassed, by Perry. We have a lot to go on already, including the extensive list of names my dad was compiling in his exposé. Half of the list is comprised of names matched with incidences Dad witnessed or heard about firsthand, and the second half is of incidences posted anonymously, and Dad's guesses about who they are. Ms. Roth is going to work quietly and carefully, and we're not going to out anybody against their will, but when the case is fully built, Perry will have even more problems than he does now.

Nita, Kat, Tiffany, Brianna, Matt, Kyle, and I, meanwhile, are going to write a new chapter for the server training handbook with the help of Dahlia Brennan, and we're also planning a "customer re-education" campaign for the restaurant. We're going to use humor whenever possible—colorful and funny but pointed signage, a code of conduct, and so on. Dev is on board so long as we don't shout at, soak, or otherwise harm the customers, and has already given me a glowing reference to use in the future.

Emma, Yaz, and I met with Nita to ask if there's some way we could help regarding the racist graffiti, which has lessened further, but not stopped. (Catch them in the act and make them volunteer at the restaurant is one of Emma's suggestions.) Nita's going to talk to Dev and Maya and let us know whether they're up for changing their strategy, and whether they want our help.

On the college front, I have declined five of my six (six!)

college acceptances and accepted but deferred one. It's my original first-choice school, and Emma is going there, and it also happens to have good social work, and psychology programs that I could switch to, if that's what I decide to do after my gap year.

In my spare time, between studying for finals, serving tables, meeting with Dahlia for talk therapy, checking my rising bank balance, and helping my dad paint and work on his résumé, I am slowly kissing Noah, and researching the architectural wonders of the Mediterranean. And every day I'm working on the new me—the calm but relentless me; the me who stands up for herself without going off the deep end, and who knows how to think *and* say.

ACKNOWLEDGMENTS

Huge thanks to my agent, Emmanuelle Morgen, who encouraged me to write this book. I am so grateful for our long partnership.

I could not have told this story without my extraordinary team of editors from Viking Children's and Penguin Teen Canada. I had two fantastic editors at Viking—Kendra Levin for the bulk (and it *was* a bulk!) of the edits, and Dana Leydig for the final stages of editing and crucial process of getting the book into the world. Both pushed me to do my best work and helped me with their keen observations and attention to detail. Thank you.

Meanwhile at Penguin Teen Canada, the wonderful Lynne Missen saw this story through every stage, from that first rough manuscript and all the way through to publication, working hand-in-hand with my New York editors. Lynne is endlessly insightful and encouraging, and really helped shape this story. Thank you.

I would be remiss not to also mention Leila Sales, the editor of my previous book, who read the first manuscript of *He Must Like You* and made sure it was in good hands (Kendra's) before she left Viking.

Massive props go to Theresa Evangelista for designing our fabulous cover, and to Sarah Herranz whose sketch of Libby is its sassy, furious centerpiece.

I'm fortunate to have the fantastic Kaitlin Kneafsey at Viking for my publicist, as well as Debra Polansky, Emily Romero, Janet Pascal, Marinda Valenti, and everyone else on the New York team from formatters to sales reps. In Toronto I'm in Sam Devotta's extremely capable hands for publicity, and have had great in-house support from Tara Walker, Vikki VanSickle, Peter Phillips and Kelly Glover. Every one of these people is fantastic and I thank them, and their teams (again, in every department!), for their passion, savvy, and hard work.

Thank you also to everyone at my agency, Stonesong Literary, for your contributions and support, and to my wonderful foreign rights agent, Whitney Lee, at the Fielding Agency.

And now for the people who have helped me with research, and/or reading and giving feedback at various stages. Thank you to:

- Bev Katz Rosenbaum, Maureen McGowan, Adrienne Kress, Michael Wacholtz, Tish Cohen, Sanaa-Ali-Virani, Samantha Steiner, and Kim Lindman for reading and feedback;
- Karen Krossing for helping me brainstorm plot and structure;
- Elyne Quan, Jing Kao-Beserve, Reshma Younge, Anjula Gogia, and Aneeka Kaliafor help with cultural authenticity and detail;
- Judi Fairholm, the National Director of RespectED: Violence, Bullying, and Abuse Prevention for Canadian Red Cross, for research and discussion regarding consent and healthy relationships;
- Stephanie Saville, whose insight and work with teens always inspires me;
- my (surprise!) Star Trek authenticity readers, Elyne Quan, Jing Kao-Beserve, Leslie Klein-

berg Zacks, and Jonah Zacks, for the most feedback, not to mention the most contradictory and passionate feedback, that I've ever received on such a short scene.

Anything I get wrong is on me.

Shout-out to some of my many buddies, online and off, from the world of publishing—everyone at Torkidlit, CANSCAIP, the Canadian Children's Book Centre, plus Amy Mathers, Helen Kubiw, Jenn Hubbs, my buddies from Backspace, Karen Dionne, Jon Clinch, Elizabeth Letts, Renee Rosen, Sachin Waikar, Keith Cronin, Lauren Baratz-Logsted, Darcie Chan, and Jessica Keener, Kelly Mustian, Sam Bailey, Bev Katz Rosenbaum, Maureen McGowan, Adrienne Kress, Leslie Livingston, Caitlin Sweet, Joanne Levy, Karen Krossing, Eileen Cook, and the many others I've been lucky enough to connect with over the past few years—I'm horrified that I don't have room to list you all . . . but I love you.

Eternal thanks to Laurie Halse Anderson for taking the time to share the experience and wisdom she's gained from years of talking with (and listening to) teens about sexual violence.

Cindy and Gary Ullman, plus Michael Wacholtz, and our daughters, Tessa and Scarlett, deserve extra props this time. They fed me, listened to me, gave me time alone, (and/or helped me hide out at a secret, distraction-free location), and helped me get to the finish line.

My excellent family—Cindy and Gary Ullman, Jim and Beatrice Wacholtz, Brian Younge, plus the larger Saville, Ullman, Wacholtz, and Younge branches—is always cheering me on, spreading the word about my books, showing up for events, and buying (perhaps) more copies of my book than they technically need. Thank you.

Thank you to booksellers in bookstores large and small, for your enthusiasm and commitment to books and reading, and the support you've given my work.

Thank you to the teachers and librarians who invite me to schools and libraries and conferences, and who do so much to instill a love of reading in students.

Big thanks, also, to the many wonderful book clubs who've hosted me, and to the incredible community of online book people—bloggers, booktubers, bookstagramers, and reviewers who help keep literary conversation alive.

Finally, thank you to all my wonderful, smart, passionate readers. I do this for you, and I could not do it without you.

RESOURCES

In the United States:
RAINN: 1-800-656-HOPE (4673); rainn.org; operates a
National Sexual Assault Hotline, has a website with many
helpful resources, and is partnered with thousands of
local sexual assault service providers. It is the largest
anti–sexual violence organization in the US.

National Sexual Violence Resource Center: nsvrc.org;
provides information and tools to prevent and respond to
sexual violence. This site has resources for survivors,
friends and family, advocates and educators, and media.

End Rape on Campus: 202-281-0323; endrapeoncampus.
org; works to end sexual violence on campus through
support of survivors online and via their hotline. They
also focus on prevention through education, and advocate
for policy reform at campus, local, state, and federal
levels.

Safe Horizon: Rape or sexual assault help: 1-212-227-3000;
All crimes hotline: 1-866-689-HELP (4357); safehorizon.org;
a national survivor assistance organization. Their site has
many resources and they provide support online and/or
over the phone. Their mission is to help survivors find
safety, support, connection, and hope.

The Trevor Project: 1-866-488-7386; text START to
678678; thetrevorproject.org; provides crisis intervention
and suicide prevention to LGBTQ people under the age of

twenty-five through resources on their site and through their helpline, which can be reached by phone, text, or online chat.

Suicide Prevention Lifeline: 1-800-273-8255; suicidepreventionlifeline.org; provides free and confidential emotional support, twenty-four hours a day, seven days a week, for all ages, and there are helpful resources on their site.

In Canada:

Kids Help Phone: 1-800-668-6868; text: 686868; kidshelpphone.ca; a national, 24/7 support service providing professional counseling, information, and referrals to young people age twenty and under. Their phone, text, and chat lines are free and confidential.

Crisis Services Canada: 1-833-456-4566; text: 45645; crisisservicescanada.ca/en; CSC is a national network of distress, crisis, and suicide prevention lines. They provide free support via their talk lines, and other resources on their site.

Below are websites that have gathered links to more hotlines, resources, and support across Canada:

- Support Services—Canadian Women's Foundation: canadianwomen.org/support-services

- Ontario Coalition of Rape Crisis Centres: ocrcc.ca

- TeenMentalHealth.org

- Youth Mental Health Canada: ymhc.ngo